The Alexandria Seal

By

C. E. Gauss

C.E. Gauss
El Cajon, CA

ISBN 10: 0692594434
ISBN-13: 978-0692594438

Printed in the United States of America

Cover image provided by C.E. Gauss
The World Factbook 2013-14. Washington, DC: Central Intelligence Agency, 2013.
Bacon, G. W. (George Washington), *Bacon's standard map of Europe*. Map. Library of Congress, Geography and Map Division.

First Edition: (November 2015)
10 9 8 7 6 5 4 3 2 1

When dining with wolves, you can never be sure if you are

the guest or main course.

Old Sicilian Proverb

There are no great men – only great challenges that ordinary

men are forced by circumstances to meet.

William F. Halsey, Admiral, U.S. Pacific Fleet – World War II

Acknowledgements

I would be remiss if I didn't thank a few people who helped me with this project. First I would like to thank my good friend Bud Kelly for giving me the confidence to bring the book inside me to the surface. An extra-big thanks goes to the group at Shell Creek Publishing. Without their help and guidance with the editing and formatting, the task would have been even more daunting than it was. Great people, great attitude and great to work with, I can't say enough about Tamara and her group.

Brave we were to anchor together under the moonless sky,

but we shared this compass and followed those stars, and here

we found our harbor. - Freya

To my wife and parents: You have been and always will be

my compass and anchor.

Table of Contents

Prologue: August 11, 1943 – 30,000 Feet Above Britain

As the last of the cotton-white clouds evaporated into a deep blue metallic sky, the pilot banked slowly to the right and flashed over the British countryside at nearly 700 miles per hour. At that speed and altitude, the land and water below blended into a brown, blue and green blur.

A short time earlier, he had taken off from a hidden airfield in the German hill country to the west of Heidelberg near Bergheim, streaked undetected across the English Channel, passed over the British Isles at nearly 30,000 feet and back out over the blue expanse of the North Atlantic. The experimental twin turbojet aircraft zoomed out of the darkness and disappeared as quickly as a bat – a creature it eerily resembled.

Its speed alone was like a rush of pure adrenalin, but the implications made the pilot's heart beat even faster. The twin Junkers turbojets were nestled on either side of the cockpit, and the groundbreaking design resulted in an aircraft more maneuverable and with twice the speed of any plane in the British Royal Air Force. The pilot's mind raced at the thought of how this newest creation could sweep the Allied bombers from the skies over Germany.

The plane's shape and coatings were truly innovative, and the pilot's eyes darted every few moments to an indicator light next to the altimeter. The lamp, which was connected to the plane's primitive radar detection system, started to flicker as he streaked over the Netherlands and toward the English Channel. He had checked and double-checked the system before takeoff, but even the most basic of male engineering tests simply overwhelmed him. He tapped the light and looked for the faintest sign of what might just be a bad connection, but it only brightened as he approached the coast. He flew directly into the path of the British radar and made no effort to avoid it. The test was not to see whether he could detect an energy pulse from the British ground stations, but rather if they could detect him.

As he approached the English coast, the real test was about to take place. All the theoretical calculations from the best engineers wouldn't matter if a squadron of British Spitfires or American P-51 Mustangs had been scrambled and were waiting for him. He knew his aircraft had the capability to outrun anything the Allies could put into the air, but their mere presence would signal instant failure. As it was, the evening had been perfectly clear. He scanned the skies and searched for any reflection off a metal surface made by British defenders in the last fading light before dusk. But he was quite alone as the sun slid below the horizon and he streaked into the twilight.

Walter and Reimar Horton, the two German brothers who authored the design, were correct: The plane cast no radar footprint – or to put it more simply, he was flying the world's first stealth aircraft. Invisible to British radar, he smiled as he realized what this monumental new design would mean to the German war effort. Their new weapon could still save his beloved motherland.

But even beyond this, the brothers had a much more ambitious plan in mind – and it was about to be tested. Leaning back, the pilot flipped a toggle switch next to his right hand and an array of instruments appeared as a crude hologram on the windscreen.

He closed his eyes, breathed deeply and concentrated, just as they had practiced so many times before. He felt the plane bank to the right, climb and then bank to the left. His heart pounded as he opened his eyes just in time to see these words floating above the hologram:

PILOTLESS CONTROL ENGAGED

Chapter 1. May 25, 2008 – San Diego, California

This was a morning on one of those days you never forget. You sit around the patio with friends and share an adult beverage, and the conversation always seems to come around to "do you remember where you were the morning of 9/11" or "where were you when JFK was shot?" Some events affect you so strongly that they become etched into your mind and part of the very fabric of your being. This morning was in no way as dramatic or important to the rest of the world, but it was for me.

For thirty-two years, I worked as a writer, investigative reporter or whatever else needed to be done at a local radio and television station. I don't mind saying that I was pretty damned proud of my body of work. No one would ever mistake me, Mark Arroyo, for a choirboy, but I did try to maintain a certain vigilante form of ethical behavior. If there was a story buried somewhere, I would do my best to obey the spirit – if not the letter – of the law, and make sure the tale was told.

By walking this fine line, I eventually generated one problem too many for the corporate office in Chicago, and on my sixty-fifth birthday, at 10:37 a.m., I was told that this might be a really good time to consider retirement. I remember it like it was yesterday.

At first, I felt a wave of relief that the pressure of an almost unbearable workload had been lifted from my weary shoulders. I had found myself in the same situation a number of times as a young man, but this one somehow seemed different. I always thought when I did call it quits that it would be on my terms, but now my walking papers were being handed to me by a management trainee who hadn't even been on the job long enough to qualify for the company health plan.

I did receive a severance package and there was a good chance I could be brought back with reduced responsibilities – with lower pay, of course. I've seen this scenario played out so many times before: My workload would slowly increase over time and I'd find myself back in the same old grind, but with only half the money.

Like any mature adult, I decided to ponder my situation with a heavy dose of culinary therapy. Most people suffering from depression might consider alcohol at this point, but my carbohydrate of choice was a large *carne asada* burrito at a Mexican cafe called Miguel's. With *mariachi* music blaring over the sound system and my personal food coma already in progress, I wasn't even aware of the guacamole slowly running down my wrist.

"Hey Mark, are you going to get some of that green slop in your mouth, or are you going to let it all fall into your lap?"

I looked up in surprise to see an old neighbor who had moved away several years earlier. "Alex, I thought you moved to Virginia or some place on the east coast," I replied as I hurriedly wiped my hands clean. "What are you doing back out here in Southern California?"

Alex McCormick had been something of a mystery when he lived in the old neighborhood. A large, muscular man with short-cropped red hair, he said he was a contract diesel mechanic working on long-range tuna boats and offshore oil-drilling rigs. He drove a large two-and-a-half-ton, dual-rear-wheeled Ford truck that doubled as his rolling machine shop. Meticulous in attire and the condition of his equipment, he presented an image not of a rough-and-tumble working man, but instead of a white-collar professional. In fact, many of his neighbors commented that his tools looked as if they had never been used.

At all hours of the day or night, a flatbed truck with a shipping container would pull up to his home and he would load his vehicle. Then Alex would often be gone for weeks at a time. Upon his return, he would host a huge neighborhood barbecue, complete with fresh fish and tall tales from his latest adventure.

"Oh, I'm just cleaning up a few loose ends from one of my business trips," he answered as he passed up an opportunity to shake my slimy green hand. "You still working at the radio station?"

I paused for a second before answering. "I was until this morning. They let me go."

"You're kidding!" he exclaimed. "Everyone knows you in San Diego. In fact, I'll bet your old station's competitors are already beating a path to your door with offers."

"Well, it just happened this morning," I returned. "In fact, I haven't even told my ex-wife yet. Pretty sure that's not going to go over very well. With the alimony and all, the money is going to be really tight. For me, it's not so much about the money, though – it's more of a shock and a blow to the ego to be let go this way. I really wasn't expecting it."

"Number thirty-seven, your take-out order is ready," a man behind the cash register called out.

Alex started to move to the counter, then turned and asked, "You planning on getting a job at another station, or have you ever considered trying something new?"

"I haven't thought much about it," I replied. "Like I said, I'm still trying to get over the shock."

"Ever thought about writing a book?" Suddenly, Alex sounded deadly serious.

"If I had a nickel for every story coming across my desk that would make a great subject for a book, I'd still be counting those coins as they slid me into my coffin," I said as I popped a hot-and-spicy carrot slice into my mouth.

"How about one that spans two thousand years, but is still relevant and influences today's events?" he queried. "You say you've seen stories come across your desk, but what if I could tie a bunch of them together? Sometimes I wake up in the middle of the night trying to make sense of things. Almost feels like I'm trying to read a treasure map without the code. Maybe with your investigative-writing background, we could work together and you could catch something I missed. You interested?"

"So why don't you write this bestseller of the past two millennia yourself?" I inquired.

Alex bit his lip as he carefully considered his answer and finally replied, "Well, it's complicated."

"Hmm, complicated," I parroted. "That usually means illegal."

"As I remember, you told me more than once that it's only illegal if you get caught," Alex returned. "I've tracked down some of the details, but a number of them took place so long ago that I can only make an educated guess as to what really happened. For some of the other things, I can only supply you with clues – you know, let you follow the trail and then draw your own conclusions. Anyway, if you're interested in hearing about my story, give me a call."

Alex pulled a tiny translucent cell phone from his pocket, held it close to his lips and whispered two sets of numbers. After the second set, the device glowed for a moment.

"There's a number on your phone where I can be reached twenty-four hours a day," he said. "I'll try to return your call within a few minutes. The second number is for a shipping company in Lisbon, Portugal. If you're curious, call it and ask if they ever operated any cargo vessels in the South Atlantic around March of 1944. Tell them you are especially interested in one particular ship, the *Southern Cross*. If they ask you why, tell them you are trying to track down relatives with the last name of Friedrick who fled Europe near the end of the war. It's really important that you get the names right."

"So you'll answer the phone in just a few minutes from anywhere in the world," I respond. "I have to get the names Friedrick and *Southern Cross* correct, or I don't get some kind of message. I just want to make sure my ears are catching exactly what you're throwing."

Alex smiled and said, "I know on the surface this might sound a little screwy, but I need to see if you're up for the job." He paused for a moment and added, "Just to show you what I'm bringing to the table, here's an example: What if, let's say for discussion's sake, my phone could get up close and personal with your phone. And then, for discussion's sake, let's say, like a giant sponge, it sucks up the contents of your memory chip and everything you stored – including any missed calls.

"By the way, that call you missed was from your ex-wife. I believe her exact words were, 'Hey, loser, just because you lost your job doesn't mean you can stop paying alimony.' You might want to get back to her for a little damage control. Seems she called the station to leave a message and was told you don't work there anymore. You are so on-the-money with this one, old buddy. She's not taking it very well."

After picking up his order and starting toward the door, Alex returned to my table one last time.

"I answer my phone in just a few minutes," he said, "because the receiver is in here." He tapped the side of his temple. "Here, I'll show you."

Placing the palms of both hands flat on the table, Alex smiled as my phone dialed a number all by itself. My ex-wife's land line rang five times and the answering machine came on. After the tone, I heard a message that sounded just like me – except I wasn't speaking.

I looked at Alex and said, "How the hell did you do that? Anyway, she knows me way too well to believe that load of crap."

He smiled and shrugged. "Oh, she'll believe it after some of the things you've written and done in the past. It is so far-fetched that no one could possibly make up a story like this: a sixty-five-year-old unemployed reporter working undercover while infiltrating a white supremacist group in Idaho. Yeah, she'll buy it – especially when she sees the pictures. And the best part is this: Now you don't have to explain to your ex- why you weren't at work. With that out of the way, you can concentrate on our project full-time."

"So, are you the reason I was fired?" I asked suspiciously.

"Nah, you didn't need my help with that," Alex assured me. "I didn't push you out the door, but I just might be able to get it reopened after we're finished. Who knows – I might even be able to help out with your alimony problem. But we only have two weeks to get this done."

Alex continued with renewed enthusiasm. "There's an address and directions on your phone to a cabin in Big Bear Lake just northeast of Los Angeles. Our little mountain retreat doesn't exactly show up on commercial GPS systems.

"At the entry on the front porch is a carved life-size wooden cigar store Indian. Around our office, he's known affectionately as Chief Snake Eyes, but officially, he's been designated as Alfred CS-26. I think a guy named Alfred was the technician who thought of putting the cameras in his eyes.

"Anyway, it's more than a tradition and always good luck to shake Alfred's hand when entering and leaving the cabin," Alex went on. "When you grasp his hand, be sure to look him squarely in the eye. This will give the security system a chance to read your facial profile, unlock the front door and make the house fully functional. Inside, you'll find everything you need to start writing 'The Great American Novel.'

"Cell phone coverage is really spotty up there, so your computer has some real nifty software that allows you to use it like a phone and send e-mails in the same conversation. It has a satellite link and is very secure. Oh, one last thing: It's really important that you shake Alfred's hand every time you enter or leave. You have to understand – he's a little sensitive and he can get pretty bitchy if he feels like he's been slighted. If that happens, some very bad things can start to happen really fast."

After his diatribe, Alex glanced at his watch. "It's almost two p.m. now, and since you're getting a late start with the traffic and all, it will probably take you at least six or seven hours to get there. If you figure on stopping for dinner, you should get to the cabin no later than ten o'clock. That will make it six tomorrow morning in Lisbon. Someone there will answer the phone."

Chapter 2. May 26, 2008 – Big Bear Lake, California

The smell of freshly brewed coffee wrenched me from my dream world. My curiosity had gotten the better of me the night before, so I drove straight to the cabin. Without stopping for dinner, I reached Big Bear around nine-fifteen. If I had been forty years younger and single, this hideaway in the forest would have been a slice of pure heaven.

At the end of a two-mile-long dirt road, an A-frame cabin nestled in a low-lying valley. The two-story glass entryway framed the tall ponderosa pines in the pale moonlight. When I turned off the ignition and stepped from the car, the sudden silence revealed a slight breeze rustling above me through the forest canopy. Alfred's eyes followed me intently as I climbed the three steps to the front porch and approached the door.

I grasped his carved wooden hand and a faint click signaled that the door was open. Stepping inside, I entered a small seating area that faced the front deck with a kitchen, single bedroom and bath located beyond it on the first level. Oversized rough-sawn beams supported the roof, while tongue-and-groove cedar panels covered every inch of wall space. Above the bedroom, an open loft held six bunk beds with three aligned on each side. To the east, a triangular window sat just below the massive ridge beam. A three-foot-wide staircase cut from native stone led to the loft and formed the upper portion of the interior fireplace. In all, the downstairs area could have been no more than a cozy seven hundred square feet.

A single bed and desk with a computer occupied the cramped lower bedroom. The monitor displayed the Lisbon phone number in its queue.

I walked back to the kitchen, opened the refrigerator and was pleasantly surprised to see that it was well-stocked. The basics were all there, including a case of my favorite beer, Blue Moon Belgian White Ale. Six a.m. might have been too early to start drinking in Portugal, but not here in America – and certainly not for me. I popped the cap off and took a long pull from the cold bottle, then tossed my coat on the bed, walked over to the computer and hit Enter on the keyboard.

The voice on the other end of the phone sounded confused as to why I was calling. Between the language barrier and my puzzling over exactly why I dialed the number in the first place, our conversation was punctuated by long, uneasy moments of awkward silence. I tried speaking to him in English and Spanish, but he was only fluent in Portuguese. Finally, through my broken Spanish, I was able to convey who and what I was trying to locate. When he realized that I was just looking for family members who fled Europe in World War II, his tone changed. He would begin a sentence and then trail off as he labored to find the words that also conveyed his own pain.

Then, on a hunch, I typed in Spanish, "By any chance, do you speak German?"

A single word appeared on my monitor, followed by a torrential response. "*Ja!* I understand it, but I don't speak the language *per se.* I learned to read it from old schoolbooks. It was a tragically painful part of my education – that is to say, I needed it to research the German archives. Their language was so different from ours, and since there was never anyone around to teach the pronunciation, I never learned to speak it. But I do understand it." Then, as an afterthought, he added, "To this day, I don't understand the people, but I do understand the language."

By keeping my German grammar and language as simple as possible, I helped to bridge our communication gap with a running series of e-mails.

"I only hope you are more fortunate in your search than I was," he wrote. "Our family was originally from Poland. When my sister researched our family tree, she tried to trace known living relatives from before the war. Many who were not able to leave Poland simply disappeared with no record.

"Most people are under the impression that only the Jews suffered. Our family is Catholic, not Jewish. I had a famous uncle who was a mayor, an important landowner, and a proud supporter of a free and independent Poland. He and his family were very outspoken, and as such became an inconvenient nuisance to the German political process.

"There are Jewish Holocaust archives available in many countries. These registries list names and nationalities. In our case, since we are not Jewish, we had more luck searching exit-and-entrance visa records of any countries that accepted refugees during those years."

As I thought about his last comment, three final sentences came across my screen.

"I'm sorry, but I see no record of a ship with that name or registry operated by our company in 1944. That is all I can tell you. Good luck."

After the call, I jumped from one website to another in an effort to piece together this most perplexing puzzle. Two more beers and seven hours later, I finally dozed off – that is, until the wonderful aroma of morning coffee pried my eyelids open.

"Hope you like it strong," Alex said as he blew the steam off of his cup and handed me another. As I leaned back in my chair, I yawned, stretched and rubbed the back of my neck to loosen the knotted muscles.

I took a sip and let the flavor of the steaming brew punctuate the bitter bouquet and high octane content. "Wow, that is strong. But don't get me wrong – strong is good. I really needed something this robust to remind me that I wasn't dreaming or imagining what happened last night."

"A good reporter is willing to dig deep enough for the *real* story," Alex declared. "This might take you down a different path than you're used to traveling, but you've been here before."

"That's not what I'm talking about," I returned. "I'm talking about this damned computer system. The database is far more extensive than anything I've ever had access to up to now. I found shipping schedules, immigration records in foreign countries, and even registry documents dating back seventy years. Who keeps records and information this extensive? This stuff is so old you'd almost expect to find it in some dust-covered box in an abandoned warehouse – not in a modern database."

"Well, I sure am glad the office equipment meets with your approval," Alex shot back with a grin.

"It's not just that it meets with my approval," I replied. "It's more than that. I've never worked with a connection this fast or an operating system this intuitive. It almost scares me to use the word 'smart,' but that's what this damned thing is.

"As fast as I can type in a search, the sites not only appear, but they do so in the exact order I need. My initial reaction was that maybe I'm smarter than I thought and I was just becoming more precise with my search parameters. But as the evening wore on, something even stranger happened: I would start typing a sentence, and before I could even complete my thought, the site would appear on the monitor. It's a frightening concept, but I believe your machine was learning how I think."

I took another long swallow from my mug. "Yep, strong is good."

"I think I know who these people are and how they're connected with the *Southern Cross*," I went on. "Oh, one other thing: Did anyone ever mention that you have an uncanny resemblance to Alfred on the front porch?"

"Oh yeah – it's a standing joke in the office," Alex laughed. "Good old Alfred is the last of the red-haired Irish Indians. So what did you find?"

"I took some advice from the clerk at the shipping company and searched for any visas with a last name of Friedrick," I answered. "I found a few, but the names and dates didn't match.

"Then, while I surfed another site, a new link popped up on the screen. I didn't understand the language, but it was followed by an English translation. What I ended up with was one hundred thirty-seven pages of names and information. Most were listed as German nationals or Eastern European. And each name had a last known location, date last seen, and case open or closed.

"Finally, after I got halfway down page fifty-seven, I found Carl and Elaine Friedrick and their two children. Their last recorded sighting was on March 23, 1944, when the *San Carlos* arrived in Buenos Aires, Argentina.

"At the bottom of the last page was the scribbled signature *Theocrat*. I did a search of code names, and I'm guessing by the look on your face that you already know who *Theocrat* was: Simon Wiesenthal, the famed Nazi-hunter. This isn't just a list of immigrants – these people are suspected war criminals!"

"Go on," Alex responded, now with a bit more enthusiasm.

"Okay, now you've given me a real mystery to solve," I declared. "So where did these people come from, anyway?

"Where do I start? One thing I was sure of was the ship's name. I looked up the specifications of the *Southern Cross* from its original blueprints. In April of 1931, construction was completed on the *Southern Cross* and her sister ship, the *San Carlos*, in Portsmouth, England. The two ships, built on contract and registered to a company in Panama, were identical in all respects except for one detail: The *San Carlos* had four passenger cabins located just behind the wheelhouse on the upper deck.

"Ten-and-a-half knots, or about twelve miles per hour, was the top speed of this older design," I continued. "Considering the distance from Buenos Aires to Genoa, which is a little over 2,500 nautical miles, the trip would have taken about nine days."

Alex laced his fingers together and let out a heavy breath. "You've lost me. Why do you make the assumption that they sailed from Genoa? They could have originated from any number of ports in occupied Europe."

"This is where I started guessing," I replied, "and your machine filled in the blanks. I researched the best escape routes from Europe to South America in World War II, and from which port the *San Carlos* was most likely to embark. Genoa popped up as the number one result 57% of the time.

"Then I looked for old newspapers from Buenos Aires dated March 23 and from Genoa on the fourteenth." After taking another long gulp from my morning brew, I smiled and said, "Then I hit the jackpot: The Buenos Aires newspaper *Clarin* had published an article and pictures about a German ship, the *Admiral Graf Spee*, that sank in the main channel off Montevideo in late 1939. Photographs showed part of the superstructure still visible above the water. The main thrust of the article referred to efforts to keep the channel as safe and navigable as possible. In the background of one of the photographs, a cargo ship could be seen entering the estuary. It was too far away to make out the name, but the silhouette with the four cabins matched that of the *San Carlos*.

"My obvious problem," I continued, "is that Argentine port-authority records show the Friedrick family disembarking from the *San Carlos*, not the *Southern Cross*. But here's the kicker: The exit visas show that they left Genoa aboard the *Southern Cross*."

Alex raised an eyebrow at this latest revelation. "You see my problem?" I asked. "They embarked on one ship, but debarked from another."

I continued with more confidence than ever, now that I had Alex's undivided attention. "At the time, because of military censorship, there were no newspaper photos available of the harbor at Genoa. But while scouring the British Air Force archives, I found a series of reconnaissance images. Nine days earlier, on March 14, a ship that matched the description of the *San Carlos* could be seen docked in Genoa at Berth 11.

"Using the British archives photos, I searched for a similar-shaped vessel in other ports. On March 9, I found the identical ship docked in Lisbon. Photos from the following day revealed that the ship had sailed with the outgoing tide.

"If we are to assume that the ship was capable of twelve knots, it would take about four days to reach Genoa. The British photos show this ship in Genoa on the fourteenth. All available Italian paperwork indicates that the *Southern Cross* was the ship in port at that time, yet it's clear from the photos that this ship was not the *Southern Cross*, but the *San Carlos*.

"Also, at that time, there was something odd going on with the German attack submarines in the South Atlantic," I went on. "Ships and their crews were normally rotated out for maintenance, so at least two-thirds of their U-boats were always on patrol. However, in March of 1944, Germany's entire South Atlantic fleet – except for one U-boat – was withdrawn for refitting and resupply. In all fairness, this can be the stormiest and nastiest time of the year, but the Allied convoys were still sailing.

"Then, a memo to Admiral Donitz, commander of German undersea boat operations, appeared in the German archives. It came directly from Heinrich Himmler, the head of the Nazi Party's secret police. Himmler ordered that there be no attacks in the South Atlantic between March 10 and March 22. Admiral Donitz strongly protested, but was overruled. Furthermore, only one U-boat was to remain on patrol, and that was *U-977*. That submarine was referred to in the memo as *Mitgehen-977*. Roughly translated, it means 'escort.'

"Then, on March 19, *U-977* reported that it sank a cargo vessel, the *Southern Cross*, and left no survivors. Once again, I repeat: Argentine records show the Friedrick family arriving in Buenos Aires on March 23."

"Anything else?" Alex inquired.

"Just one more detail," I replied. "At the beginning of the hostilities in World War II, there were only two ships with Panamanian registry bearing the name *Southern Cross*. Both were sunk within a few months of the United States entering the war. One was an inter-island steamer operating in the Philippines. It was sunk by the Japanese in January of 1942. The other, the sister ship of the *San*

Carlos, was sunk off Cape Hatteras, North Carolina, by *U-166* on March 11, 1942.

"Personally, I believe the *San Carlos* sailed from Lisbon on March 9 and, while at sea, someone changed her name to the *Southern Cross* before arriving in Genoa on March 14. Then, between Genoa and Buenos Aires, her name was changed back to *San Carlos*, and on March 19, the *Southern Cross* was reported sunk with no survivors by *U-977*. The *San Carlos* then arrived in Buenos Aires, and its passengers disembarked and disappeared into the local population. Obviously, the disappearance of whatever or whoever was on the *Southern Cross* was very important to someone."

I leaned back, interlaced my fingers behind my head and asked, "So, did I pass the audition?"

"Not bad," Alex responded with a nod. I knew I had made an impression. "There are clean clothes in the closet and you know where the shower is. I'll throw together some breakfast and we'll get started."

"Now, to make sure we're completely clear about this," I reiterated, "you did say I would get full publishing rights and credit, correct?"

"Yeah, we will need to check it before the final release," Alex replied, "but you were picked for your reputation. You have talent and credibility. The book, articles, personal appearances, you name it, along with the story of a lifetime … it will all be yours."

"See, that's exactly what I'm concerned about," I returned. "You make it sound so simple. So far, from what I can see of this story that you're allowing me to discover, it appears to have the possibility of irritating some really important and powerful people."

"Oh, we really hope so," Alex declared. "In fact, we're counting it. Is there a problem with that?"

"Not so much a problem," I said, "but it would be nice to know who I might infuriate."

Alex chuckled, "That's exactly what the other writers used to say at first – but they got over it."

"In that case, " I returned, "I'll take my eggs over easy."

Chapter 3. May 26, 2008 – Big Bear Lake, California

"Your story is simply about a journey," Alex explained as he moved the last of his eggs to the side of his plate. "It's not about people or ideas, but a substance.

"Originally, it was known as Greek fire," he continued. "The first record we have of the substance is around six hundred B.C. There it was used successfully as a weapon against the enemy fleets attacking Constantinople in what is now modern Istanbul, Turkey. By our best estimate, it was made from tree resins, sulfur, naphtha and other flammable substances which allowed it to burn underwater. We aren't really sure of the exact proportions or how it was produced – only that it was important enough at that time to be considered a state secret, so the formula was closely guarded.

"As more modern weapons were developed, the interest in the formula faded. It was lost, found and then lost again until, some nine hundred years later, it showed up in Alexandria, Egypt. From there, it somehow wound up in Germany just before the beginning of World War I.

"Mark, I need you to write me a fictitious, yet plausible, account of how this could happen," Alex clarified, "and we definitely have a deadline. I'll be back tomorrow morning and we'll pick up the story from there."

As Alex left me alone with my thoughts and my breakfast, I began to wonder what the hell I had gotten myself into. I walked back into the bedroom, pulled the chair up to the desk and stared at the blank screen. I tapped Enter on the keyboard and the plaintive query WHY appeared on the monitor. "Why am I here?" I asked myself aloud. "Why am I doing this?" Then it added a second word: ALEXANDRIA. Now the display read, "Why Alexandria?" Why, indeed ...

I decided to search for the history of Alexandria, Egypt. Around 331 B.C., Alexander the Great defeated the Persians, who had been the hated oppressors of the Egyptian people for two hundred years. After his victory, Alexander decreed that a new center of culture and learning would be established, and that the city would bear his name: Alexandria.

Now, I knew how my story would begin, and I also realized that my imagination would probably run wild as I fleshed out the framework. History, according to Carl, was about to be written.

* * *

After that night's victory celebration, as Alexander and his men slept, a vision came to the conquering hero: Before the great general stood Athena, the Greek goddess of wisdom, and Thoth, who occupied a similar position in the Egyptian pantheon. The two spoke as one.

"Alexander, tomorrow the first rays of the sun will reveal the location of your new city. The light of our wisdom will shine down upon it, and be its guide and protector. Make it worthy."

Alexander arose at dawn and, with his most trusted general and friend Ptolemy at his side, stood on the shore of the Mediterranean Sea. As they looked to the east and saw the sun creep above the horizon, its first rays broke through and illuminated a valley on a small, offshore island. The brilliant shafts of morning sunlight shone like a beacon, highlighting a small fishing village named Rhakotis.

"There, Ptolemy," the conqueror declared. "There you will build my city."

Alexander left Ptolemy in charge of the entire construction process. However, he would never set foot in the city that would bear his name. At the tender age of thirty-two, Alexander – the greatest conqueror the world has ever known and the only undefeated leader in history – died in Babylon, in what is now Iraq.

The great city, with its library and bustling economy, became the center of knowledge and commerce in the ancient world. Any ship entering its harbor was required to turn over any scroll or manuscript in its possession. A team of scribes carefully copied each document and returned an exact duplicate to the original owner, while the library took possession of the original.

This was how the formulae and writings of many of the great minds of the ancient world made their way to Alexandria. Among these works were those of a Greek mathematician and philosopher, Archimedes. The chronicle of that journey begins here.

Chapter 4. 415 A.D. – Alexandria, Egypt

Abianus stood in the colonnade of the great library. It was so much more than the first reference center in history. Not only was the Library of Alexandria an archive of the most gifted writers and arcane knowledge of the ancient world, but here in these hallowed halls, the greatest minds of the day also studied and debated science, religion, philosophy and mathematics. Palladius strolled past ornate fountains, fed by underground springs which flowed down from the mountains, and greeted his friend.

"Ah, I see you have decided to seek respite from the company of all your dead associates and give the living a portion of your time," Palladius said with a smile.

"You may be the living," Abianus retorted, "but you hardly have more to say – and in your case, it is hardly more entertaining."

"Now, don't get a broomstick up your tunic," Palladius countered. "I have as much respect for the masters of old as I do for the brilliant minds of today. Perhaps you should also widen your outlook. I realize that scribing duplicates and translating the writings of the followers of Jesus consumes your every waking hour, but here also are the works of the greatest minds of all time. A well-rounded and open mind could perhaps make you even more appreciative of your author of the universe."

"Ah, you never stop trying, do you, my friend?" Abianus asked.

Palladius chuckled and, with a more serious air, broached the subject that had plagued him since that morning. "You know I have the deepest respect for you, and for your philosophical and moral courage. Even more than that, I envy you for your blind faith. I know you, as a leader in the Coptic Christian community here in Alexandria, are completely devoted to your religion's teachings, but I also know you are from the soil of Egypt. For thousands of years, our ancestors tracked the sun, the moon and the stars in all the heavens, and worshiped them as their gods. We know they learned to predict the flooding of the Nile, and that their gods would appear in a certain place and time in the heavens. They filled their calendars, planted their crops and waged their wars by the positions of the stars. And they became the most powerful and dominant nation on Earth. They flourished for more than two thousand years, conquering their enemies by watching the skies. I ask you – was this an accident, or is there perhaps a system and an order to the universe?"

Palladius knelt to pick up a pebble from the courtyard. He rolled it in his fingers while observing its every curve and texture. "In your Bible, it says that your God created the heavens and the earth. Must he then have not also created the system which controls their movements? Abianus, I am your friend, and I say with all sincerity that we seek the same thing: the answers to all the eternal questions. Many different roads lead to Alexandria or Rome, but each path in its own way results in the same destination. There are great minds today and in the past that have struggled with these very questions. The power that you believe created the heavens also created our minds. We are not competitors, but simply travelers on that same journey. The door is open to the theater of great minds and thoughts here in Alexandria. At least take a seat and hear what they have to say."

Abianus took a long, deep breath, thought about his answer and finally replied, "As you ask, I will at least listen and consider their views."

A wry smile creased one side of Palladius's wrinkled face. "By all the gods of the universe, whatever their names, today I have made wondrous strides. The great Abianus himself has let the door open but a small crack, and perhaps allowed a little light to enter. You will see."

"I only said I would listen," Abianus cautioned. "Nothing more."

"You are aware of the smaller library annex near the Serapeum," Palladius continued.

"I know of the Serapeum," Abianus replied. "It is the temple of Hypatia and her cult."

"Hypatia is a great mind," Palladius explained, "and her cult, as you call it, only seeks the truth. Where you clash is that they seek this verity through intellect, not faith. You should view her as a fellow traveler, not a competitor.

"In the annex, there is an area that only the most trusted and select scholars may visit. Unlike the rest of the library, which is always open, it is locked and guarded at all times. Here, nothing may be removed or transcribed."

Palladius held his hand at eye level and revealed a golden ring. "Each item in this area has the mark of this ring, the Seal of the Library of Alexandria. There are writings in this room that have moved far beyond theory and philosophy. They now exist in the real world. You know of the legend of the fire that burns under the water?"

"That legend is common knowledge, like dragons and unicorns," Abianus scoffed. "This fable, it is said, twice destroyed the Roman and then Persian fleets, and saved Alexandria."

"I tell you, it is real and not a myth," Palladius defended. "Within the four walls of this chamber lie secrets and knowledge that the common man simply cannot imagine."

Palladius allowed a moment for this tidbit to sink in, then continued. "I can arrange for you to have access to this room. When the great Pharaoh Ptolemy, the direct heir of Alexander the Great, founded the library, he did so for the pure beauty and love of knowledge. But Ptolemy, and those who followed, also understood that knowledge was power. There is knowledge and the power that goes with it in this room. The secrets locked away in these confines could be used for good or for evil. The power there is that great. Here, there are secrets that the world may not as yet be ready to hear."

"But why?" Abianus inquired. "Why would you take the personal risk of allowing me to enter such a potentially dangerous place?"

"I sense a growing hatred in Alexandria," Palladius revealed. "The beauty and freedom of thought is beginning to vanish, slowly but surely replaced by bigotry and intolerance. Many of your Christian brethren are not as, shall we say, enlightened as you. Perhaps a highly respected man such as yourself could persuade others that differences in thought can be tolerated. Just because you do not believe in a particular ideal does not justify its being extinguished. Hypatia has said, 'Reserve your right to think, for even to think wrongly is better than not to think at all.'

"You will see a series of guards at various gates on the second level near the far left wing of the annex," Palladius continued. "The inscription above the door will read, 'The Place for the Cure of the Soul.'" He handed his ring to Abianus and said, "Show my signet to the guards and tell them Palladius has had cause to send you."

Palladius started to leave, but first he turned to face his colleague. "There are many texts in this room," he observed, "but you will be especially interested in the writings of the Greek mathematician Archimedes. They are carefully stored in a white stone box. Place the ring in the space on top where it fits and turn it to the right. It will unlock the box and all of its secrets.

"The text itself is written not on papyrus, but on thin hammered sheets of copper. You see, his words were meant to withstand the ravages of time. You will also find five coins in the box. They are reputed to be from a necklace worn by Diana, the Greek goddess of the hunt. It is said that whoever is in possession of all five of the coins has power over the forces of nature. Lightning, wind, storms, floods and even volcanic eruptions could all be controlled or used as powerful weapons.

"But be careful, my friend," Palladius concluded. "As you continue your journey, realize that there is a sublime beauty to mathematics and science when it unlocks a secret. You will see." With that, he left Abianus to his devices and his thoughts.

Abianus would not give his friend the pleasure of knowing that he had already stirred his curiosity. Twice already in the last two weeks, he had listened to speakers in the great hall. Today he was especially interested in a particular demonstration.

The floor-length curtains dropped as he entered and the light faded as though it were dusk. A fire danced in a small pit while a bellows kept the embers glowing brightly. An open cone had been placed over the pit and produced a beam of light which became more intense as the room darkened.

A curious array of spheres of various sizes hung from the ceiling on cables, and a hand crank connected to a number of different-sized gears sat directly below them. When the floor apparatus was engaged, it caused the orbs to rotate on tracks at different speeds and along different paths. With a single turn of the orator's handle, the spheres revolved around the center orb on different journeys at the same time! Abianus watched in amazement as the event took place. He was so fixated on the machinery and the shadows it cast that he barely heard the speaker's words.

While the complex mechanism shifted, the shadows changed shape and all the parts moved as in an elaborate dance. Each time the bellows pumped, sparks erupted from the cone like shooting stars. Then he saw it: The shadows on the orbiting spheres were not merely random shapes, but something he recognized. In that instant, as the dark silhouettes revealed the different lunar phases, a connection between the sun, the moon and the earth flashed before him. He didn't understand it completely yet, but Palladius was correct – there was a sublime beauty to this unlocked mystery.

Abianus hurried to the library annex next to the Serapeum. Along the way, he noticed crowds milling and gathering on side streets. He couldn't hear what was being said from where he was, but the reaction of the masses told him that some emotional chord had been struck.

At the rear of the annex, a guard armed with a long spear stood at attention in front of an ornate iron gate. As soon as Abianus began to speak, the guard's eyes flashed nervously from side to side while he watched the gathering crowd moving toward the temple entrance.

"The captain of the temple guard has ordered that no one should pass this day," the guard barked as he brandished the spear across his body and widened his stance to block any passage.

Placing his hand across his chest in a universal salute and show of respect, Abianus made sure that the sentinel saw his ring. "Son and protector of Egypt, I did not come here to question your captain's authority. Palladius has sent me and I have come with the blessing of the seal."

As soon as he noticed the embossed symbol on Abanius's finger, the defender of the gate came stiffly back to attention, moved aside and raised the iron crossbar. As he passed the sentry and entered the stairwell, Abianus whispered, "May the gods of Egypt and other lands watch over you."

As he stared straight ahead, the watchman answered, "And to you, sire. May the same gods watch over you, over all the wisdom and knowledge that you seek, and over this sacred athenaeum, which we will defend with our very lives."

* * *

Abianus hugged the side of the narrow stairwell as he made his way up to the second-story corridor. The low din of the crowds massing outside the temple was quickly turning into a roar. Splinters of sunlight spiked through elevated windows and pierced the shadows of the dim hall. As the light beams bounced off the stone columns, Abianus's movement caused tiny specks of dust to swirl and dance in the thin rays.

The chaotic sights, sounds and smells of a restless crowd began to drift up through the stairwell. Guards rushed past Abianus toward the stairs as he detected the first telltale scent of smoke. The Place of the Cure of the Soul was unlocked and unguarded.

In a room where Abianus would otherwise have wished to linger for hours, the gathering smoke reminded him that he had only minutes. His eyes darted around the room until he spotted what he was looking for. High on a shelf, like a white dove waiting to take flight from its lofty perch, the glistening alabaster box awaited. A beam of light from a window slit bathed it in a soft glow.

Standing on a bench, he carefully retrieved the box and slipped it under his cloak. Making his way through the rampaging crowds, Abianus immediately left to seek the refuge of his monastery deep in the Sinai Desert.

Chapter 5. 647 A.D. – Wadi El-Shaerel Taumi, Sinai Desert

Ibrahim slowly chewed the date and savored its sticky sweetness for as long as possible. The only water for miles up the *wadi*, or gorge, supported a small grove of date palms, and this was the last of the fruit. After today, the only food left would be the flat barley cakes. As the youngest of the Coptic monks, he had not yet developed the disciplined mindset needed to push aside all human needs and desires. While castration had provided a complete physical, if not mental, remedy for his carnal needs, the pangs of hunger in his stomach never completely dissipated.

It had been a twelve-day round-trip journey to the Gaza Strip on the Mediterranean coast from their monastery in the heart of the desert and the caravan returned late that afternoon with only meager supplies. The Moslem armies of Caliph Omar were laying siege to and taking control of all the major cities of Egypt – even the small villages. With numerous high-profile executions and no real defenses, there was almost no resistance. Markets were closed or confiscated by the conquering troops, and food was in short supply for inhabitants and strangers alike.

Ezra, a blind cleric in charge of the monastery, summoned Ibrahim later that day after the caravan's return. "My son, our brothers have returned with some very disturbing news," Ezra declared solemnly. "People on the coast from Gaza to Rafah are being given a dire choice: Become a Moslem convert or die a martyr's death for their faith and beliefs. Many have embraced the new religion, but a number of our brethren have refused. Their butchered bodies and sun-bleached bones line the coastal roads of Gaza as a reminder – and a warning. I believe they will search for us next, because of who we are and what we have."

The old man leaned over and picked up several scrolls, each three hand-lengths long and about one hand-length wide, wrapped in a golden cloth. "I have been informed that the caliph's men – the handmaids of the devil – burned the great library in Alexandria. Original versions of many mysterious and wonderful writings have been lost forever. In our possession are the exact translations made by Abianus, our founding patriarch, of some of the writings of the original twelve disciples and other great minds of the past. Almost three hundred years ago, Abianus carefully translated those writings into Greek and Coptic while in Alexandria, and brought them here for safekeeping."

Ezra closed his wrinkled eyelids for a moment to gather his thoughts before continuing. "This evening, as the sun sets, I need for you to climb up into the rocky cliffs and place these into one of the burial chambers. Near the top of the ridge, you will find an alcove chiseled from the solid rock. You will know it by the inverted cross of Saint Peter carved into the stone above the entryway. Inside, you will find a stone sarcophagus, carved from the rock itself, with the engraving *Abianus the Great.* Below the seal of our abbey's founder is this inscription: *The Place of the Cure of the Soul.* While the chamber was being dug, quartz crystals embedded in the ceiling and walls of the chamber were exposed. It was as if the very stars in the heavens had fallen to Earth all around you. This is where you will know to hide the scrolls."

"As you request, sire," Ibrahim said obediently, "but must it be done tonight? There is a strong wind building which will turn bitterly cold after sunset, and even though there is a full moon, the path is narrow and more dangerous in the dark. I can go now and …"

"No, it must be done tonight," Ezra interrupted. "As the full moon rises, light will spill through cracks in the wall and in turn illuminate four of the crystals above the sarcophagus. It will take only a few minutes, but as each becomes its own tiny star, you must place your hand on that crystal and press against it when it glows. After you have placed your hand on the fourth crystal, the engraved panel will slide open. You must move quickly once this happens. It will close in a short time and the mechanism will not allow it to be reopened until the next full moon. After it is done, you will return and speak nothing of it to any of the brothers.

"Come back at dusk and you will find the scrolls wrapped in an old cloak inside the back entrance," he concluded. Even though Ezra was quite blind, Ibrahim felt the old man's gaze as if the vacant pupils were staring into his very soul.

"You must swear to never tell of the existence of the chamber, even under the threat of death," Ezra warned. "For more than three hundred years, only the abbots of this monastery have known of the chamber's secret, and each of them has only revealed it once in their lifetime to their successors. It is only because of my blindness and what I fear is coming that I now break this vow."

* * *

Abdul-Aalee, which means "servant of the most high," took his name and duty quite seriously. He traveled the coastal road while converting the masses with his sword – all at the behest of his master, Caliph Omar.

When the Moslems captured the city of Alexandria, Abdul-Aalee asked what to do with the library's collection of writings. Omar's answer mirrored Islamic doctrine: "If the writings agree with the Koran, they are not needed. If they do not, they are heresy. Either way, burn them all."

To save his own life and curry favor with the caliphate, a tax collector in Gaza told Abdul-Aalee of the legend of the monks in the heart of the Sinai who were protectors of the true word of the apostles. Exact transcriptions and translations of the original writings in the people's own language were said to be housed in the desert monastery. As in Alexandria, these were also to be destroyed.

While trailing the small caravan during the six-day journey, Abdul nearly lost them twice – once when the sands gave way to the stony soil of the wadi, and again when the wind obliterated their trail. But when he noticed the birds, he was able to follow them through the maze of canyons. Now, as he looked down at the small oasis where the gorge spilled out at the base of the red sandstone cliffs, he saw local inhabitants clothed in their simple garb, as well as the distinctive Coptic crosses that adorned their mud-and-stone buildings.

The sun was just beginning to paint the walls of the wadi crimson with its evening glow. Red hues on boulders faded into shades of pink and orange, and as the sun sank toward the horizon, the shadows lengthened and colors morphed like an evaporating sunset. It was then that he spotted a lone figure making his way amongst the rocks.

His young lieutenant, Usaamah, or lion, came up beside him and whispered in a low voice, "There is but one God, and the men are prepared to do his will."

Abdul whispered, "I have dealt with these Christian monks in Gaza before. I know them – they would choose death rather than forsaking their beliefs. We will kill them quickly where they stand. While they are distracted with preparing their evening meals, or when they kneel to pray, we will strike. Look, there is one in the rocks, making his way up into the cliffs," he said as he pointed to the movement halfway up the sandstone face. When Ibrahim's head emerged from behind a boulder, Abdul cautioned, "Conceal yourself in the shadows and make sure he does not escape."

The lion slid back down to where the remaining soldiers had gathered, then delivered his master's instructions and hurried off after his victim.

It was over quickly. As the brothers knelt for their evening prayer before dinner, the Moslem assassins sprang silently from the shadows. Ezra stood in front of his flock with his hands raised toward the heavens, but the blind cleric could give no warning of the impending massacre.

* * *

Ibrahim made his way past the many openings which served as the final resting places of the men who had so faithfully served the monastery in years past. Ordinary monks such as himself were buried in the lower caverns, while the summit was considered the most holy, and as such was reserved for the most important leaders. Although they were Christians, old beliefs from their Egyptian heritage still lingered and so figured into their daily practices.

There were no pyramids with elaborate burial chambers in which to inter the honored dead, so they used the mountain as their sepulcher. The elevation at which you were laid to rest on the holy mountain was a testimonial to your importance and stature. After all, who could doubt your prominence if you were closer to the heavens – and therefore to God?

As Ibrahim ascended the narrow rocky path, he noticed that many of the openings appeared to have been formed naturally by the wind and occasional rain. When he reached the summit, he came upon it: a narrow opening that faced to the east. He stood at the fissure and looked out upon the fading light of the desert and the wadi. Ibrahim turned his body sideways and slid through the aperture. Stone chips, remnants of the original craftsman's labor, still littered the floor. He stepped into the chamber and there, carved out of the living rock itself, lay the sarcophagus.

The square room was no more than fifteen feet on a side, with an uneven ceiling about eight feet high. As Ezra had said, small quartz crystals covered the entirety of the natural stone surfaces.

Alone in the chamber, Ibrahim felt the approaching darkness wrap him in its murky blanket as he waited for the moon to rise. The wind built in intensity and created an eerie whistling sound as it blew through the openings. How was he to see in this blackness? The answer came soon enough.

As the moon rose above the desert horizon, its pale light flooded through the entrance and crept across the stone floor in a steadily advancing beam. When it reached the rear wall, the rising stream of moonlight climbed up the angled panel below the sarcophagus and exposed the words: "The Place of the Cure of the Soul." When fully illuminated, the panel reflected the light toward the ceiling. Crystals captured the reflection and glowed like a thousand glimmering lights in the night sky.

The dark, forbidding hole in the ground was transformed by a pale golden radiance and – as Ezra had explained – one by one, the crystals on the wall began to gleam as the moon began its journey through the heavens. The higher the moon rose, the more its light found different openings in the wall, splinters of moonlight each illuminating individual crystals above the sarcophagus.

Ibrahim marveled as the elaborate mineral formation glowed in an array of vivid colors, each a little different from the rest. When he placed his hand over them and pressed as instructed, the crystals felt warm. Light would slide between his fingers and give his hand a pink, fleshy glow. He couldn't help but think how fortunate he was to even be here and to view what only a select few had ever witnessed before.

As Ibrahim placed his hand over the final crystal, the stone panel slid to the side with a low, grinding growl that he could hear even above the whistling din. As the pale moonlight reflected from the ceiling and illuminated the interior of the chamber, Ibrahim placed the two scrolls on top of the others stacked neatly to one side. It was then that he saw the box and the ring. They were objects of such beauty that he couldn't resist touching and then removing them for closer examination.

Ibrahim slid the gold band onto his finger. He had never before worn jewelry of any kind, and was surprised by the weight and feel of the precious metal. Carved from alabaster, the box had a soft, almost oily, feel and texture. The stone was of a thickness that didn't reflect the moonlight so much as it absorbed the rays. In fact, it very nearly appeared to glow.

Ibrahim had just started to raise the lid when the scraping sound of a footstep on the stone chips behind him caught his attention. Time had run out for the startled acolyte and his recently acquired mechanism. As the stone panel slid back into place, the lion's sword slashed downward and through Ibrahim's exposed neck. Death was almost instantaneous, and as his lifeless body slumped face down and away from the assassin's blade, the alabaster box came to rest under the corpse, where it would lie untouched and undetected for more than 1,200 years.

Chapter 6. March 1890 – Wadi El-Shaerel Taumi, Sinai

Desert

As they drove their camels even harder, Anai and Mered El-Mouggi kept glancing over their shoulders at the approaching wall of windblown sand. They raced to escape the *sirocco* and seek the protection of a wadi or canyon – any shelter from this deadly desert nightmare.

The two brothers spent many a day and night exploring the arid Sinai wilderness, and were keenly aware of the danger bearing down on them. These sandstorms or El Khamisin winds, with their gusts up to ninety miles per hour, blew intermittently in the spring. Swirling winds came from the south and whipped up choking clouds of dust from the desert. This dust was so fine that it would make its way into the slightest opening. It dried the mouth, accumulated on the mucus in the nostrils and lungs and, worst of all, dried the eyes. The grating pain of simply blinking with a layer of grit under one's eyelids was almost unbearable and was known to drive grown men insane.

As spring gave way to summer, the weather patterns began to change. The wind would blow in from the north off the Mediterranean Sea and even bring with it an occasional rainstorm.

The brothers' knowledge of the area was almost legendary. Their cousin, who worked at the recently completed canal through Suez, introduced them to a newly formed British company exploring for oil in the Sinai. The young company, Anglo-Egyptian Petroleum, had made its first substantial discoveries in the Gulf of Suez. Samuel Marcus, the young German engineer they escorted, was their responsibility and represented their ticket to a bright future. Here was a real job with an important foreign company paying in British pounds. This was better than any dream.

The fair-skinned European was nice enough, but he wasn't much for conversation. "Mr. Sam," as they referred to him, was only truly interested in his rocks and sand. When he did speak, it was about the location of certain types of rock formations or the coarseness of the local terrain. If he wants sand and gravel, Anai thought, he'll have more than his fill if we do not soon find shelter.

The wadi descended to a flat plane, with sand dunes stretching to the horizon in both directions. Directly in front of the entrance, the steep wall of advancing sand rose to over seven hundred feet high and curved into a colossal horseshoe shape by the funneled winds of the canyon.

This was the site of the fabled wells of Wadi El-Shaerel Taumi. Centuries of neglect and drifting sands had obliterated nearly all signs of the well and human habitation. Here and there, a few exposed rocks and scattered mud bricks broke the endless expanse of sand that lay before them. Wind and occasional flash floods had eroded the walls of the sandstone gorge in many places, leaving pockets large enough for a man to find shelter.

The brothers noticed the depressions in the sandstone as they quickly unloaded and hobbled the camels. The animals knelt and instinctively turned their backs to the approaching storm. Samuel turned and was about to speak when he realized that the men had knelt for their evening prayers. However, the timing seemed a bit odd. So far on their journey, the brothers did not seem particularly concerned with religious observances. Obviously, given the current circumstances, the approaching storm served as a grim reminder of their own mortality.

As they arose, Mered seriously observed, "We only have enough food and water for six days. If this is a strong storm, the wind could blow for weeks. In this place, we prayed to Allah and all the ancient gods of Egypt. At one time, there was even a Christian monastery here. You should also pray to your Christian god."

Samuel put one of his blankets into a depression to cushion against the rocks, then covered himself head to toe with his other blanket. He wiggled and squirmed to push himself as far back into the opening as possible. Finally, he took his guide's advice and, for the first time in many years, he began to pray.

At first, the sandstorm reminded Samuel of a whisper in the distance, but suddenly it was upon them with all the sound and fury of a herd of stampeding animals. Then came the wind. Sand and small pebbles pummeled the blanket mercilessly as he tried to shrink deeper into the crevice. Samuel squeezed the blanket until his hands cramped, and he made a silent promise to himself to be a better person if only the fury of the winds would stop – and if only he'd survive.

After several hours, the intensity of the black blizzard diminished. Samuel could still hear the howl of the raging wall, but now it sounded different. It seemed to come from a different direction. He kept his blanket snugly wrapped around himself until the first faint glow of the approaching dawn crept under the edges.

As he peeled away the blanket's edge, the accumulated sand slid off like a miniature avalanche. In just one night, the landscape had been changed completely. The choking tempest still gusted, but now it came from the north.

The events of the past evening had been quite traumatic, indeed. However, the transformation of the dunes at the canyon entrance was even more startling. No longer a massive sand structure with occasional exposed rock, but now red sandstone cliffs that the shifting winds revealed had been buried below. The intermittent patches of sand reminded Samuel of Germany in the spring, when the warm days melted all but the last few remaining pockets of snow sheltered in the shadows.

Anai and Mered pushed aside their blankets and stretched. Their smiles reflected the simple pleasure – and relief – of having been spared from the sirocco's wrath. The two laughed as they pointed at Samuel's shoes. Where leather was exposed to the elements, the tanned finish had been sandblasted away.

The two brothers set about preparing breakfast and, after the previous night's escape, all three agreed it would be a good idea to head back toward the coast.

Ever the geologist, Samuel stretched while surveying the formerly hidden sandstone cliffs. Near the top, an opening in the rock face caught his attention. As he examined the area, his eyes kept returning to the same spot.

Samuel had learned to trust his instincts. That feeling in the pit of his stomach was, after all, how he had stumbled upon those oil deposits at Suez. If something didn't feel or look quite right, young "Mr. Sam" believed it deserved a closer look.

Grabbing a canvas sample bag and shovel, he began making his way up the face between the boulders. Several times, he stooped and shoveled sand off the path where it had been sheltered from the wind.

Anai and Mered squatted and ate barley cakes as they watched him pick his way between the rocks.

Near the top, Samuel stood for a moment to admire the view. The early morning heat was already causing objects to shimmer in the distance. He was just about to toss aside the next shovelful of sand and continue onward when the inverted cross carved above the opening in the rock caught his eye.

Squinting to look through the exposed opening, Samuel saw what looked to be a large object with unnaturally straight lines against the back wall. Geology and his own observation had taught him that certain shapes could be formed by the elements, but others required the use of tools.

A rush of adrenaline shot through Samuel's body as he hurriedly pushed the sand aside. A man accustomed to the exhilaration of discovery, he still could not help but feel a sense of euphoria. Sliding through the opening, he closed his eyes tightly to acclimate them to the darkness. In the faint light, he squinted and realized that the straight line was actually the edge of a large stone box. Could this be a coffin?

Shuffling his feet while slowly feeling his way forward, Samuel bumped against something on the ground. Moving aside to allow more light from the opening, he discovered human bones protruding from the sand. The spinal column just below the head was severed and inside the ribcage, partially buried in the sand, the square corner of what appeared to be a small box was barely visible.

Samuel reached down for the tiny container, trying not to touch the ribs, but they fell aside with the slightest contact. He lifted the coffer into the small shaft of light and blew away the sand from the top to more clearly see the words carved into its lid.

The writing was Greek, or similar to it. Of that he was certain. Samuel recognized this form of writing from his visits to the museums in Alexandria and Cairo. For the most part, the words and symbols were a complete mystery – except for one.

Samuel was a geologist and they paid him to make discoveries, but this was different. In his hands he held an object from a different time, a different culture and a different way in which the world was viewed. The word he recognized was *Bibliothekai* – Greek for repository or library.

A seal was carved into its lid. It appeared to be of Greek origin. A classical human facial profile was flanked by a cobra and a vulture.

Samuel knew that these were the symbols of the two ancient Egyptian kingdoms of the upper and lower Nile. The upper kingdom included the highlands of Ethiopia with its wealth of gold, while the lower contained the Nile delta with its agricultural bounty bordering the Mediterranean Sea. Together, their treasures of gold and grain made them two of the most powerful kingdoms of the ancient world. This seal was a symbol of Greek dominance and the uniting once again under its rule of the two ancient Egyptian kingdoms.

Bending over to pick up the canvas bag, Samuel noticed the sunlight reflect off something to the side of the skeleton. Carefully brushing away the sand, he saw a ring resting on a bony finger. He carefully removed it and held it up to the light for closer inspection. Moments earlier, he had seen this exact same image. He placed the signet into the depression on the alabaster box's lid. It fit like a baby in a cradle.

Chapter 7. 1911 – Essen, Germany

Erhard Biermann III had become an embarrassment to his family. His father and grandfather were driven men with distinguished backgrounds in politics, the military and, last but not least, the art of brewing. However, at fifteen, young Erhard could think of nothing better than to sneak off for a wild roll in the hay with any one of the numerous young women employed at the estate.

His favorite, however, was the cook's helper, a forty-eight-year-old widow who thought the boy's amorous advances cute at first – until she realized how serious he had become. At the very least, a secret affair with the master's son would guarantee her job security as she dreamed of a chance at the real prize: the widowed patriarch of the family, Erhard the Eldest.

She smiled to herself as she remembered the first time she slipped away with the youngest Erhard down to the wine cellar. He was so energetic and excited. It was over almost before it began. Over time, she taught him focus and, more importantly, the concept of discretion. With his youthful exuberance channeled, she hoped to control her young lover.

But being a Biermann had made young Erhard headstrong, so he never quite grasped the idea of such prudence. He was, after all, his father's son, so he had come to view the estate's employees like any of the family's other possessions.

The final straw came when his father caught him in the tackle room with the stablemaster's daughter – and the following day with the stablemaster's wife! Sleeping with commoners – the help, no less – finally pushed Erhard II over the edge.

That night at dinner, the elder Erhard ate in somber and deadly silence. Before the table could be cleared, young Erhard arose to leave.

"Sit down!" the father barked at his wild child. "I have something to say to you." Looking toward the maid as she entered the room, he said, "Leave us."

When the two were alone, he continued. "Some of these people have worked here for twenty years and I consider them more than employees. They are not only personal friends, but almost family. I will not have you taking advantage of them and embarrassing me in the process. You are on notice, young man. If anything ever happens like this again, I'll send you off to the naval war college in Denmark so fast you won't know what hit you. Is that perfectly clear?"

Without waiting for a response, he went on. "Tomorrow I will be leaving for Berlin with Herr Horton and we will be gone for two days. While I am away, you are in charge of this estate. I expect you to conduct yourself with the dignity that befits a head of this household.

"The pheasant hunt will occur two days after I return," he concluded, "and Herr Horton has supplied an additional thirty birds from his personal flock to help stock our fields. While I am on travel, your only duty is to watch over the birds. I have given the help those days off – and that includes all of your dalliances. No one will be here, so there should be no distractions. You will be alone with your thoughts. You may leave now."

As he exited the room, Erhard heard his father's parting comment. "I hear Denmark is very cold this time of year. It is said that there are only two seasons: winter and May 25."

* * *

Sitting up in bed, Erhard remembered his father's words and a chill ran down his spine. He hadn't even thought about the birds for almost a day-and-a-half.

When Herr Horton's driver came to pick up his father, the cook's helper came out of her hiding spot in the wine cellar. What had begun as a morning frolic ended as a full eighteen hours in his father's bedchamber.

Erhard reached for his bathrobe as he rolled over and pulled back the bedclothes. The rustling covers awakened the cook and she reached over for him. He pushed her away and finished throwing on his robe, then ran out to the pheasants' holding pen behind the stables.

As he stood in the bright moonlight, Erhard could only shake his head in disbelief as he uttered, "Ich werde so geschraubt (I am so screwed)." Dogs or marauding wolves had broken into the holding pens while he frolicked with the help. All that remained were a half-dozen carcasses, some scattered feathers and a blood-stained enclosure. Any remaining pheasants escaped or were carried off.

Pacing back and forth with his hands on either side of his head, he kept muttering, "What am I going to do, what am I going to do? I've got to replace those birds before my father returns tomorrow."

Erhard reluctantly decided to ask for help from Herr Horton's two sons, Reimar and Walter. Since their father had provided the original birds, the brothers could help him obtain replacements.

Since he was not exactly on the best of terms with the Horton boys, he knew that any help would cost him dearly. Erhard gathered a few items for barter – or bribe – and raced across the moonlit fields toward the Horton estate.

He was right – it was not going to be an easy sell. Besides being stubborn and bullheaded, Erhard was also quite large for his age. He had been the schoolyard bully since their elementary days and the Horton brothers were two of the main targets of his torment. Small for their age, and with a love for academics and science, they were easy prey.

Breathing deeply from the run to the Horton house, Erhard gently rapped at the brothers' bedroom window. After the third knock, the shades parted slightly and Reimar, seeing who it was, whispered, "Go away, *ungeheuer*." They had taken to calling him "monster" while in school.

"I've got to talk to you right now," Erhard begged. "It's important."

"Come back in the morning," Reimar replied as the shades closed.

Erhard persisted. "No, this is really serious. It can't wait until tomorrow."

Reluctantly, Reimar agreed. "Very well – go to the back entrance."

When the Horton boys emerged, Walter put his finger to his lips and they walked with him behind the stables.

"So what is so important for you to come over here at this time of night?" Walter demanded. "In fact, what brings you to come here at all?"

The words flew out of Erhard's mouth like water from an open ball cock as he told his incredulous tale. "Then father said if anything else happened, he would send me away to a military school – a naval academy! No more women, and I'd be seasick for certain. I get queasy if I even watch someone stir a cup of tea. If I can't get you to help me, I don't know what I'll do. I know we've had some mild disagreements in the past, but I really do need your help."

The brothers stood silently and tried to keep from smiling. Were they finally about to rid themselves of this pompous pain-in-the-ass? The more Erhard talked, the more desperate he made his situation sound. The Hortons could hardly wait to hear how he planned to get out of this one.

"So what I really need is for you to give me another thirty pheasants," Erhard said in a matter-of-fact tone.

"You are joking," Walter said while trying not to laugh out loud. "Our father would skin us alive if thirty birds went missing. Not a chance."

"Listen, I need those birds and you're going to give them to me!" Erhard spouted as his face turned beet red. "Do you understand?"

"What are you going to do – beat them out of us?" Walter asked as he smiled at Reimar.

Erhard clenched his teeth and took a deep breath. "You're right – I can't expect this to be a one-way exchange. I brought some things to trade." He held out an old three-ring binder. "This is the secret brewing recipe for our family's beer. It has been handed down for nearly ten generations."

"Unless you've forgotten, our fathers are the best of friends – and business partners as well," Reimar reminded the desperate Erhard. "Your father supplies us with beer as part of one of their agreements. If that's all you've got, you're out of luck." The boys were really enjoying the sport of grinding down their childhood nemesis.

"I also brought this," Erhard said as he extended a white stone box toward Walter. The brothers looked at it for a moment and handed it right back to him. "No, just wait," Erhard pleaded. "It's really old and has strange things inside. It was in a storage trunk at my uncle's house and this ring was tied to the top. It has to be worth a lot of money."

"So now you want to bribe us with something you stole from your uncle?" Walter inquired.

"He won't need it," Erhard replied. "He died more than twenty years ago from some kind of fever he caught in Egypt. His sister, our aunt, cared for him when he returned from Cairo. After he passed away, she continued to live in his house in the south of Spain. She died last month, and all of their belongings were shipped here and put into storage in our basement. I bet it's really old and rare. Here, take it," Erhard said pushing the box back toward the boys.

Walter stared at the box and then at Reimar. Then he looked up at Erhard and slowly spoke. "This is the deal: You give us the box and the brewing procedure," he said as he took the brewer's notebook from Erhard. "For that, we will bring you thirty pheasants in the morning."

Erhard nodded in agreement – and sighed in relief.

"That's not all," Walter continued. "If you ever bother my brother or me again, we will tell your father the whole sordid story." Holding the book up to Erhard's face, Walter smiled and added, "And this book is our proof. That's the deal. Take it or leave it."

Erhard concurred eagerly and said with controlled anger, "I'll expect you early in the morning."

"You know, Erhard, if you don't keep your end of the bargain and they send you off to military school in Denmark, the fact that there are no girls around won't make much difference," Walter mused. "For ten months out of the year, it is so cold up there that your manhood will probably look like a tiny blue robin's egg in the spring. Just keep that in mind."

As Erhard walked away, Reimar smiled at his brother. "'A little blue robin's egg' – that was a nice touch."

Walter punched his brother on the arm and grinned. "We won't go over with the birds too early. He still needs to sweat a little for all of the grief he has brought upon us over the years. Now, let's see what is in this box."

Chapter 8. May 27, 2008 – Big Bear Lake, California

The phone rang twice before the receptionist answered.

"Assistant Director Wood's office," came the crisp salutation. "How may I help you?"

"Alex McCormick to speak to the A.D."

"He's been expecting your call," the receptionist responded, "and he asked me to put you through immediately *if* you were in a good mood. Otherwise, I was to leave you on hold."

"Well, I think you can put me through, Natalie," Alex returned with a grin. "You already know what kind of mood I'm in after being up all night."

After a few seconds of dead air, another voice greeted me. "Hey, how's your mystery writer doing?"

"Actually, it's a pretty compelling story he's got going so far," Alex answered. "If I didn't already know the ending, I'd be tempted to read it myself."

"Well, don't go overboard," Mr. Wood cautioned. "Have you been able to find out who put that bug in the computer?"

"Not yet," Alex replied. "The encryption is really first-rate. It has some form of floating code that changes and fluctuates several times per second. If you don't have their 'magic box' with the specific algorithms, reading the thing is impossible. Not to mention that it's embedded in a BBC news broadcast going out all over the world. At any one time, there could be as many as twenty million people listening. Tracing it is just not an option."

"Wow, I feel better about this already," Mr. Wood mused facetiously. "You don't know who they are, where they are or how they bugged your computer. Just humor me with the Cliff Notes condensed version: What *do* you know?"

"Well, we know that someone is reading our unfolding novel," Alex said, "and my bet is they are becoming extremely interested.

Someone hacked into the fictitious database we set up and the only way they would have known about certain details is if someone on their end had actually read the transcript. We'll just keep laying out clues from the database our author is using to see who reacts to them. The trick is, like a little bird, to keep them following the bread crumbs down the path until they show their hand."

"Well, that's just fascinating, Mr. McCormick," Mr. Wood said. "Are you meeting with Ryan Lessley tomorrow?"

"Yep, bright and early at eight a.m.," Alex replied. "I'm sure we'll both be on our best behavior after flying all night."

"Now, you two boys play nice," Mr. Wood warned. "I really don't care what you have to do, but you get Lessley on board and get him moving. As for your other mystery friends, this is *my* condensed version: You find them, and you find them quickly."

Chapter 9. May 27, 2008 – Big Bear Lake, California

Alex walked slowly into the cabin. He was still wearing yesterday's clothes. It looked like someone had had a long night.

I looked at him and smiled. "So, you have a good night's sleep?

"Just about the same as you," came the curt reply.

"So, Alex, you want to see what I have so far?" I inquired.

"I've already seen it," he answered. "A little bird gives me an updated copy. I think you're catching on to this writing thing. You might even have a future with it."

"I've got to say, Alex, it really warms my heart to hear you heap all this praise upon my unworthy shoulders," I razzed. "It just really fires me up."

"Well, it's good to know you're a self-starter, because I did really like it," Alex countered. "But we do need to stay on schedule.

"The next part of the story deals with the Friedricks and how they escaped from Europe with the formula," he continued. "I also need you to come up with a plausible reason for why our formula is now able to block different wavelengths in the electromagnetic spectrum. Things like standard communication radio frequencies, radar, sonar … maybe even X-rays, too. You know, just common, everyday, run-of-the-mill stuff. I don't need you to explain how it works – just give me a believable story of how someone might have stumbled onto it."

"That's all?" I asked. "Don't I need to come up with a cure for cancer – or herpes, maybe? Perhaps in my spare time I could throw in a solution to world hunger?"

"Nope, and I'll even give you two days on this one," Alex responded to my sarcasm with his usual aplomb. He even managed to sound magnanimous about the deadline. "You might want to fit in some sleep along the way, but it's really important that we make as much progress as possible."

"Well that is kind of you, I must say," I shot back. "Hey, can I get some more of those spicy chicken wings? Those suckers are really addictive."

"Sure, I'll have some sent over," Alex said. "Oh, there is one other thing: If at any time your screen starts flashing the message *ALFRED SAYS IT'S TIME TO GO*, that means our security has been breached. I'm not saying that it's ever happened, but you should be prepared."

As he walked over to the closet, Alex slid the door open. "I don't know if you noticed or not, but the downstairs bathroom is actually inside the bedroom. In case of an emergency, the bedroom door will close and lock automatically, and a floor panel will slide open under this wooden box here in the closet. In case you are in the can, we don't want you to get locked out.

"There is also an air line and an emergency exit chute leading down to a tunnel. Motion-activated sensors will turn on a row of lights as you move through it. The shaft itself is about two hundred yards long and ends at a large metal door in the back of a maintenance room for the ski lifts. Don't bother trying to open the door, though. It can only be opened from the inside. If the alarm is triggered, someone will meet you there. And lastly, once you start down the tunnel, you can't go back. It will completely seal behind you in a matter of minutes."

Leaning back in my chair, I mused, "Funny that you mention security. I pictured you folks as more top-of-the-mountain, hold-the-high-ground kind of guys. I'm not really complaining, though. This secluded valley is really beautiful, but you can't see anyone until they're right on top of you."

"Don't worry," Alex said. "We have our electric eyeballs working twenty-four hours a day. Anyway, for us, this valley has other hidden benefits."

"Well, I'll certainly try to keep my bathroom breaks short," I replied, "and I'll keep an extra pair of shoes next to the closet."

"That's probably a good idea," Alex offered. "Alfred is extremely efficient, but his timing is lousy and he has absolutely no sense of humor."

Chapter 10. May 27, 2008 – Big Bear Lake, California

I paced back and forth in my bedroom like a caged lion. I just couldn't get that tunnel out of my mind. Why didn't Alex tell me about the escape route on the first day? He said we had two weeks, but had something changed? When he left, he said he would return in two days. From my end, nothing was different – as far as I knew. I couldn't put my finger on it, but something didn't seem quite right. Then an unnerving possibility occurred to me: What if Alex had told me about the tunnel not because we have two weeks, but only two *days*?

Up until the last few moments, I had assumed that I was insulated from whatever was going on around me. If my guardian angel Alex McCormick could read my story, maybe someone else had access to it as well. Driven with a new sense of urgency, I quickly sat down at the computer, more determined than ever to pound out my story as quickly as possible. But I now had the unshakable feeling that I had somehow become the bait in some kind of twisted trap. That would be a great title for my book: *Good Things Don't Happen to Bait.* The only trick now would be to live long enough to see the manuscript make it to print.

Chapter 11. January 21, 1923 – Essen, Germany

At first, the flames glowed with a faint flicker. Then, like a brook winding through a stream bed, the fire followed the trail of black liquid down the main hallway and into each room of the old mansion. When it reached the foot of the curved staircase and the large puddle of the inky substance that awaited, it erupted with an audible *whoosh*. The blaze quickly ignited the stairway's carpet runner and centuries-old wooden railing. Area rugs in adjacent rooms were devoured by the conflagration, and as the fire grew, the intense heat caused the matching rugs and curtains to smolder and catch even before the inferno reached them.

While the exterior of the three-hundred-year-old structure had been built out of stone from local quarries, the interior held little more than wood covered with plaster. It was only a matter of minutes before the intense heat made its way through this meager cover and to the heart of the downstairs walls.

For the French Army officers who commandeered the house as living quarters, the smoke and clamor of collapsing walls caused absolute panic, and the now-raging pyre on the staircase had sealed their easiest avenue of escape. Slow to rise from a night of drunken revelry with select vintages in the old estate's wine cellar, they began to realize the sobering thought of burning alive.

Furniture flew through upstairs windows as the men cleared away jagged shards of broken glass dangling from the window frames. They jumped to safety some twenty feet below and huddled together. Some with broken bones from the fall and wounds from the shattered windows, they stared in disbelief at the old building now engulfed in flames.

A loud crash signaled the collapse of the second-story floors, so they turned to each other to take a quick head count. Two of their comrades were missing. As they stumbled and limped around the outside of the burning building in search of their absent friends, a lone figure standing fifty yards away at the edge of the forest smiled in grim satisfaction.

Claus von Duckworth was the youngest of three sons. His elder brothers had died in France on the Western Front in the second battle of the Marne in September of 1918. News of both of their deaths reached his parents on the same day – a traumatic event from which they never recovered.

As was the custom in families of the German landed aristocracy, the eldest son inherited the complete estate. Because of their family's history and influence, Claus and his brothers chose careers in the military. After their deaths, as the last remaining male heir to the Duckworth holdings, Claus was given less dangerous assignments so as to perpetuate the family name.

Nevertheless, he had still seen more than his share of carnage. In 1916, while serving as a company commander outside Verdun, Claus witnessed events that would shape the rest of his life. The German high command was switching to a new and deadlier way of doing business: Long artillery barrages were replaced with short and intense fire, followed by poisonous mustard gas. Claus's original company of 239 men had been chewed up in the meat grinder of attacks and counterattacks until only 113 remained. Striding through the trenches, Claus reminded his men to "be prepared for a counterstrike – and make sure your gas masks are tightly strapped in place."

Deafening barrages marked the fusillade as they marched through the French lines. After what seemed an eternity, there was silence. The shells could still be heard streaking overhead, but now there was no bone-shaking explosion upon impact. The silent killer was on its way.

"Ready, first platoon!" Claus screamed through his mask. As they climbed to the top of the trench, a wave of orange mist washed over them. The wind had shifted.

Piercing screams could be heard from beyond the deadly fog as its choking vapors took their awful toll. An Imperial German Army corporal's head exploded as a bullet from a British Enfield rifle slammed through his right eye. British and French soldiers took full advantage of the fickle winds and attacked under cover of the Germans' own gas barrage. In the July heat, perspiration accumulated inside the faceplates of the German troops' gas masks, burning their eyes and obscuring vision.

The gas passed over them in what seemed only a few moments, but when Claus rallied his men to attack, the British and French descended upon them. Hand-to-hand fighting erupted with both sides struggling for a small piece of muddy, blood-soaked French real estate.

To his left, a newly arrived recruit panicked as a French hand grenade flew into the trench and lodged in the ankle-deep mud and human excrement. With his hands covered in sludge from climbing into and out of the trench, the dutiful soldier lunged for the lethal projectile, but it slipped from his hands. He groped for it in the muck and found it just as the geyser of mud and shrapnel tore through the line. The force of the explosion threw Claus against the back of the trench and left a pink froth on the front of his mask. Eventually, the insurgents were beaten back as more members of his company rushed in to repel the onslaught from adjoining trenches.

Unconscious from the blast, Claus lay sprawled on the dismembered bodies of two of his men. Their corpses kept him from sinking into the quagmire and were the only reason he did not drown in the dreck of the French countryside.

* * *

Claus was transferred from a field hospital to Berlin and eventually to his family home, where he was recuperating when the news of his brothers' deaths reached his parents. While still in Berlin, he heard the attending physicians discussing a difficult decision: To stem the infection, his left arm and right foot would have to be amputated. After he returned home and as he lay in bed healing from his wounds, Claus grew increasingly angry and bitter day by day. His shredded right boot was placed on a shelf between his dead brothers' pictures as a grim reminder of the events that changed his life.

On his last assignment of the war, Claus had been assigned to Field Marshall von Hindenburg's staff. Walking with a single crutch, he was part of the delegation on that fateful morning in 1918 when the Imperial German Army surrendered to the Allied forces in the Compiègne Forest.

Claus had been a member of the German honor guard, but in his opinion, *dis*honor guard was more appropriate. He felt that the military and the motherland had been stabbed in the back by German and European politicians. When the day for armistice arrived, not a single statesman was present; the German army stood alone to carry the burden of national disgrace. In men like Claus von Duckworth, these seeds of hatred took root and festered.

His brothers could have died at the hands of the Americans, the British or the French; Claus would never know. But there was one thing of which he was certain: They died fighting on French soil. To these officers who took his family and now his home, the war had ended four years earlier – but not for Claus von Duckworth.

The Duckworth claim to this land could be traced back more than five hundred years. Records showed the Springersbach Monastery deeding large tracts of land to the nobility of the day. Over the decades, these tracts would be carved up and parceled out as political plums to buy loyalty from other powerful families.

When Napoleon invaded Germany in 1800 and seized the Rhineland for the French, he dissolved the centuries-old agreement between the Roman Catholic Church and the German landed nobility. Ever in need of more funding to finance his wars, Napoleon decreed that the Rhineland region would be required to send a large portion of its farming and industrial production to France. This policy would be repeated a little more than 100 years later – with the same negative results.

In need of still more hard cash and growing tired of administering the German lands, Napoleon auctioned these estates back to the Germans in 1804. The Duckworths, having been bled dry from their payments to France, could only raise enough money to retain a portion of their original holdings. Their total estate now consisted only of the family home, two barns, stables and about 650 acres. By the early 1900s, it had shrunk to less than half that size.

Then, in 1923, when Germany became unable – or unwilling – to pay reparations from World War I as outlined in the Treaty of Versailles, the French once again seized the Rhineland – this time also taking in the Ruhr Valley in exchange for non-payment of war damages. These French officers who had commandeered the Duckworth estate were the living image of that policy.

Two months after the Versailles Treaty was signed, Claus's father Heinrich suddenly passed away. Even though he was barely in his early sixties, the doctors listed the cause of death as old age – but this was only partly true. Claus watched his father visibly age, but the true cause of death was a broken heart – broken by a treaty and the demise of his first two sons.

Late in January of 1923, Claus had been stationed in Berlin and attached as a liaison officer working on plans to deal with the French reoccupation of the Rhineland. On January 19, he received the news of his mother's death. He was immediately granted leave and took the train to Essen near his family home. Claus was met at the station by his longtime family friend, Reimar Horton. They had grown up as neighbors, so it was only fitting that Reimar send the cable to Berlin.

"I wanted to meet you here before you had a chance to go home," Reimar said. "Your mother is at the mortuary in town. You can see her before the funeral."

"I'll see her tomorrow, Reimar," Claus replied. "Today I only want to go home and remember her as when she was alive."

"I'm afraid you can't go just now, my old friend," Reimar whispered. "The French officers have taken over your house as living quarters."

Fire erupted in Claus's eyes. "My mother isn't even cold yet and they move in!" he hissed as he spat out his uncontrolled hatred of these French squatters.

"Actually, she was alive when they first arrived," Reimar said. "You may not know this, but your mother became increasingly ..." he hesitated as he chose his next words carefully, "... elderly. Since your father's death, she would put on a good act for you when you came to visit. We took it upon ourselves to have the housekeeper move in and stay there full-time."

"Why wasn't I told of this?" Claus lashed out. "I could have been there to help, to care for her."

"You know how fiercely independent she was," Reimar countered, "and so she said the thought of being a burden or bother to anyone would have killed her. But couldn't you see? She became a shell of her former self since your brothers' and father's deaths?"

"I thought she was just slowing down – you know, getting older," Claus said in disbelief.

"That's what she wanted you to think," Reimar tried to assure his friend. "You were her last baby. The very last thing she wanted was for you to be tied down taking care of her and not having a life of your own."

"How did she die?" Claus demanded. "You said she was alive when the French arrived." He struggled visibly to keep his anger under control.

"She was on the front porch when the soldiers drove past the main gate. She ran into the house screaming that the French were coming to kill her last remaining son. The housekeeper heard the noise and found her lying at the foot of the stairs. She never regained consciousness."

Staring off into the distance, Claus said, "My friend, I need a favor."

* * *

Later that night, as Claus slipped into his house through the cellar door, he realized that this would be the last time he'd ever visit his lifelong home. There was nothing left for him here – not anymore. He had no family now, and the shame he felt at not realizing his mother's condition would haunt him for the rest of his life. He would soon be a man on the run, a fugitive wanted by the French authorities in his own country. And the real crime was that his own German government was too weak to offer him any protection.

Claus had heard rampant rumors about South America, with its large German immigrant population and governments with their liberal, open-arm policies. His mind was made up: He would strengthen his resolve to rebuild his life and his honor in a new country, far away from politics and European bureaucrats.

But before he could accomplish any of this, there was one last thing he must do. So, with the last of the accelerant he had obtained from Reimar, Claus saturated the foot of the stairs where his mother had taken her last breath. He dropped a single match to ignite the black stream as he slipped out the front door. If these French trespassers were going to sleep in his house, he would make certain that it would be a long rest.

Chapter 12. May 27, 2008 – Fairfax, Virginia

As he pulled into the parking lot of the warehouse complex, Ryan Lessley had reached the end of a twenty-four-hour work day. It was quite a damp and drizzly morning for this late in May. In fact, the weather felt more like fall than spring. He felt sick to his stomach from lack of sleep and not having eaten for such a long stretch, and the drive only made the climate seem worse than it actually was.

Just the day before, he had basked in the warm sun at the top-secret McDonnell Douglas test site in the Mojave Desert. He dearly loved this place – not only because it signaled the end of the journey for one of his projects, but the stark landscape of rocky bluffs had become his personal sanctuary. He truly enjoyed the rock-climbing in the area, and exploring the hidden gorges and trails that the general public never got a chance to see only served as an added perk.

It was not so much that Ryan was an introvert or a hermit, but at the age of thirty-eight, this committed bachelor came to cherish these moments alone in the wilderness almost as much as his work. Whenever asked where he was, someone on his team would invariably smile and say, "Oh, he's probably out with his second wife."

This was not said entirely in jest. His "second wife" had been the unseen benefit of his high security clearance and he took full advantage whenever possible. Out at the test site, whenever he had a free moment, Ryan would slip away into his private world. More than once, when an unexpected problem arose, a search party would have to go looking for him.

Since the opportunity might present itself at any time for Ryan to wander off and enjoy the wilderness, he made what seemed to him a simple and logical choice: His working wardrobe became a pair of hiking shorts, climbing shoes, assorted T-shirts, a down vest for the chilly desert mornings and the ever-present baseball cap of his beloved University of California Golden Bears. This eventually become his signature style of dress — not only at the test site, but back at the office as well. A visiting senator once made a surprise inspection for one of his tests and Ryan had been told to wear long pants for the occasion. A curt reply of "I don't own any" ended that discussion forthwith.

His undergraduate degree in computer engineering from the U.S. Naval Academy and master's degree from Cal Berkeley helped to get his foot in the door of his other passion: building large-scale test model aircraft. After leaving the military, he went to work at the McDonnell Douglas facility in Palmdale, California, and soon gained a reputation for his meticulous attention to detail, ability to work with *prima donna* designers, and uncanny knack for dreaming up new and simple solutions to complicated problems. One morning, he even found a carved walnut plaque on his desk that simply read, "Ask MacGyver."

Abandoned as a baby, he had no memory of his biological parents. After bouncing around three foster homes, five-year-old Ryan Lessley finally beat the odds and was adopted. Newborns are the easiest to place by the agencies. However, the older the child, the tougher the task. Typically, like many orphaned and abandoned children, Ryan partially blamed himself for his parents not wanting to keep him. "If I had only been better, more perfect, this would never have happened," he told himself over and over again. With the fear of rejection always in the back of his mind, Ryan Lessley grew up with the attitude that he would accept nothing less than perfection as a standard for himself and everyone around him.

At McDonnell Douglas, he started by working on a team that built models for wind tunnel testing. As his expertise improved and clearance level increased, stealth technology became his focus and passion. With the urging and financial backing of upper management, Ryan formed a small company and began subcontracting some of his more complicated fabrications.

His passion for rock-climbing and fanatical attention to detail established his new company's name, Can't Take It For Granite Industries, as a catchy *double entendre*. He met contract deadlines and budgets, and eventually complete projects were dropped into his lap. And he did not disappoint.

On the day before his drizzly drive and while he was still at the desert test facility, his latest creation had been put under the microscope. Besides their ever-evolving fuselage designs, new radar-absorbent coatings were always being developed and tested. His babies, which could be up to fifteen feet long, would be hoisted up onto a one-hundred-foot platform and bombarded with radar waves from all directions. The resulting signature would then be recorded and his months of work would either pass or fail in an instant.

Even though Ryan oversaw the building of dozens of such models, there was always a sense of anticipation and personal connection. His report card was laid out in plain sight for everyone to see, but what made him so special was the fact that he never let his ego influence the way he viewed the test results. This is not to say he wouldn't be sorely disappointed if something failed, just like anyone else in his position would. Rather, he described his reaction as his "analytical ego." He cared deeply for what he did, but when it failed, Ryan Lessley was less concerned about covering his own rear end than finding out the "why" and the "how."

For that reason, he was handed a plane ticket for a red-eye flight to Washington, D.C., and told to arrive in Fairfax, Virginia, no later than eight o'clock the next morning.

Chapter 13. May 27, 2008 – Fairfax, Virginia

Thinking the late flight from L.A. to Dulles International Airport wouldn't be crowded, Ryan gave his first-class ticket to an extremely pregnant young woman who seemed to be having difficulty maneuvering down the aisle. In her current state of great discomfort, she just seemed to need it more than he did. In exchange, he took her seat in coach. His consideration did not go unnoticed: A man in his mid-forties seated across the aisle had even more room on his side, so he swapped chairs and took Ryan's recliner in 4C.

But as the plane filled with passengers, Ryan realized he had committed a major miscue. With the economy struggling, all the major carriers were cutting down on the number of flights in favor of the bottom line – their profit margin. This was a full flight with few, if any, extra seats, and as the night wore on, a large man in the spot next to him began snoring and claiming more and more of his area. It's not that Ryan would have slept anyway. He simply hated red-eye flights. No good deed ever goes unpunished, does it?

The only thing Ryan detested more than late flights was causeway traffic. The twenty-five-mile drive through the Beltway to Fairfax always put his nerves on edge. He had considered stopping and getting something to eat, but the lack of sleep and time change had put his stomach in knots.

As he pulled up to the security kiosk at the entrance, Ryan gave the guard his name and identification, and was directed to the far corner of the lot, where a black Cadillac Escalade was parked. A tall, lean man with a steely gaze leaned against it with arms folded. At first glance, haircut and physical appearance indicated military.

As Ryan drove up, the man approached and asked, "You Lessley?" Ryan nodded and handed him the letter that was in the envelope with his ticket. Ryan noticed the man's hands were large and scarred. Perhaps he was a butcher or a carpenter.

The tall stranger read the letter, pulled a picture from his pocket and compared it to Ryan's face. He then passed a non-disclosure agreement through the window, the kind Ryan had signed dozens of times in the past. Ryan scribbled his initials in the spaces highlighted with yellow marker and handed it back. Returning to the Escalade, the stranger climbed in and motioned for Ryan to follow.

* * *

Like Ryan, Alex McCormick had spent a long day and night of travel from California to Virginia. Even though the agency's private jet had eliminated any annoying layovers from his flight schedule, traveling west to east always wreaked havoc on his internal clock. During the flight, Alex took the time to peruse the dossier of one Mr. Ryan Lessley: headstrong, intelligent, thinks on his feet … exactly the reasons he was chosen – and precisely why he could be a major pain-in-the-ass.

Driving through the complex, Ryan counted a dozen warehouses whose size he guessed were at least 100,000 square feet. The entire area was protected by ten-foot-high block walls with electrified razor wire and surveillance cameras every fifty feet. Nothing much out of the ordinary here – just a bunch of individual storage units with a whole crapload of security.

At the ninth structure, an overhead door opened and the two vehicles entered. As the portal closed behind them, Ryan's eyes began to adjust to the darkness. He saw what appeared to be a long, narrow storage space with nothing more than household items and boxes stacked all around them. As the outer opening slammed shut behind them, a wall that appeared to be made of cinder blocks slid open in front of them to reveal a large, brightly lit warehouse with crates stacked to the ceiling.

The lead vehicle pulled forward and Ryan followed until it came to a stop at the rear of the building, directly in front of a small enclosed area about the size of a three-car garage. Several armed men in military fatigues stood guard and watched them as they passed. The man in the first car walked over to Ryan as he climbed out and stretched his legs.

"Mr. Lessley, my name is Alex McCormick," he said with a twinkle in his eye as he stuck out his right hand. "Welcome to our little storage area. I want you to know how much we appreciate you coming out on such short notice."

"Well, the way it was presented, I didn't think I had much of a choice," Ryan answered wryly as he shook hands with this mystery fellow.

Alex smiled and continued. "You're probably wondering why we asked you here. Three months ago, The Smithsonian Institution notified us that they were putting together a display of World War Two-era experimental aircraft. They wanted to know if we had anything unique to add. As you can see, in this building alone there is a huge amount of inventory. Some was actually captured from the Germans around 1944. Much of it has never seen the light of day, since it was crated prior to being shipped. In those days, we grabbed everything we thought might be valuable – you know, before the Russians could get their hands on it.

"Many of the items in these warehouses have never been inventoried beyond the original shipping manifest," he continued. "Each building in the complex is similar to this one, and there are probably thirty sites like it spread across the country. So of course it was a stroke of sheer luck that we even found Item #GR44-4426964 on an inventory list from 1944. The first two letters and numbers designate Germany 1944. There were three crates – two with the wings and other assorted parts, and another with the fuselage. On the shipping manifest, they were listed as 'Flugzeug Fledermaus.' In German, that roughly translates to 'The Bat Aircraft'."

Chapter 14. May 27, 2008 – Fairfax, Virginia

Alex pulled a key from his pocket and reached for the lock as Ryan asked, "So, since you don't work for the Smithsonian, who exactly are you?" McCormick slid the key into the lock and turned the handle so the tongue disengaged the striker plate in the door jamb, but left the door closed.

Without turning around, he replied, "Let's just say we have a mutual friend who suggested that perhaps you could help solve part of a puzzle."

"That's not a good enough answer," Ryan said as he probed for a deeper meaning to why he had been shanghaied to this place. "Why do you need a mock-up of a sixty-five-year-old aircraft when you could ship the original and be done with it in three days?"

"Mr. Lessley, you're correct," Alex acknowledged. "We didn't ask you here today because we need someone to build a test model. With your clearance level, we can speak openly. What we need from you is your insight and opinion. You might even say we think you are wired a little strangely, but in a good way.

"When you walk through this door, you are going to see a World War Two-vintage aircraft unlike any other you have ever examined – but at the same time it will be very familiar. Frankly speaking, there are some aspects of the aircraft's design that …" Alex paused for a moment to search for the proper words. "... well, I don't know how else to put it: We're not quite sure what the hell they are."

"You know, Mr. McCormick, as you say, to be real frank, I took a red-eye to get here, haven't slept in about thirty hours, and I'm not in the mood for cryptic answers," Ryan said testily. "So why don't you just cut the crap and tell me why I'm really here? Because if you can't or won't tell me, one of two things is going to happen: Either you get someone here who *can* tell me or I walk out that door."

Alex gave him his best deadpan stare and said, "Actually, there is a third option: We could just shoot you."

Ryan glared back and was about say something he was sure he would probably regret, but just then he caught some movement out of the corner of his eye. The two Marine guards had disabled the safeties on their weapons and were now moving closer.

"Mr. Lessley, can I tell you a little story?" Alex said as he leaned back against the unlocked door. "After you hear me out, if you want to leave, you can walk out the main gate and never hear from us again." The implied threat, of course, was that Ryan's security clearance, and his career, wouldn't be worth a plugged nickel after today.

"By late 1943, the Germans had become desperate," Alex began. "To the east, the campaign against Russia was going badly. The Allied invasion from across the channel was about to take place, and the British and American bombing raids were destroying not only the means of war-material production, but also civilian cities and their morale. The Germans were frantically looking for a miracle weapon to turn the tide of war in their favor."

"I know my history," Ryan answered sarcastically.

"Good," Alex said in an even tone, "then I'm sure you'll find the rest of the tale very interesting."

With that, he turned and opened the heavy steel door. A rush of cool air blasted Ryan's face as he was led into the blackness of the hangar. When the door closed behind them, he heard someone flip a switch as soft halogen lights drew a halo around the object in the center of the room.

Just as a child might see his own facial features in old pictures of his grandparents, Ryan Lessley's eyes now fixed on what appeared to be the grandparent of the American F-117 stealth aircraft.

Chapter 15. August 11, 1943 – Bergheim, Germany

The hidden airfield from where the bat-like aircraft had departed was a technological marvel in its own right. Pear and apple orchards surrounded the two-story farmhouse. Grape arbors arched over hillsides surrounding the main building, giving it the appearance of an old, rural family farm in the rolling hills of Germany.

Here, far from the never-ending bombings of German cities, the tranquility seemed bucolic by comparison – almost from another century. Nothing appeared out of the ordinary for this rustic dwelling, but as evening approached, that would quickly change.

Darkness brought a quickened pace and purpose to every movement of the farm's employees as they headed back to the main road. Just off the dirt path that led up to the house, a diesel generator hidden under a thick canopy of trees came to life. Sections of ground on the path started to separate as geared teeth pulled them apart. Underneath it all, a concrete runway stretched away from the front of the house. Panels covered with trees and shrubs melted into the forest, and farmhands began setting out lanterns to illuminate the runway's outline.

This structure had been painted to look in every way like a weatherworn old farmhouse – and it certainly fit the bill. The main hangar door then began to raise and, with barely an inch of clearance on either side, The Bat emerged from its cave.

By any standard, this machine was different. With no tail, the plane was shaped more like a boomerang than a conventional aircraft. Its two recessed Junkers turbojet engines and smooth, rounded shape gave it an almost unearthly appearance.

The fuselage was composed not of metal, but multiple thin layers of wood veneer over a metal tubular frame, all laminated together with each layer's grain running in different directions for added strength. It was just as much a work of cabinetmaking art as was its original purpose: a sophisticated attempt to confound the British radar. A dull black coating covered the exterior. It felt slick and almost greasy to the touch.

The Bat, as it came to be called, was the brainchild of two brothers, Reimer and Walter Horton. Previously submitted proposals for research funding on an impressive list of imaginative inventions were rejected. All of their requests were turned down until a chance meeting with Air Marshal Hermann Goering gave them their opportunity. Now, the aircraft they hoped to make invisible to British radar was about to be tested.

Even with all of these groundbreaking innovations, there remained several glaring problems with the early German jet. It could be unpredictable and, at times, difficult to fly. Engines could develop a vapor lock in a steep dive or sharp turn and stall – not to mention that early jet fuel was highly unstable. On the previous day, this latter problem had spelled the end of one of the experimental planes in a fiery explosion during fueling. As a memoriam, yet another name was added to the long list of adventurers and explorers who sought to push the battlefield envelope.

Even with its groundbreaking technological advances, the bat-like plane's days were numbered. By 1943, German leaders were convinced that the war could only be won with a bold plan. As a result, projects such as The Bat had taken a back seat to grander schemes.

With the stealth project on permanent hiatus, the German High Command set its sights on a new plan: a transatlantic bomber capable of attacking the American heartland. With a new and terrible weapon which he was assured would be available within the next year, Adolph Hitler felt certain that a nuclear strike against major cities in the United States would force America into a quick surrender.

A plane this large would require the newest, most cutting-edge alloys. Only the lightest and strongest would do. Wooden planes simply could not stand the stress of a transatlantic flight. So, since the technological baby had been thrown out with the bath water, and because of The Bat's structural limitations, funding from Air Marshal Goering froze due to political pressure from above.

Feeling that The Bat was too unreliable, undependable and unsuitable for attacks on the Americans, Goering ordered that the research information and blueprints be put aside. Eventually, they would catch the attention of an art dealer – or thief, depending on one's point of view – on Goering's personal staff.

Chapter 16. 1943 – Colonia del Sacramento, Uruguay

A one-lane road running west from Montevideo to Colonia, Uruguay, skirts the banks of the muddy Rio de la Plata River. The trip itself takes only ninety minutes, but the two cities might as well be light-years apart.

Located just a three-hour ferry ride across the river from Buenos Aires, the town has its sights set firmly in the past. A charming maze of cobblestone streets and areas the locals call "red lantern districts," it is a place where people who want to be left alone go to live in peace. As residents of the big city of Montevideo often say, "When a person from Colonia walks into the room, you get the feeling someone just left."

Located where the three countries of Argentina, Paraguay and Uruguay share common borders, this area was historically the stage for strained political relations and intrigue. Over the centuries, landlocked Paraguay continually fought border skirmishes with neighboring Uruguay to gain access to the sea by way of a port on the Rio de la Plata.

At the onset of World War II, all three countries declared themselves neutral. But with the heavy influence of their large German immigrant populations, both Paraguay and Argentina made no secret of their support for a German-dominated world.

On the other hand, Uruguay, with its deep harbors and access to the South Atlantic, was an instant magnet to the British. Large amounts of investment capital flowed into the country and the shadow of the British Empire quickly spread throughout the land.

Another reason the British needed access to ports in the area was their claim over and habitation of the Falkland Islands off the coast of Argentina – an assertion the Argentinians dispute to this day. A barren collection of rocky outcroppings and alpine meadows resembling Scotland, the Falklands were settled and inhabited by the British for more than two hundred years. To England, it was not only of strategic value, but also symbolic of their once vast and now fading empire.

It was here in Colonia that Claus Von Duckworth began building his new Germany. With the brewing recipe and coal-to-oil procedure that the Horton brothers gave him before he left, Claus set about presenting himself as just another hard-working immigrant from Europe who wanted to make a new start.

These three countries were also pressured by the Allies, who publicly stated that they did not want South America to become a sanctuary for German war criminals. At the same time, Americans and British alike had been sheltering and protecting Germans whom they thought might be useful to their cause. The Cold War had begun.

No matter what concerns were voiced at the time, by this juncture it was too late to stop the German exodus. Although these stories were dismissed as merely sensationalist journalism by South America's government-controlled press outlets, the exploits of Israeli Nazi hunters in later years told a different tale. To this day, there is no absolute proof that any organized methodical escape organization such as the infamous ODESSA ever really existed.

But this much is known: At a time when getting away from Europe was almost impossible, waves of Germans were able to flee to South America and start a new life. With the help of sympathetic governments and German nationals already ensconced there for years, all but a few were able to live out in the open without even so much as the need to hide their identities. But not just the rich and notorious war criminals made it out of Europe at this time. Somehow, ordinary citizens as well were finding a way to make their escape.

In early 1944, Carl Friedrick, his wife and their two small children slipped out of Germany and escaped through Italy with the help of a string of safe houses and Catholic monasteries. Booking passage on a tramp steamer leaving from Genoa, they arrived in Buenos Aires and melded with the local population.

* * *

Carl met his future wife in the spring of 1936. Elaine first ran into the young *leutnant* while he was on an inspection tour of the Olympic training facility in Berlin. Carl recently had been appointed as a junior officer to the staff of General Ernst von Landendorf, while Elaine was an Olympian on the German women's track team.

Elaine, the first alternate on the 4x100-meter relay team, was in training for the Eleventh Olympiad to be held that summer in Berlin.

She practiced and attended all events as a team member, but unless there was an injury or she could shave a few tenths of a second off her time, her goal of representing The Fatherland in the Olympics would remain only a dream. Akin to any other spectator in the stadium that day, she would only have a much better seat.

As the officers moved among the athletes and made small talk, Elaine approached Carl, introduced herself and slipped him a small, folded paper with her address and phone number. At the time, affairs and unwed mothers were not frowned upon in Germany. In fact, they were encouraged by the government as a way of producing more children for the Fatherland – that is, of course, as long as one fit the proper racial and social profiles.

At fifteen, Elaine was one such young, unwed mother. Her own mother was horrified when informed of her daughter's pregnancy, but Elaine defiantly informed her that it was every young woman's duty to produce children for the future of Germany. When Elaine's daughter was born, a couple unable to have children took the baby. It wasn't until five years later, after the birth of the twins, that the full impact of her loss and never knowing her first child eventually set in. As far as she knew, the child was alive and well, but as a mother she still grieved the loss.

Elaine watched the touring officers as they talked among themselves. More than once, General von Landendorf turned to the young lieutenant and spoke with him. Instead of a simple nod, which would have been the proper reaction of an officer of his rank and age, he would engage the general in lengthy conversations. Clearly, this was a self-confident man of considerable substance.

As a little girl, Elaine spent many long and wonderful summer days fishing with her grandfather. In his eyes, the simple act of casting a line into the water was a metaphor for life itself, and he taught her many colorful phrases – most of which were unacceptable in polite conversation. One such expression that came to mind as she watched Carl was, "He might be a keeper."

It took Carl three weeks to build up the courage to meet this pushy and forward young girl. Not even the company of men his own age and officers much more his senior had challenged his confidence as did Elaine. Carl took pride in knowing that he rarely, if ever, had been caught at a loss for words. On the other hand, making small talk with women always proved difficult for him. When in the presence of officers of much higher rank and prestige than himself, he felt self-assured and relaxed. However, this skinny and freckle-faced young lady had him stammering and searching for even the simplest turns of phrase. That knowing smile of hers as she cocked her head to one side told him things would never be the same.

That first evening, they only went out for coffee, after which they walked through the training facility's Olympic Park. As they returned to Elaine's apartment, Carl shook her hand at the front door. Her wrist went limp as she looked at him with curious surprise. Carl leaned over, kissed her on the cheek and said, "Even wild birds make a nest before they lay their eggs. When I become a father, I want to be a part of my children's lives, not just some stop along a production line." Carl didn't realize it then, but he had just stated to perfection the one phrase Elaine's grandfather emphasized above all else: "Be sure to set the hook."

Throughout the summer, whenever their schedules allowed, they spent as much time together as possible. Exploring each other's hopes and dreams, they both realized that this tall and slender tomboy had stolen his heart. Carl decided on the first night that she was the one, and planned to find the ideal and perfect moment to propose.

The German women's 4x100 relay team was one of the favorites to win the gold medal. The semifinals would be August 8, with the finals held the next day. Carl was torn with the timing of this race. If Elaine's team won, he didn't want to play second-fiddle to the event, yet he wanted to be part of a memorable day. If he could only drum up the courage to ask her. The ring he bought was simple, yet beautiful – like his future bride. There was one thought, however, that he could not reconcile: The stadium would hold more than 110,000 people that day. What if she said no?

On the morning of August 9, the day of the finals, the German women's team was in high spirits. All four members of their relay team had reached the finals in the individual 100-meter event, and they won their semifinal relay heat in world-record time. The possibility of sweeping the 100-meter race and winning the 4x100-meter relay was the talk of all media in attendance. Rarely was there the possibility of one country completely dominating the two highest-profile women's events in any of the Olympic Games.

With a stunning time of 48.9 seconds, they eclipsed the existing world mark by a full second. In track and field, that did not merely break the record – they shattered it! The United States, Canada and

Great Britain represented other nations in the final heat, but it seemed only the Americans posed a serious threat.

Ansell Kirsch, the German women's track coach, sat at his desk as the last member of the women's relay team exited his office and closed the door. He shut his eyes and hoped an answer to his dilemma would appear. With the women's relay finals a mere five hours away, he still had not submitted his final list of runners for his country's team.

The German and international press just couldn't get enough of these four young ladies racing for the top spot on the podium. Kirsch knew the landslide of gold wouldn't stop on the platform where the medals themselves were presented. The influence and propaganda value provided by the victory would showcase the new Germany to the world.

So why was he this troubled? The girls' times for the 100 meters were relatively close, but there was a distinct gap between Elaine and her teammates who ran in the semifinals – that is, until this morning.

Elaine, experimenting with a new stance, exploded out of the blocks and shaved a full .11 seconds off her time. When she ran a second practice heat, they clocked her at .16 seconds faster.

Elaine now had recorded the third fastest time for any of the German girls. Ansell always pushed the girls to compete. "A country's uniform does not win races," he admonished. "Only with hard work and determination will you achieve your goal." And now the sisterhood of runners was turning up the pressure. One by one, each of the girls came to his office and offered to let Elaine take their spot. They all wanted her to experience the once-in-a-lifetime chance to compete in the Olympic Games.

Knowing the public-relations significance of the four name athletes, Coach Kirsch discussed the problem with Hans von Tschammer, the head of the Reich Sports Office.

Within fifteen minutes, they heard a knock at the door and, before he could even open his mouth to answer, an attractive blond woman barged into the office. Ansell Kirsch recognized her immediately as Leni Reifenstahl, Adolf Hitler's personal choice to document the Berlin Olympics.

She did not mince words. "Under no circumstances are you to change the runners in the race. This decision comes from above." Coach Kirsch knew now that his hands were tied. No matter how fast Elaine ran, she would never be on the track that afternoon.

Standing on the infield of the stadium, Elaine searched the massive crowd for Carl. Tickets had been sold out for months, but she managed to get him one from an old boyfriend on the men's track team. Although Carl's seat was located in the upper section, German architect Albert Speer had so masterfully designed the complex that not a single fan's view was obstructed. As the women positioned themselves in the starting blocks, the huge crowd rose in anticipation.

After a clean start, the German team began to pull away almost immediately. Located on the inside lane and staggered so as to appear behind, they drew even with their American counterparts as the first leg of the German team passed the baton at the 100-meter mark. At the end of the second leg, Ilse Dorrfeldt – the third German runner – was clearly pulling away and threatening to smash her own team's world-record time.

Ilse ran smoothly with long, fluid strides, but as she prepared for the final baton exchange, the unthinkable happened. Hundreds of hours of practice and thousands of repetitions of the most basic maneuver in the relay event now failed her. As she pumped her arms and reached forward to make the pass, Ilse stumbled.

Kathe Kraub, running the anchor leg for the German team, was already sprinting with her right hand extended for the baton's delivery. As Ilse fell, she lunged forward and the baton just grazed Kathe's fingertips. As if in slow motion, runner and baton tumbled to the track.

Silence settled over the stadium like a fog. Ilse lay face-down on the track as if frozen to the ground. For several seconds, her stunned teammates stared at her as they also felt unable to move. First Elaine, and then the other three girls, rushed to their fallen comrade. They knelt beside Ilse and tried their best to console her.

In the stands, Carl blinked his eyes several times in disbelief, but his attention had been drawn away from the miscue on the track by the large board on the infield that listed the order of finish. A subdued voice droned from the public address system and announced the results – first in French, then English and, finally, German. Flashing lights at the center of the track reflected the same results. The gold medal went to the United States, with a time of 49.9 seconds. Silver went to Great Britain and the bronze to Canada. At the bottom of the leader board, the message flashed decisively: "Deutschland – DQ," or "Germany – Disqualified."

As the four American runners took their victory lap, each in turn knelt and gave Ilse and her teammates a short hug as a sign of respect and consolation for a fellow competitor and human being. They couldn't even begin to imagine her pain and humiliation. At one time or another, each of them had failed or come up short in competition, but few had done it on such a grand stage as this – in front of the entire world.

Moments later, two men in brown suits made their way onto the track and escorted the German team away to just a smattering of applause. Elaine arose to leave with the team, but one of the men stood directly in her way, making it clear that she was not invited to this party.

As the infield cleared and the throng of stunned spectators left the stands, Elaine stood alone and stared at the large board that displayed the final standings.

In the chancellor's private box, Adolf Hitler witnessed the entire event. Summoning the team to his exclusive viewing area, he would play the role of the caring and understanding national leader as he consoled the women's team in front of the world's newsreel cameras. It would be the job of Leni Reifenstahl, the Reich's official film and propaganda genius, to snatch the team away from the precipice of gloom and turn this moment of defeat into victory. This unforgivable failure of discipline could still be turned into a publicity coup. This time, she would make him appear to the masses as almost divine as he demonstrated his capacity to forgive.

A dark sneer curled under his mustache. There was almost no applause when the team left the field. His vision of a Germany that would no longer accept losing had come a long way, indeed. Domination of Europe – and beyond – would require a country with a backbone of steel and a people with a spirit that refused defeat.

Away from the press and the public eye, Coach Ansell Kirsch would be relieved of his duties. He would never again coach in Germany. It was not important for the public to know the details of his dismissal. It only mattered that the German people knew what was expected of them at all times.

Carl made his way down to the field and, with military bluster, managed to persuade the security guard to allow him onto the track. He walked up behind Elaine and was about to put his hand on her shoulder when she lamented, "We were so close – so very close. I feel so badly for Ilse and all the girls. This was our chance. This was our time."

Feeling her disappointment, Carl whispered, "You can still compete in the European games, and also in four years for the next Olympiad."

"Four years!" she snapped as she spun around to face him. "Do you know how old I will be in four years?"

As a matter of fact, Carl had no idea exactly how old she was at the time, much less in four years. But the look in her eye told him that this was probably not the best time to explore the subject.

"Besides being past our prime," she continued in a tone he had not heard before, "do you really think they would let any of us be on the team as a reminder of this monumental failure?"

"If you were still the best, they would have to let you on the team," Carl reasoned logically.

"I *was* one of the best," she wailed, "and that didn't matter. They will just develop new runners. This is, and always has been, about the politics. Can't you see that? It's just ..." she let out a deep breath, bit her lip and wiped away a tear as she tried to think of something to say. "I'm sorry I spoke to you like that. You were here and the words just came out," she cried as she threw her arms around his neck.

She felt something small in his coat pocket pressing against her breast. Elaine leaned back and placed her hand over his heart so she could feel the tiny box. "What is this?" she inquired coyly. When Carl looked uneasy and didn't answer immediately, she stepped back, cocked her head and put her hands on her hips. "Carl Friedrick, is that little box for me? Were you going to propose?" The stunned lieutenant could only stare blankly as she smirked.

After several seconds, Elaine gave him an impish grin. "Well, since you aren't going to answer, perhaps I should go to dinner with that cute young captain who keeps asking me out."

Tossing the top of her warm-up jacket over her shoulder, Elaine spun around and began walking to the women's locker room. As she strutted away, Carl heard her say, "But if you had asked, I probably would have said yes."

* * *

On August 23, a week after the closing ceremonies of the 1936 Berlin Olympics, Carl and Elaine became husband and wife on the field of the very same Olympic training facility where they first met.

With the death of his parents in an auto accident two years earlier, Carl's only living relative, cousin Wilhelm, acted as best man.

The wedding party was a photographer's dream. Carl and Wilhelm were resplendent in their military dress uniforms, while Elaine and her sister wore simple summer sundresses with flower garlands in their hair. The remainder of the bridal party, with Ilse Dorfeldt as maid of honor, wore their Olympic warm-up suits. It was the last time they would all be together on or off the field. Dark clouds of war were gathering over Europe and there would be no Olympics – or games of any kind – in 1940 or 1944.

Deciding to leave Germany was not an easy decision for Carl. A dedicated member of the Hitler Youth Organization, he displayed an almost fanatical love for the Fatherland. As a young boy, he contracted polio and was condemned to desk duty – not a true soldier's calling at all. Bright, efficient and tireless, he handled his job with a mechanical efficiency that defined the young German mind. Do your best with tunnel-vision commitment to the party and ask no questions. With this attitude and work ethic, he quickly rose to the rank of captain on General Landsdorf's staff.

But as the war dragged on, bulletins from the Eastern front crossed his desk that made it more difficult to follow the party line. Glowing newspaper reports of battlefield exploits stood out in stark contrast to the numbers of dead, wounded and missing in the many classified documents that he saw every day.

A mind trained to deal with details becomes haunted by questions and loose ends. If the eastern campaign was going so well, why were so many troops being pulled from the west? Carl saw those classified reports on the buildup of men and materiel in England. If a captain dealing in logistics could draw the conclusion that an invasion from the west was imminent, surely the German High Command must know it as well.

As time passed and more troops were deployed, he noticed another alarming trend: The transferred troops were not being sent deeper into Russia, but instead stationed nearer to the Fatherland itself. He remembered the exact moment when the realization washed over him. These new troops were no longer the point of an attacking spear – they were a defensive perimeter. The Russians were coming.

More and more trains had been scheduled to take more and more prisoners to the detention camps in the east. Even with more people scheduled for internment, there was no increase in food or supplies allocated for the burgeoning populations. Carl would occasionally hear pieces of conversations in the hallways of the chancellery. "Only war stories," he told himself as he shut the rumors out of his mind. A true believer in the Fatherland and the Reich, he found it impossible to even contemplate such horrible innuendo.

Chapter 17. 1934 – Berlin, Germany

Even as his was always a tight-knit family, Carl was especially close to Wilhelm, the son of his mother's older sister. About the same age, the two were immediately drawn together and became as close as natural brothers. The two boys resembled each other in stature and looks so closely that from a distance one was often mistaken for the other. Tall, willowy and with complexion and hair that spoke of hours in the summer sun, they were inseparable. After Carl contracted polio and eventually learned to walk again with a slight limp, Wilhelm would hobble and stumble along with his cousin so he would not feel so self-conscious.

Carl and Wilhelm, or Willie, were the spoons that stirred the pot. Even if they weren't the culprits, their mothers and fathers would naturally assume the worst. Never mean or malicious, they were merely filled with too much energy – and constantly looked for ways to channel it.

When they reached the age of fourteen, they became eligible to join the Hitler Youth movement and gradually drifted apart. Carl soaked up every aspect of the program like a sponge and threw himself fully into the new regime. Willie just wanted to know why, which inevitably led to more and more arguments – until the boys finally stopped speaking altogether.

In 1938, Willie enlisted in the German Navy and was assigned as a cook on the battleship *KMS Admiral Graf Spee*. Feeling a sense of German duty and ingrained obligation to the Fatherland, Willie felt that the naval branch of the services still was the most honorable.

The commanding officer, Captain Hans Langsdorff, was a man filled with a sense of great moral pride. A strict follower of the statutes of the Geneva War Convention, *der kapitan* felt that his actions represented the honor and image of his beloved Germany. His ties to a bygone era even included the use of the original German naval salute instead of the Nazi fist thrust into the air.

When attacking unarmed merchant ships, Langsdorff made every effort to remove their crews before destroying their vessels. The hospitality he extended to his captive guests became legendary, as he felt a sense of responsibility for the welfare of all captured military and non-combatant personnel. Numerous documents from captured officers detailed his humane treatment of their crews. Many of these same officers later honored him by attending his funeral.

In 1939, the *Admiral Graf Spee*, while raiding the South Atlantic shipping lanes, ran into resistance from British warships and was severely damaged in a running engagement. The German warship was barely able to limp into the neutral port of Montevideo, Uruguay to make repairs. Then the old precept of The Golden Rule came into play: He who has the gold makes the rules. Pressured by the British, Uruguay threatened to take control of the *Graf Spee* if she did not leave port within seventy-two hours.

Under the Uruguayan government's interpretation of international law, non-combatant vessels were to be given at least a twenty-four-hour head start before a warship could leave a neutral port. Numerous British cargo vessels were docked in Montevideo at the time, so the Brits staggered their departures to keep the still-dangerous German battle cruiser at anchor. This allowed the Allies to gather an even larger force at the river inlet to meet the German ship when it eventually did sail.

Just as in politics, war is a game of chess. Even with additional time, the British simply could not amass enough "capital" ships – battleships, cruisers and carriers – to be certain that they could defeat the *Graf Spee* when she tried to break out into the South Atlantic.

Now the game was on. The British fleet remained just beyond the horizon so the Germans could not determine their exact strength. By adding extra oil to their boilers, the British produced more smoke than normal. This gave the impression that a much larger and more formidable force awaited the Germans.

After the Germans' defeat in World War I, the Treaty of Versailles stripped their military of all offensive weaponry. However, ever-resourceful Germany skirted the treaty in a number of ways. *This is not an infant air force. It is merely a recreational flying club*, they reasoned. *A training program for a future army? Oh no, this is a summer athletic camp for our young men.*

Also at this time, a secret agreement with the Russians allowed Germany to conduct military research deep in the Ural Mountains, far from the prying eyes of the Allied powers. In exchange, the Russians gained access to advanced technology and modernization of their existing factories. At these research facilities, two German brothers – Reimar and Walter Horton – met Russian physicist Pyotr Ufimtsev, who had been widely acknowledged as one of the founding forefathers of stealth-technology theory. He would have a profound impact on the Horton brothers' vision of an aircraft's possibilities. Their design for The Bat would be decades ahead of its time.

The Treaty of Versailles also heaped numerous constraints and limitations upon the German navy. Through clever negotiation, the production criteria were changed from the number of ships allowed to restrictions based on weight. The naval engineering arms race had officially begun.

At the time, conventional shipbuilding technology consisted of riveting overlapped metal plates together. Power was supplied by steam-driven coal engines. The German war machine demanded new methods and designs to remain within the letter – if not necessarily the spirit – of the treaty.

The first change was revolutionary and would have far-reaching ramifications. The ship's joints were now welded instead of riveted. This allowed for a much higher vessel-to-weight ratio and also streamlined the construction process. But the largest leap forward by far was the change from coal to diesel fuel. These new diesel engines generated more energy, were more efficient, and required less fuel and manpower to operate.

But a new wrinkle came along with this advancing technology: The diesel engines required fresh-water cooling and state-of-the-art desalinization systems. Without proper temperature regulation, these huge engines would overheat and grind to a halt. The changes allowed the Germans to build much larger and potentially more dangerous warships than would otherwise have been allowed by the treaty.

During the *Graf Spee*'s engagement with the British, an incoming shell had disabled the fresh-water cooling system. Captain Langsdorff realized that the damage was far greater than anyone understood. Without extensive repairs, he knew that the pride of the German navy would not be seaworthy for a long voyage to a friendly port, much less a running battle against what he presumed to be overwhelming odds.

The captain also knew that he could not allow his prized command to fall into the hands of the enemy. So Langsdorff cabled Berlin and asked for further instructions. He was told that the honor of not only the German navy, but the Fatherland itself, required that he fight to the death. Unwilling to sacrifice his crew in a futile effort, Langsdorff decided to go against orders and scuttle his beloved *KMS Admiral Graf Spee* in the river channel.

On December 17, 1939, he ordered all vital equipment destroyed so as to render it useless to the enemy. Then all captured seamen and non-essential crew members, of whom Willie was one, were sent ashore. As the ship pulled away from its moorings around 6:15 on the morning of December 18, reporters and crowds lined the waterfront.

The massive vessel pulled away from the dock and steamed into the river channel. As she sailed out to the shipping channel, the huge battleship suddenly shuddered as scuttling charges exploded below decks. The mighty *KMS Admiral Graf Spee* belched a plume of thick, black smoke and slowly settled into the muddy waters of the Rio de la Plata.

The next morning, knowing that he could never return to Germany, *Kapitan zur See* Hans Wilhelm Langsdorff wrote a letter to the German High Command that detailed his actions, then wrapped himself in a naval flag and took his own life. It was only fitting and proper that he commit himself to the same fate as was realized by his last sea command.

Willie, along with his fellow shipmates and onlookers, was caught completely by surprise. British officials in charge of the German prisoners were overwhelmed by the throng as the crowds rushed forward to gain a better view of the sinking ship. As he stood silent and still, the teeming mass of spectators surged past Willie and before he knew it, he was standing at the rear of the mob. Knowing that he must make a quick decision, Willie turned and walked away from the dock through the oncoming deluge of people. It was much better to be free and hiding in a strange country than interned in a British prisoner-of-war camp.

Chapter 18. May 27, 2008 – Fairfax, Virginia

Ryan Lessley strolled past Alex McCormick and around the plane, stepping in and out of the light to gain different perspectives. He ran his hand along the edge of the wing to feel for any exposed heads of sheet-metal screws, but only detected the seamless, curved edge of a work of art. The flat black paint – if it even was paint – felt more like a wet sheet of plastic. It concealed the joints so well that the plane appeared to have been poured from a mold. Ryan stood in front of the aircraft, half-bathed in the light, and let out a deep breath. "Man, this is really beautiful," he praised. "So how did she fly?"

"We only found four references to it in any official records," Alex replied. "We think they only built three prototypes originally. There's a passing reference to a fire and an explosion during fueling due to static electricity that destroyed one. Another document detailed a test flight and mock air-combat competition with a Messerschmidt Me262, which was the first operational jet fighter in the war and at the time still in the developmental stage. According to the account, the plane showed excellent speed and exceptional maneuverability. Another source mentioned a high-altitude test flight over England, but the plane disappeared over the North Sea."

"I thought you said there were *four* references," Ryan said absent-mindedly as he concentrated on the matte black finish of the aircraft. "What is this coating made of, anyway? It feels thicker and smoother than paint."

"We're not sure," Alex answered. "I know what you mean, though – it's more like Teflon than actual paint. It's one of our many mysteries. We shouldn't call it The Bat. We should call it The Onion. Every time we answer a question or solve another of the plane's riddles, it seems like a whole new one appears. It's just like peeling layers off of an onion."

Then Alex shifted gears. "Do you know what a mass spectrometer is?"

"Sure," Ryan answered, "it's one of those high-tech machines used to identify unknown chemicals and compounds."

"Close enough," Alex conceded. "With all the new search engines and databases, we can compare the results to almost any known organic or inorganic compound in existence. As long as the substance is in some directory, the spectrometer gives us a good chance to know what we're dealing with. We found residue in the fuel lines, ran it through mass spec and made test batches of the German fuel. All I can say is this: That was some really nasty, volatile shit. It's a miracle that most of their planes didn't just explode. You really have to hand it to those early test pilots – they were some brave cowboys.

"We also examined a piece of the plane's black coating. There's one extremely large carbon-based molecule that doesn't appear in nature and is not in any database. Today, as you know, our modern stealth aircraft use coatings with carbon fibers to help absorb radar waves. Right now, some really smart people are beating their heads against a wall trying to figure out where this coating comes from and how it was produced. At the moment, it appears to be one of those pieces of knowledge lost to the ages."

"Well, I'm no chemist," Ryan returned, "but why can't you just break it down into component parts, put them together in correct proportions and just whip up a batch in your chemist's kitchen?"

"Like I said, it's not that simple," Alex countered. "It's a process that has been lost to time. You remember the old saying, 'The devil is in the details'? Well, that one certainly applies here. It's a huge molecule with thousands of interacting pieces and, to put it simply, we just don't know the exact process to make them come together and bond in this exact order."

Ryan almost laughed out loud. "Are you trying to tell me that you can't replicate something that was manufactured way back in the 1940s?"

"In the time of Alexander the Great," Alex replied as he tried to deflect the question, "the Greeks developed a weapon which could burn even while underwater. Homer and Archimedes described it, and yet to this day, what exactly the substance was is open to debate.

"Ancient Greeks writing narratives 2,500 years ago is one thing, but this plane is for real. But I digress. Let me get back to my story. We were stumped until we realized another old saying: It's better to be lucky than good. One of our lab technicians has a passion for beer. His brother was in South America on vacation – Uruguay, to be exact – and while walking through a flea market, he noticed some old brown beer bottles from the 1940s. Two brothers were selling a local beer out of their delivery truck. After a sample, even though he thought he was really getting screwed, he bought their last eight bottles for twenty-five dollars. He thought they would make the perfect birthday gift for his brother back home. Back at the hotel, he cracked one open to make sure they were the same ones he tasted, and therefore good enough for his brother's birthday. They turned out to be so good that by the time he got home there was only one left."

"What's this have to do with the plane?" Ryan asked impatiently.

"Better to be lucky than good," Alex answered. "On a slow day at work, the technician ran a sample of his last beer through the mass-spectrometer during his lunch break to see what that aromatic fragrance and unique taste were. And yes, to answer the question you're about to ask, this probably was not the proper use of a government lab."

Alex McCormick smiled as he patted The Bat's shiny fuselage. "Can you guess what was on the printout? Our mystery compound was found in minute quantities in the beer itself – parts per billion, to be exact. The amount was so small that it indicated a contaminant, not an ingredient, but it's in there just the same. Wherever this beer was brewed, our mystery chemical was in close proximity."

Chapter 19. December 22, 1943 – Berlin, Germany

By late 1943, Allied air raids over Germany had become a daily occurrence. The war had now come home to the Fatherland. For Carl, worrying about his family's safety had evolved into an all-consuming monster. Only last week, a young lieutenant three offices down had lost two cousins in an air raid over Dusseldorf. Now the sorties targeted not just Berlin, but areas across the heartland as well. Carl knew that he must bring his family to safety, but that ultimately meant taking them out of Europe. Without the proper transit papers, that would be impossible.

As boys, Carl and Willie allowed their imaginations to take them to fight duels, battle dragons and rescue fair young princesses. The Germanic legends of Lohengrin fueled their imaginations, so naturally, dragons and black knights alike kept their distance in the lads' neighborhood.

The two would concoct codes for secret messages and delighted in hiding them inside their parents' correspondences. All they needed to see was a small smudge from a dirty finger on the lower left corner of the envelope to know that a covert message awaited within.

As they grew older, Willie would say with a sly smile, "That good-looking young princess over there needs to be rescued." Even though their childhood friendship had grown strained, Willie made a point of approaching Carl at his wedding and whispering, "Take care of your princess." This simple reminder of a bygone era haunted Carl's every waking hour. He wished now more than ever that Willie was here. Secret missives, a fair princess, childhood fantasies … all would become even more real with each passing day.

Chapter 20. December 18, 1939 – Montevideo, Uruguay

Slipping quietly away from the waterfront, Willie slowly made his way up a side street. Old two-story tenement buildings lined the cobblestone alleys and eventually gave way to run-down, single-story shacks along a few dirt roads. He stood out like a sore thumb, but then what did he expect? After all, he was a stranger in a country where he didn't dress or look like anyone else.

First of all, Willie thought, he needed to do something about his clothes. A few feet past a short stone wall, he spied his new wardrobe flapping in the breeze on a nearby clothesline. He glanced around furtively. Everyone was running past him down to the docks to get a better view of the sinking ship and not paying the least bit of attention to the stranger at the side of the road.

This was his chance. He climbed the wall, pulled the pair of old faded trousers and shirt off the line and over his uniform, and grabbed a straw hat from a nearby post. Watching the people rush past him, Willie tried to emulate how they dressed: shirttails out, hat cocked at a certain angle. The pants and shirt were too small, but he at least felt he could blend in until he could concoct a plan. He and Carl had always been able to dream up one crazy scheme or another. Letting out a deep breath, he finally said, "I wish Carl were here right now." Willie would have even welcomed hearing his cousin's stern reply, "What the hell were you thinking?"

Sliding into a thicket of palms, Willie stared at the ground and tried to collect his thoughts. The soothing, rhythmic buzz of the insects contrasted sharply with the booming explosions coming from the harbor. What would Carl – good old practical Carl – do right now? he thought.

Willie knew that many South American countries contained German immigrant communities. If he could just make his way to one of them, he could blend in – or perhaps find someone willing to help.

But then, if there was a German town in Montevideo, where would he find it?

He grabbed a low-hanging branch and pulled himself up into a tree, then climbed to the top to try to get a sense of where the center of the city was located. With his back to the water, he studied the horizon for any clue. He had heard that many German immigrants constructed buildings more reminiscent of the Alps than the tropics to remind them of their old homes, so he searched for the distinctively Alpine architectural form. Steep roofs stood ever-vigilant against the threat of the next tropical snowstorm. Off in the distance, Willie saw taller and more modern buildings and decided to start in that direction.

Sliding down from the tree, he stepped out onto the dirt road. In the distance, a figure walked slowly toward him. Willie pulled the hat down over his face and moved as far to the side of the road as he could without actually stepping into the grass. As the man approached, Willie was surprised to hear him say in perfect German, "Nice shoes." As he glanced down at his own feet and saw the spit-polished naval footwear of the Fatherland, the flaw in his disguise was immediately apparent. He stopped, looked up and saw hazy blue eyes with European features staring back at him.

"You look lost," the man said. "Perhaps I can help." Without another word, he turned and walked back in the direction from which he came.

Glancing quickly over his shoulder and seeing no one else around, Willie followed. The mystery man turned right at the corner and out of sight. With a lump in his throat, Willie quickened his pace. A dust-covered, older-model sedan sat at the side of the road with the passenger door wide open. Willie climbed in and, as the car pulled away, the driver – without taking his eyes off the road – said, "You were the only one to escape."

Chapter 21. May 27, 2008 – Fairfax, Virginia

Ryan was absolutely fascinated with the aircraft. With its finish, look and clean, flowing lines, he wouldn't have been surprised to see it on display in some modern art museum. When he put his hands on the fuselage, the coating gave him the feeling that it was almost alive.

Bringing himself back to Earth, Ryan muttered, "Since it's apparent that you don't work for the Smithsonian, I'm guessing you're with one of the alphabets – maybe ATF, NSA, FBI, CIA or DEA. I'm going to go out on a limb and bet you know or have people who could find two brothers in some backwater town in Uruguay."

"Oh, they were easy enough to find," Alex said with disgust. "Their company was named Papagayo Hauling. That's Spanish for 'parrot.' The truck's cab was painted in bright red, yellow and blue feathers – looked just like a *papagayo*. Made quite an impression on the technician's brother, too. He told us it was just about the ugliest damned thing he'd ever seen."

"So what did they say?" Ryan asked eagerly. "Where did they get the beer?"

"Don't know," Ryan came back. "They weren't able to tell us."

"What happened to your vaunted reputation of being able to squeeze information out of a rock?" Ryan teased.

"Remember what I told you about the onion?" Alex asked. "The two brothers are dead. They were found about two hundred meters from an old farm building at the edge of a small river that flows to the Rio Plata. In the wet season, it floods its banks, but most of the time it's just what we back home call a creek."

"What happened?" Ryan quizzed.

"Local police just wanted it to go away, so they quickly wrote it off as a methamphetamine lab that went bad," Alex answered. "A lot of that stuff goes on down there. It's easier to get the ephedrine and other chemicals in large amounts where they live, and no one asks too many questions when a little money gets passed under the table."

"So what made them suspect it was a drug lab?" Ryan wondered. "Did they have a reputation of cooking or dealing?"

"No, it's *how* they died that's the real mystery," Alex replied. "They were literally cooked from the inside out by some sort of chemical burn. One was just sitting on a stump, his eyes rolled back in his head, mouth wide open, tongue and throat all blistered. His brother was found lying at the edge of the stream. He choked from all of the mud he swallowed trying to put the fire out inside him.

"If a batch of meth goes bad and the cooks are careless, they can die from inhaling white phosphorus fumes. Symptoms look similar to what happened to the brothers, except there was one odd difference: In these forested areas, anything that dies is quickly scavenged by animals and insects. The brothers hadn't been seen for three days. The bodies were bloated, but the animals didn't even touch them. In fact, you could see footprints in the muddy stream bank where the local varmints nosed around and just turned away. Whatever killed them was nasty enough that even the local fauna had enough sense to keep back."

"You mentioned an old farm nearby," Ryan remembered. "Who owns the place?"

"An old German family that immigrated in the 1920s," Alex said. "Small produce farmers – and they have a great reputation as local brewers as well. Supposedly, when they came here from the old country, they brought recipes, yeast and techniques that had been handed down for generations. In fact, one of the brothers regularly hauled truckloads of coal out to the hacienda. It all fits. So at that point, we began to discretely ask around."

Alex's facial expressions and body language did not indicate that he had just solved a puzzle – more like he had snatched defeat from the jaws of victory.

"Sounds pretty cut-and-dried to me," Ryan declared. "So what is it you're not telling me?"

"Well, about a week ago, I was getting my morning coffee at Starbucks," Alex began. "Lots of empty seats everywhere, but this stranger sits down directly in front of me. Before I could ask if we had met, he wanted to know why I was interested in Colonia. I couldn't quite place the accent, but if I was a betting man, I'd wager that he was Israeli. Not absolutely sure, but I'm usually pretty good at those things.

"He must have seen how surprised I was by the look on my face, and taking advantage of that moment, he said that it would be better for me to just drop it.

"Then, as he stood up, he said something really odd. 'You should drink your coffee before it gets cold. A man like you never knows when he might get an important phone call. Here, I'll leave the tip.'

"I watched him walk out of the coffee shop and turn down the sidewalk. Then a cell phone in my pocket began to vibrate. I did *not* have a cell phone in my pocket before that meeting took place!

"I went to answer the call, but my attention was divided between the stranger walking past the plate glass window and the coin that he left on my table. A voice on the other end of the phone snapped me back to reality. I immediately recognized the North Carolina drawl – it belonged to the assistant director of the CIA!"

Then, effecting his best quasi-Southern accent, Alex recounted his conversation with the fed. "'Mistah McCormick, this is Gerald Woods. I just need to know: The gentleman you were speaking with – is he still present, or has he departed?'

"'He left only a few moments ago, sir,' I answered, 'and he seemed to know you would be making this call. What exactly is going on?'

'Did he leave anything on the table?' the assistant director then asked me."

'Yes, sir,' I answered, 'there is a small ...'

"But before I could finish my answer, Mr. Woods interrupted me. 'Suh, this line may have been compromised and therefore no longer secure. Take whatever the gentleman left, leave Stahbucks, and walk in the same direction as he did. Someone will contact you. Hang up the phone – *now*!'

"Then the line just went dead," Alex continued. "In one smooth motion, I folded the newspaper over the coin and slid it into my other hand – with my new cell phone. I pressed the red button on the Android device and stepped out of the coffee house. I glanced left, then right, then briskly headed in the direction of the mystery man.

"Half a block later, I saw a cab idling by the curb about a hundred feet away. It displayed a sign that read OUT OF SERVICE. Suddenly, the driver flipped the placard on the roof and pulled up to me. He looked Pakistani, which is not exactly a rarity in Washington. I climbed in and asked, 'Where to?'

"Chuckling as if I didn't already know, the driver said, 'Langley.' Then he screeched away from the curb and it was on like NASCAR!"

Chapter 22. December 19, 1939 – Colonia, Uruguay

Wilhelm was driven up the old highway bordering the Rio Plata till it came to an overgrown gravel road winding inland away from the river. Perhaps a half-mile up the road stood the gates to an old and luxurious hacienda. Banana palms bordered the large, circular driveway, which also served as a central courtyard.

Seated on the front porch was a gray-haired man. Even though his eyes flashed with a youthful fire, he somehow seemed old beyond his years. The white paint on the rocking chair had all but peeled off, revealing the gray and weathered wood beneath. A carved walking stick lay across his lap and a ceramic mug of beer rested on a small table to his right. His left shirt sleeve hung empty and limp. At first glance, he looked more like a southern plantation owner during the Civil War than someone in charge of a German safe house.

As the car approached the front steps, the driver spoke. "That man's name is Claus von Duckworth," the driver instructed. "From now on, if anyone asks, you are his nephew from Vienna. Try to learn as much Spanish as quickly as you can. Don't talk to strangers, and above all else, don't leave the compound."

Stepping from the car, Willie walked across the gravel drive toward the porch where the old man was seated. At this latitude, heavy tropical rains could turn roads into an impassable mess, and a mere twelve inches of gravel was all that kept the driveway from becoming a swamp. If one were even slightly paranoid, anyone approaching the house and not being careful would also be heard. Low-tech, but effective.

Reaching the top of the stairs, Willie smiled, held out his hand and said in German, "My name is Wilhelm, and ..."

Claus cut him off quickly. "I know who you are. This is the last time you are to speak to me in German. Do you know any Italian, Portuguese, or Spanish?"

"When I was young, we would go on skiing holidays in Italy and France," Willie replied, "so I still remember a few phrases."

"Good – build on that memory," Claus said as he arose from the chair. Steadying himself by placing his hand on the table, he paused for a moment before continuing. Now that they were face-to-face, Claus stared directly into Willie's eyes.

"Official records will list you as a casualty on the *Graf Spee*," Claus declared. "Your family will mourn their loss and eventually the pain will pass, but you now have a chance for a new life. In time, you may even come to embrace this place and think of it as your home. Other young men like you are here in our new Germany – and more will come. Don't ask too many questions and do all that is requested of you. For now, the less you know, the better it will be for you if anything should happen. Miguel, show my nephew to his room."

Willie's room was located at the rear of the hacienda's ground level and appeared at one time to have been a storage room of some kind. The floor was six inches lower than the main building, indicating it had been added at a later date. The ceiling dipped and sagged in so many different directions that Willie felt the need to lean against something just to keep his balance. Judging by the differences in texture and inconsistency of materials, it appeared that the walls and ceiling had been repaired over a span of time by different work crews. One wall even had straw mixed in with the plaster, its strands sticking out in all directions like an unkempt beard.

Outside the two small windows grew massive clumps of thorny cactus. A natural barrier to keep intruders out – or was it to keep him in? A stone's throw away, several buildings nestled against the verdant jungle. At one structure, several farm workers smoked leisurely on the covered front porch, and on the other property was some sort of storage building with a coal chute or cellar entrance in the back. A single bed sat centered between a wash basin and mirror, and a small dresser held a bowl of fruit and several books.

Willie turned in surprise to see Miguel still standing in the doorway to his room. As his eyes became adjusted to the dim light, Willie noticed for the first time the man's chiseled features, darting eyes and leathery skin – darkened not so much due to race as from countless hours in the tropic sun.

"Dinner is served promptly at seven," Miguel announced. "Do not be late. There are books on your table. You would be wise to learn what you can and bring that knowledge to dinner tonight."

He turned to leave, but looked back and raised a single finger as if to emphasize one final point. "Never again mention the French – *never*. Señor Blanca was a staff officer with Hindenburg when Germany surrendered in that damned French railroad car in 1918. He has never forgotten – or forgiven – that tragic event. And do not be deceived by what appears to be his frail appearance. He is iron – he is Germany." With that, he walked away and closed the door behind him.

Willie stood alone and stared at the door while digesting Miguel's parting comments. He turned to the books and noticed that they were texts on translation and grammar. German translated to Spanish, German to Italian, and Italian to Spanish. Judging by the worn covers and dog-eared pages, they had been used many times before.

At the bottom of the stack lay a copy of Adolf Hitler's autobiographical manifesto, *Mein Kampf*, meaning "my struggle." Detractors referred to it as 780 pages of grammatical errors, but there was no debating the profound impact that it had on the German people. Willie chuckled and thought, this is like having the Nazi version of the Gideon Bible in your hotel room.

Opening the book to a turned-down page, he immediately noticed an underlined sentence. "A man does not die for something which he himself does not believe in."

In broken Spanish, Willie said to himself, "Well, it seems that after all, Mr. Hitler and I do have something in common."

Chapter 23. August 9, 1943 – Colonia, Uruguay

The news was not good. In Europe, the tide of battle was turning, and Willie felt powerless to help Carl and his family escape. Willie spent many sleepless nights staring at the ceiling, watching lizards race up and down the walls and as he wracked his brain to think up a plan for their rescue.

Over the past four years, Willie had worked himself into a trusted position as a "family member" on the farm. Given more and more responsibility, he even became the appointed courier for the monthly trip to Buenos Aires. After he delivered coded messages to the German embassy, which in turn would then transmit them to Berlin, he would return with their instructions. It was on one of these trips that the blueprint for his plan began to take shape. Willie didn't realize it just then, but his opportunity would arise within the next two weeks.

At dinner every evening, the only topic of discussion was the war in Europe. Claus von Duckworth's hatred, which until now had been reserved exclusively for the French, now spread to all the Allied forces. The mere mention of Churchill, Roosevelt or especially Stalin would send him into a screaming frenzy until saliva frothed at the corners of his mouth.

With each new report of the fighting in the East, Claus would become even more furious. Stalin and the Russians were not only holding on, they now advanced toward Germany. His eyes wild with rage, he would pound on the dinner table and end his tirade by screaming, "I hope there is a special place in hell for Uncle Joe!"

It always seemed like a passing fever. After he let it out of his system, a more calm and rational discussion invariably followed, with a wide range of ideas being mutually exchanged. It was at one of these dinner sessions that Claus mentioned plans to smuggle party faithful and vast resources out of Germany – resources to rebuild and establish a new German Reich.

A shadow group known as ODESSA, or *Organization Der Ehemaligen SS-Angehörigen*, had been established for exactly this purpose. Untraceable Swiss bank accounts were opened and monies transferred. These funds would then become available if the war came to, as he put it, an "unacceptable outcome."

Willie finally asked the burning question. "But where can they possibly hide so many people *and* set up a new government at the same time?"

Claus answered with one word. It burned into Willie's very soul. "Here."

The following Thursday, as Willie prepared to make his monthly trip to the German embassy in Buenos Aires, Claus handed him the courier envelope and took him aside. Claus looked very grim.

"Today, when you arrive at the embassy, they will have a simple but extremely important task for you to perform," Claus instructed. "It is imperative that you follow their directions precisely. Do not – I repeat – do *not* deviate at all from their instructions."

As the ferry churned through the muddy waters of the Rio de la Plata, Willie felt his blood rush in anticipation. Although merely a glorified messenger boy, he might now be in a position to finally help his family escape.

As he entered the embassy, the uniformed and plainclothes security personnel watched Willie closely while he made his way down the hall to the consul's office. At the door, he was stopped, placed against a white screen and photographed.

After entering the office, Willie was surprised to see not the normal array of bureaucrats, but the German ambassador himself and two other men whom he did not recognize. He didn't know any of them personally. However, their uniforms were unmistakable: Dressed completely in black and discussing paperwork with the ambassador, they wore the distinctive uniform of the *Waffen-SS*.

They were German secret police! One wore a ring turned so it appeared as only a silver band. However, when he reached for his coffee, one could clearly see the distinctive skull-and-crossbones emblem on the underside. Although Willie had never met or spoken to the ambassador before, he was well aware of the significance of the man's presence.

The ambassador spoke first. "And you must be the Wilhelm our friend Claus has been telling us so much about. A cup of coffee, perhaps?"

"*Danke schoen, mein herr,*" Willie thanked him in his most respectful tone. "Black, if you please."

"I trust your ferry crossing wasn't too rough," the ambassador said. "It can be quite windy and the waters quite choppy this time of year."

Before Willie could respond, the ambassador continued. "Did Claus tell you we have a small errand for you to run?" Willie nodded and one of the strangers in black stepped forward to hand him an envelope. Even as he took the parcel, Willie couldn't stop staring at the ring.

"We are conducting a very simple test," the ambassador explained. "We just want you to act like you are entering the country, just like any normal traveler. There is a steamer from Marseilles arriving this afternoon and you are going to play the part of one the passengers. In your envelope, you will find your entry visa and German marks to exchange for Argentinian pesos."

Just then, there was a soft knock at the door and the ambassador's secretary entered with more documents. "Ah, here is your passport," he said as he held up the traveling papers in order to compare Willie to his picture. "I think his eyes are more brown than green – fix it." He then handed the passport back to his secretary.

"Change the clothes you are wearing to the ones in the suitcase by the door," he continued. "There are toiletries and other items in there to make you look like any other traveler arriving from the continent. Your passport will be ready by the time you change. Do you have any questions?"

"How will I get into the area where the people are arriving?" Willie inquired.

"That has all been arranged," the *SS* officer responded. "When you are standing in line with the others, simply follow directions and do as you are instructed – just like all the others." His smile caused a shiver to run down Willie's spine.

The drive to the dock from the embassy took only fifteen minutes. Willie was then led through a series of corridors and passageways. As he merged with a group of people filing into the immigration office, a policeman stepped aside to let him in.

When his turn came, he presented his passport and entry visa, then showed the cash given to him as proof of his ability to support himself and not become a ward of the state. The agent slipped a bill from the envelope and slid it aside as he continued to check Willie's papers.

Ah, the international language of a bribe, Willie thought to himself.

"Your passport was issued in Vienna," the agent snapped as he looked up at Willie. "Did you travel straight to Marseilles?" Willie nodded yes. "Please take your bag and go through that door over there."

When he entered the room, Willie was surprised to see the two men in black from the ambassador's office. Each was wearing a long coat covering his uniform, and the looks on their faces underscored the impression that something was not right. Seated next to them were two men dressed similarly to Willie.

A side door opened, after which the well-dressed and irritated head of the port authority entered. "We try to maintain friendly relations with your government and this is how you repay us. I received a phone call from our ambassador's office to cooperate fully with you, and at the same time you are attempting to walk three German nationals with fake papers right through our immigration offices? If you want them in this country so badly, make them a part of your embassy staff, or land them on a deserted beach and have them walk into town. With this mess you have created, I'll be up until midnight doing paperwork – that is, if I can even figure out which forms to fill out."

The SS officer who had addressed Willie in the office spoke first. "We have no intention of embarrassing you," he said. "We needed to see if these papers would work – and obviously there are problems." Unbuttoning his coat and revealing his uniform, his honey-sweet tone evaporated. "I need you to tell me what is wrong here."

The change in attitude was immediate. "It is not so much what is wrong, but we have learned that the little details are important," the port authority official stated. "All three are traveling here from Europe, yet none brought or made mention of staying with family members here in Buenos Aires. It is not a crime to travel alone, but it does make us suspicious and examine you more closely.

"The first two 'immigrants' also acted extremely nervous. Your first man said he traveled from Marseilles, but the exit visa stamp is blurred and smeared. It is almost impossible to read the exact date. Any competent agent would have re-stamped the papers – unless there was some other reason for the smear. He also did not have a telephone number or hotel reservations for accommodations here in Buenos Aires. And besides, if anyone comes from Marseilles, they get a closer look anyway, since they come from that cesspool of thieves.

"Your second man's papers say he was from Portugal," the official went on. "When he came to the window, he had trouble understanding basic Portuguese – or even Spanish, for that matter. First it was his hearing, then he was still feeling the effects of sea-sickness. He kept looking around, became flustered and was unsure about the simplest details of his story. At one time, he even said he came to go sport-fishing.

"Finally, your third man presented this to my agent." He then pulled a German mark from his pocket. "It is new and uncirculated, and the paper has an oily feel to it. I personally would examine it to make sure it wasn't counterfeit. Each of your three men registered small, but significant, red flags during the examination process." Willie listened intently as the phony travelers' indiscretions were brought to light.

At last, the *SS* officer spoke. "You have been most informative. Now, I need you to tell me what I should have done so we will not have any more of these little meetings."

* * *

The next day, as Claus tended his tomato garden, Willie approached him. He had lain awake nearly all night, and he realized that this might finally be an opportunity to bring Carl and his family to safety in a new land.

"How are you planning on getting people out of Germany?" Willie asked as he tried to control his burgeoning excitement.

"It's not my plan," Claus replied as he raised himself up from one knee with Willie's help. "Very powerful people are making what you might call contingency plans. We will just be one stop along the route and they are assembling the final pieces as we speak. Bankers, industrialists, even some members of the Catholic clergy … all are part of the plan."

Willie saw his opening. "Then what we need is to make a test run," he began. "Someone in the military – somebody who will leave with their family, and above all, someone who is expendable. If your plan is to be operational at a moment's notice, every safe house, every document and every possible problem will need to have been calculated and tested. We will need to know in advance …" Willie hesitated as he searched for just the right words, "... before irreplaceable assets are shipped."

"And I assume you have such a subject in mind for this test case – is that correct, Herr Wilhelm?" von Duckworth cocked his head as he asked. The answer could already be found in Willie's eyes.

"Yes sir, I have the perfect subject in mind," he replied. "He works in the Chancellery. He is a captain and it is imperative that he be discretely contacted, so his superiors are not aware. This can be done, and I am certain invaluable lessons will be learned."

Willie thought the process through and saved his most persuasive argument for last. "Above all, we will need to test how completely we can make people disappear and give them a totally new identity in a foreign country with a conquering army once again at Germany's doorstep."

Claus stared at Willie. "So you think that, once again, Germany is about to lose the war?"

"I think that this is a plan that would never be proposed by a government on the verge of victory," Willie replied. Claus grimly clenched his teeth, his eyes seeming to withdraw back into their sockets. He knelt down quietly and returned to his tomatoes.

Two days later, as Willie lay in his bed after dinner, he heard the familiar tapping of Claus's cane as he made his way down the hall. The rapping stopped just outside his room as a sheet of paper was slid under the door. The single-sentence note simply read, "Bring your people out."

Chapter 24. December 24, 1943 – Berlin, Germany

On Christmas Eve, Carl went into the office earlier than usual. Even as times became tougher, he was still able to purchase a few gifts for the children. Fresh oranges smuggled in by the Spanish consulate would be a special treat for Elaine.

Carl leaned back in his chair and thought about how much more special Christmas had become since the arrival of the twins. Then he laughed aloud at how he and Elaine had fought over naming the little ones.

He had insisted that, if they had a boy, he would be called Adolph. Elaine never liked the name, so they compromised: All the children's names would start with the letter "A." Now, if she delivered a boy, he would be Alex and, if a girl, either Alyssa or Alana.

On the night of the birth, the doctor was as surprised as anyone when first a boy and then a girl popped out! Carl and Elaine returned in one week for the well-baby checkup and discovered a minor clerical error: When the hospital staff filled out the birth certificates, the head nurse – after having completed the forms for Alex Friedrick – had meant for her assistant to turn the page on the file, so she said, "Next page." The assistant took this to mean that the next baby's name would be Paige, so she entered this errant information on the birth certificate.

As the embarrassed nursing staff tried to figure a way out of its predicament, Elaine kept repeating the name to herself – Paige Friedrick, Paige Friedrick, Paige Friedrick. Carl remembered the look on his wife's face when she said, "Honey, our son's name begins with an A, and I really think the name Paige has a beautiful ring to it. Can we just leave it that way, please? I really do like it."

Whenever she said "please" in that long, drawn-out, little-girl voice of hers, Carl would simply melt inside. Paige Friedrick it would be. Case closed.

Oh well, Carl thought. Back to work. The sooner he finished here, the sooner he could go home. One of his jobs consisted of sifting through a myriad of incoming diplomatic pouches and classified documents, and routing anything of interest or value to his superiors.

This was the easy part of his day – the fun part. His most demanding challenge was to take logistics nightmares, simplify them and design plans that could be implemented by any fool – and there certainly were more than a few of those oafs in his office.

Carl blew on his hot tea as he thumbed through the pile of reports and diplomatic communications. Everything from requests for winter clothing to cooking supplies crossed his desk. "What in the world is this?" he would mutter from time to time throughout the day. But this packet of papers was different. This is the first time I've ever received anything from the German consulate in Buenos Aires, he thought. His office had only been concerned with the European Theater up until that time. He couldn't imagine anything from Argentina that his superiors would want to see.

Carl was about to toss it aside when he noticed a small smudge in the lower left-hand corner of the envelope. He took a deep breath, licked his lips and thought about all the odd games one's mind can play when this exhausted. It had to be nothing more than an overworked mail clerk with dirty hands – or so he thought.

Carl's small, eagle-emblazoned letter opener cut smoothly through the paper and the official documents slid out onto his desk. Nothing really out of the ordinary here – just a list of all ships entering and leaving the Plata estuary. Low-level spying at the consulate was part of their daily routine. Most of the ships were of Italian or neutral registry and had left some time ago.

Carl picked up the envelope again and ran his thumb over the smudge while looking at the consulate memo in his other hand. Gazing at the top of the document, he noticed his immediate superior's name, Ernst von Landendorf, was misspelled. Instead, it read "von Langsdorff." Suddenly, Carl remembered that Langsdorff was the name of the commanding officer of the *KMS Admiral Graf Spee*.

Laying the communiqué down on his desk, he pulled out a sheet of tracing paper and placed it over the document. He strained to remember the boyhood code that Willie and he had dreamed up so many years before. As he circled the letters on the page, his mind screamed, "What kind of an idiot are you? Willie is dead. He went down with the *Graf Spee* four years ago."

But Carl pressed on. He had to know. Was this just some kind of crazy coincidence or … ? Slowly, Carl circled the letters and arranged them in their coded sequence. A group of letters stared back at him like burning coals: SAVEYOURPRINCESS.

Chapter 25. March 10, 1944 – Berlin, Germany

More than two months had passed since Carl received his cryptic letter from the consulate in Buenos Aires. Between the letter from his dead cousin and all of the troubling information that constantly crossed his desk at the chancellery, he certainly rode quite the emotional roller coaster. At once elated at the thought that Willie might be still alive, he would then plummet into despondency over what he feared might soon happen to his family and beloved motherland. The stress took a major toll on his home life. Lack of sleep had caused him to become quick-tempered, irritable and just not much fun to be around.

Because of his position, more and more time was required at the office. Every day was a workday for him now, and the distinction between weekdays and weekends had simply evaporated.

Sunday morning was especially comforting for Carl, because he could attend church with his wife and children. It reminded him of a simpler and happier time, and how sitting next to his parents and being in the presence of God had invigorated him and made him feel safe. But now he just worked every Sunday as he sorted through never-ending stacks of paperwork and cursed at the world. Instead of a protective cross on the wall, a large red flag with a black swastika – the German crucifix – had become his backdrop.

Carl meticulously sifted through papers, directives and sealed attaché folders from Lisbon, Paris and Genoa. Then he came to the envelope from Buenos Aires. Once again, a slight smudge lingered at the lower left-hand corner. Lifting out the papers one by one, he noticed that they seemed to be nothing more than mundane reports intended to give the impression that a valued source of information was on the job. He couldn't help but visualize some low-level consulate worker sitting in a local street-side café, drinking himself into oblivion as he jotted down a few notes to give his superior something to send back to Berlin.

Nothing of military significance here. The most worthwhile intel spoke of German detainees in Uruguay and what they had missed the most about their homes. Before he could pull out a sheet of tracing paper to search for cryptic messages, his eye caught the words *Graf Spee*. As he read the clipping from a local Buenos Aires newspaper more closely, he realized that those Uruguayan prisoners taken from the great German battleship lamented not being able to return home to help in the war effort, while mentioning a few of their favorite memories.

One sailor, an unidentified cook, spoke of a beloved restaurant off the *Kaiserdamm*, or underground railway, where family celebrations were often held. The oddly named German eatery Hofbrau Genoa was described more as a bar or dance hall than an actual restaurant. The sailor had reminisced, "The schnitzel was the best he had ever tasted, and the beer … well, it was so rich that you could float a bottle cap on its foamy head."

Later that morning, Carl decided to take an early lunch. February was always cold, but today was clear and he felt only a gentle breeze against his face as he left the chancellery. Thinking a good walk in the brisk air would help clear his mind, and seeing as how the restaurant was only a little more than a kilometer away, he briskly set off on his impromptu constitutional. Walking down the Kaiserdamm, he turned left on Klist Street – not exactly the type of neighborhood where one expected to find a memorable restaurant. It would seem that the German government's grand scheme for urban renewal had completely overlooked this area.

From the outside, it more closely resembled a hardware store or tailor's shop. Carl entered and was immediately reminded of the article's description – it really did appear more like a working-class bar than a restaurant.

A man in a dirty white apron mopped the floor just a few feet away. He ambled over to Carl as he entered. "We are not open until two on Sunday," the man said while sizing up Carl with a quick glance. In uniform, Carl had become accustomed to the treatment that came with his position. He thought for a moment and answered, "A friend of mine who served on the *Admiral Graf Spee* always bragged about how you served the best schnitzel in all of Berlin – and if I ever had an opportunity to eat here, that I should."

The man in the apron listened with a bemused expression. Clearly, this stranger was trying to curry favor with the owner. Presently, he replied, "Well, it's still early, but I'll see if the cook has anything ready. While you are waiting, please enjoy a mug of our private-label lager. It is especially famous for its thick, foamy head." Carl remembered the newspaper article and acknowledged, "That's what I've read."

The man ambled over to the bar and pulled a handle on the wall. Sputtering to life, the faucet under the tap filled a heavy glass *maßkrug* or beer mug, with a rich brown liquid crowned by a thick, creamy head. He reached above the tap and took something off the shelf, then placed it onto the top of the mug. It floated as if suspended on a cloud.

He set the *maßkrug* on the table and headed back behind the bar. Carl looked into the sea of bronze foam and fished a bottle cap from the top of the one-liter mug. As he rolled it over in his hand and wiped the foam away, he noticed a bright red crown and the brand name: Princess Ale.

Carl felt a knot beginning to develop in the pit of his stomach. He wondered whether an odd circumstance perhaps had put him somewhere he did not belong. He began to drain the large vessel of its hoppy contents.

A few minutes later, another man came out from behind the bar and apologized for not being ready to serve customers at this early hour. Unlike the first man, he was well-dressed and appeared in excellent physical condition.

Carl had seen men like him before: dressed in black turtleneck sweaters and dark, well-tailored pants ... he knew the look all too well. Exchange the leather dress shoes for boots, add some dark facial make-up and a satchel of explosives, and he might be ready to be dropped behind enemy lines. He could be Special Forces, or even worse – the *SS*.

Setting a menu down on the table, the gentleman introduced himself. "Captain, my name is Steinman. I am the manager. I'm sorry, but it is a bit early to serve schnitzel. We have but a few light snacks available at this hour. We are just a local diner and many of these people are retired naval personnel, so they are in the habit of dining late. In fact, our chef and his assistant are former Navy cooks. Perhaps something else on the menu might appeal to you, *herr kapitan?*"

Feeling even more uneasy, Carl reached for his wallet to pay for the beer. However, the manager immediately voiced his disapproval. "There is no charge for the beer, Captain Friedrick."

Well, this is discomforting, Carl thought. This manager – if he is in fact the manager – knows my name. Carl decided it was time to leave. As he rose and headed for the door, the man in black had a few words for him.

"Sometimes, when I need to think, I find it comforting to go to Saint Hedwig's Cathedral near Leipzeiger Street, light a few candles and think through my problems in the holy silence," Steinman stated. "I believe you know where it is located. There is something about the solitude of the old cathedral and the warm glow of the candles that allows me to sort my thoughts. I find it especially comforting and rewarding to light the three middle candles on the top row and the middle taper at the bottom." With that, the manager picked up the empty *maßkrug* and retreated through the door behind the bar.

Meanwhile, back on Kleist Street, Carl popped the collar of his coat up against the back of his neck to shield himself from the chilling wind and blew into his hands for warmth. As he glanced back at the Hofbrau Genoa, a young woman replaced the OPEN sign with one that read CLOSED. The wind blew even harder now and he felt its chill down to his bones.

Chapter 26. March 10, 1944 – Berlin, Germany

Construction on St. Hedwig's Cathedral in Berlin began in 1747. Because of the cost and often-wavering political will, it took nearly thirty years to complete. It was originally built to give the new and burgeoning Roman Catholic immigrant population a place to practice its faith. It also stood as a symbol of the government's religious tolerance and of the power of the Roman Catholic Church in Germany. It became one of the most important cathedrals in all of Europe.

In the new Germany, Bernard Lichtenberg, the bishop of Berlin, presided over his congregation and balanced the religious teachings of the church with the secular doctrines of the Third Reich. This was never more apparent than when he openly prayed for all the Jews, was thrown into prison and eventually died on the way to the Dachau concentration camp.

Carl spent many Sundays as a child in this very cathedral, attending church with his parents and pondering the deep philosophical questions that all men consider from time to time. Now, once again, he sat in the pew and searched for answers.

The memories were bittersweet as he entered the cathedral through the large arched double doors. Warm remembrances of his parents were overshadowed by those of the last time he was here. Ten years earlier, he had said his final goodbyes in this very building. The vision of their car plunging off an icy road in Switzerland and the thought of their mangled bodies would make even a hardened German war veteran shiver.

All of the pain came rushing back as he walked through that hallowed doorway and his eyes blurred as tears welled up. As he walked over to an alcove at the side of the entryway, he saw five rows of candles ensconced in shelves on the wall. Placing several German marks in the collection box, Carl lit the three middle candles on the top row and the one below it, then genuflected on the padded kneeler in front of the candles. Staring into the flickering flames, Carl thought of his parents and drifted into a distant past.

His mother had been an ever-present nurse during his long childhood illness. She was always there to tell him "no" and forcing him to learn to walk again. Realizing now that she had been right all along, he remembered her encouraging words. "Carl, your strength of will and determination define who you are and what you can do. The inflated opinions of those so-called experts do not matter."

His father insisted that his polio-stricken son participate in sports as he recovered. Lessons beyond merely winning and losing were there to be learned, but he could only play on Sundays if he first attended church. "Strength in a man is not only the size of his muscles," his father would say. "Remember, you must be physically strong to have the stamina to be morally brave." He would repeat this mantra over and over again: "Physical strength and moral courage."

Movement from across the church caught his eye and brought Carl out of his flashback. A priest in a monk's robe made his way between the pews and stood before the lit candles. Staring intently for several seconds, he made the sign of the cross and knelt beside Carl.

In the dim light, Carl recognized the priest as the one who had conducted his parent's funeral mass. "It's strange how things have a way of coming full-circle," the clergyman said as he let out a deep breath. "I presided over your parent's interment and helped them leave this earthly realm. Now I may also help you and your family escape. Many people come here looking for help, but unfortunately we must turn most of them away. However, you, Herr Friedrick, you are one of the lucky ones. Someone is looking out for you.

"Leaders of our church are more concerned with what may happen when the godless Russians arrive, instead of what is happening to our fellow German citizens today. I am afraid that this will be a burden and a stain that the church must bear for years to come."

With that, he arose and extinguished the candle on the lower row with his thumb and index finger. He then removed an envelope from inside the sleeve of his robe. Holding it like a priceless heirloom, he handed it to Carl and whispered, "Be very careful – people would kill for this." Carl cradled the envelope that now carried a black smudge from the extinguished candle in its lower left-hand corner.

Chapter 27. March 10, 1944 – Berlin, Germany

Back in his office at the chancellery, Carl locked the door behind him. He pulled out the envelope that the priest had given him and ran a finger over the smudged corner. He thought of how the cleric had extinguished the flame with his fingers and methodically smeared the lower left-hand corner of the envelope – like something from a religious ceremony during the Middle Ages.

With that thought, he opened the envelope. A key to a locker at the Grunewald Railway Station slid out, along with a yellowed page torn from an old family bible. The circled verses were from a seldom-quoted book of Sirach, a book of the Christian Old Testament and Hebrew bible. This passage came from Chapter 15, verses 15-20:

"If you choose you can keep the commandments, they will save you. If you trust in God, you too shall live. He has set before you fire and water to whichever you choose, stretch forth your hand. Before man are life and death, good and evil, whichever he chooses shall be given him. Immense is the wisdom of the Lord. He is mighty in power, and all-seeing. The eyes of God are on those who fear him. He understands man's every deed." The last sentence was underlined. "No one does he command to act unjustly, to none does he give license to sin."

As Carl drove to Grunewald Station, he repeated the verse over and over again, like a song inside his head that he could not escape. Choosing between good and evil – or life and death – was clearly a black-and-white decision. However, a little gray area would certainly help settle his mind.

Grunewald had established itself as one of the major train hubs in Berlin. During the week, and especially on weekends, it was a veritable beehive of departures and arrivals. A lone man in uniform walking through the crowd toward a locker would hardly be noticed. Less dense than weekdays, it was still packed with throngs of people returning from holidays and military men in uniform hurrying to catch their trains.

The end locker on the third aisle would not easily be noticed. Carl slid the key into the slot, turned the handle and opened the door to reveal a small suitcase. He considered taking a quick look inside when a sudden commotion outside on the arrival platform caught his attention.

Three German soldiers pushed a man toward a group assembled at the far end of the platform. He pleaded for aid from anyone who would listen. "There must be some mistake," he wailed plaintively. People were forced into boxcars like cattle. Stars of David hung around their necks and bewildered looks of resignation told more than any cry for help would ever reveal.

In the beginning, the trains had loaded their passengers from rail spurs away from public view. Now it seemed that the government no longer cared to hide its horrible secret. As Carl drove home, he kept reciting the passage that the priest had given him and remembering the scene at the train station. He just couldn't push it out of his mind.

Carl was met at the front door by his wife. For some reason, she looked much older than when he had left her that morning. She exhibited a countenance of anguish and her eyes were wet with tears, but she couldn't quite bring herself to openly cry. It was as if all the emotion and life had been drained from her.

"They're gone," Elaine whispered in short, breathy gasps.

"Who?" Carl asked. "Who is gone?"

"Mother and father," she replied in agony. "Their house, their street – there was nothing left but burning, broken houses as far as I could see. I heard there had been an air raid over Potsdam, and I couldn't get ahold of my parents, so I asked my friend Enga to drive me there. It was horrible. There is just nothing left."

"Did you check with the rescue workers?" Carl asked. "The hospitals? The shelters?"

"Yes," she replied, "there was just nothing left. I couldn't even find the house where I grew up." With that, she slumped into a corner and began to softly sob. Carl leaned over to comfort her, but she pushed him away and screamed, "We're going to die here! Our children are going to die here!" She glared into his eyes and wailed.

Standing in the doorway with suitcase in hand, Carl understood he was now the only one who could make the decisions for his family. Knowing now that Elaine had asked their neighbors, Ernst and Helga, to watch the children while she searched for her parents, he walked over to their house to explain the tragic event.

Helga was still at home with the children and said she would watch them as long as was needed. Carl thanked her and asked if she could watch his children for at least a little while longer. He told her that he needed to make some calls to his superiors to arrange a few days off to sort out personal matters. For the moment, with his family cared for, Carl turned his attention back to the suitcase.

The only room in the house that had a lock was a small study. Closing the door, Carl turned the old-style key left in the lock to the right and heard it click. He turned on a desk lamp and unbuckled the two straps on the suitcase. Inside were nothing more than travel brochures from Switzerland, Germany and northern Italy. The people in the pictures looked as though they lived in a happier time. They hiked through high alpine meadows, skied and relaxed leisurely by the sea.

Instinctively, Carl pulled at the lining and it separated from the case. He reached in and pulled out several bundles of papers wrapped in waterproof oilskin. The first sheet was all too familiar: a death notification issued by the military. He could still remember the impact it made on his family as it notified them of Willie's death after the *Admiral Graf Spee* sank.

But this one was different – it was dated three days in advance and stated that Carl Friedrick, his wife and two small children were killed in an automobile accident in northern Italy. Attached to this sheet was the directive, dated several months earlier, advising all non-essential personnel to temporarily move to rural areas for their own safety. The form had been carefully crafted to sound more humanitarian than an indictment against the German Air Force, which could no longer protect the skies above the Fatherland.

Carl flipped the sheet and pondered the notion of an official document listing his own death.

The next package contained documents issued by the International Red Cross for refugees who were left without papers due to loss or destruction. Usually, only the signature of a high-ranking German church official was necessary. However, the Archbishop of Genoa had signed this particular document. In war-torn Europe, these papers were more precious than gold. They were a ticket to a new identity in another land.

The priest was right: These forms, signed by the proper officials, *were* worth killing for.

The last set of credentials was stapled together: four tourist visas for Argentina, with boxes checked to waive health forms, financial status and round-trip ticket requirement. The final sheet contained booking passage on a Panamanian-registered steamer called *La Cruz del Sur*, or *The Southern Cross*, which would sail from Genoa in three days.

Below the pile of papers lay packets of currency – not newly printed, but circulated so as not to raise any suspicion. German marks, Italian lira and Argentinian pesos. There was enough money here to buy somebody out of a really tight predicament, if necessary.

Someone had certainly gone to a lot of trouble and expense to arrange for Carl and his family to disappear and start a new life in South America. The questions lingered and rolled through Carl's mind: Who had the means to set all of this in motion? Who benefited from these people fleeing the Fatherland? Who had the power to cover it up?

Chapter 28. March 11, 1944 – Berlin Germany

Before he left for the chancellery the next morning, Carl went next door to tell his neighbors that he would be gone for a few days. Ernst and Helga were among the first to offer condolences at the loss of Elaine's parents, and would happily continue watching the children if need be.

Having no little ones of their own, Ernst and Helga had considered Carl, Elaine and the children as their adopted family. To Alex and Paige, they were another set of grandparents.

Helga was a typical *grossmutter*, or grandmother. One might expect to see her on a poster that advertised ordinary family life in Germany. Somehow, despite the food shortages, she always managed to have a sweet or cookie stashed away for the grandchildren. She felt that it was necessary to spoil them on occasion, and they would cry out *"danke, oma, danke!"* in glee whenever presented with their treats. Helga soon discovered that one of the few advantages of the food rationing was her forced weight loss.

Ernst, now in his sixties, still carried a piece of shrapnel in his leg from World War I. It ached mercilessly whenever the weather changed. Even with Helga's cooking, he was proud to brag to his friends how he could still fit into his uniform from twenty-five years earlier. In his mind, it did seem that it had shrunk a bit over time.

Helga met Carl at the door and he told her of his plan to move them to safety. She nodded in agreement, but at the same time she looked troubled.

"Is something bothering you?" Carl asked.

"We had visitors this morning," Helga replied. "They said we were being investigated to determine if my grandmother was half-Jewish."

"Investigated?" Carl repeated in astonishment. "But Ernst is a war hero. He was wounded twice on the Western Front and still attends veteran's rallies. I assure you, I will look into it when I return."

She smiled, leaned over to kiss his cheek and whispered, "Carl, do not come back."

Chapter 29. March 11, 1944 – Berlin, Germany

Carl's superior, General Ernst von Landendorf, came from a family with a long history of military service. Having distinguished himself in World War I, he eventually rose through the ranks – a challenging feat in depression-era Germany. His penchant for perfection and meticulous planning proved to be his one fatal flaw on the battlefield, where split-second decisions were constantly required. Now he was stuck behind a desk co-coordinating supply shipments – a job which not only fit his personality, but one that he managed to raise to an art form.

Modest in stature but massive in ego, von Landendorf was certain that a coordinated effort had been established to hold him back from his much-deserved promotions. There could be no other possible explanation for his lack of advancement. He felt that he needed to accomplish something truly impressive to gain the attention and respect of his peers – and turn the heads of his superiors.

His chance had come earlier in the week during a general staff meeting, where the main topic of discussion dealt with the delays in moving troops to the Eastern Front and detainees to the work camps. General von Landendorf boasted that his logistics unit was the most efficient in the chancellery. He surmised that by tighter scheduling and with multiple usages of each train, the rail transport problem could be solved. He had set the bar high, and now his staff, headed by Captain Friedrick, would have to come through with flying colors to make him look good.

The task at hand turned out to be more daunting than he expected. What confronted him was not just a mere scheduling problem, but a logistics nightmare. The Russians, ever distrustful of the West and especially of the Germans, built their railway system to a standard which matched no other in Europe: The tracks on their rail beds were wider than those used in other areas of the world. This was by design, for it would keep an invading army from using their railroad system to drive deep into the Russian heartland.

With their rails wider than the German lines, each German train had to be unloaded and then reloaded on captured Russian trains. With a shortage of Russian-gauge locomotives and rolling stock, the partisans and Red Army saboteurs fully understood that this could be a major setback.

It took time to rebuild the rail beds, but during a discussion with Captain Friedrick on an inspection tour, Carl suggested that it would be faster and more efficient to simply add an extra rail between the existing two. They could bring the German trains into service more quickly and, when Russian rail stock was available, they also could use the same rail lines.

German locomotives also broke down more often in the cold. They had not been designed like their Eastern bloc counterparts to deal with the severe Russian winters. Captain Friedrick once again came to the rescue by suggesting a simplified train design. This would make them more reliable.

All these changes were being implemented, but the demand for war materials had slowed the pace to a crawl. The general was assured that unlimited slave labor would be available, so once again it would come down to scheduling – and Captain Friedrick was just the man for the job.

Carl was unaware of any of these details when he entered the general's office on Monday morning. "Good morning, *herr general*," Carl said as he clicked his heels together. "I need to speak to you on a subject of a personal nature."

"I'm glad you're here," the general replied as he turned his attention back to the maps on his desk. "I also need to speak to you."

Carl went first. "My wife's parents were killed in an air raid over Potsdam the day before yesterday, and she has become hysterical worrying about the children. We have a family friend living about twenty miles south of Milan in the rural countryside. I need a few days to take them there."

Without looking up, the general responded, "Impossible. We are now responsible for scheduling and routing all trains in and out of Berlin. I can't afford to have any of my staff off on a holiday."

"*Mein herr*, with all due respect, this is no holiday," Carl responded. "It is simply an attempt to save the spirit of my family."

Irritated at having his decision challenged, von Landendorf tapped his forefinger on the map at his desk, pushed his glasses up to his forehead and rubbed his eyes.

After what seemed an eternity, he let out a deep breath and muttered gruffly, "Three days – not one minute more. You drive to Milan, drop off your family and return immediately. Is that clear?"

"*Ja, mein general,*" Carl stammered his thanks as a trickle of sweat ran down his back.

With that, the general rang for his secretary. "Captain Friedrick will need a staff car," he barked. "See to it that it's fully fueled and ready in fifteen minutes." He listened for a moment and said, "No, he will be going to Milan. Make sure he gets one of the 302s, not an Opel. The 302 has a larger fuel tank and carries extra petrol cans."

Carl knew that the Mercedes-Benz 302 was the cream of all staff cars in the motor pool. Usually reserved for the highest-ranking officers and dignitaries, it had a powerful straight-six-cylinder engine and a wide stance, giving it stability for excellent handling – even on icy roads.

General von Landendorf opened a drawer in his desk and pulled out a letter of transit. He filled in the names of Carl, Elaine, Alex and Paige Friedrick, then signed it with penmanship only a doctor could have loved. Carl recognized this as the most prized of all transit documents. It allowed him to freely cross all borders under German control.

General Von Landendorf looked up as he handed Carl his travel papers. He reiterated one final time, "Three days."

Chapter 30. March 11, 1944 – Berlin, Germany

Carl returned to his office for just a moment to make sure there were no loose ends to deal with before leaving the building. He put everything in its proper place and leaned over to retrieve his briefcase. It was then that he heard an ominously familiar voice at the doorway.

"Keeping banker's hours now, are we?"

Without raising his head, Carl knew exactly who it was. "Well, Conrad – how is the air marshal's private art dealer today? Liberate anything for the war effort lately, or just some pretty pictures for an anonymous private collection?"

"Now, is that any way to greet an old friend?" Conrad chuckled mockingly. "Since I know you didn't mean anything by your little joke, I'll show you what a big man I am and overlook it."

Short and pudgy, Conrad was as physically disgusting as he was intellectually brilliant. Carl always thought that the whiny tone of his voice and his irritating laugh probably contributed to why he never married – that and the fact that he seemed to prefer the company of other men.

The two first met at the military academy in Dresden. As long as Carl could remember, Conrad had always been viewed as a somewhat shady dealmaker. Fifty years later, the great hockey player Wayne Gretzky would state his playing philosophy: "I skate to where the puck is going to be, not where it has been."

Conrad was simply ahead of his time. He perfected his art not in athletics, but in manipulation. His extremely methodical mind analyzed moves like pieces on a chess board. Move, countermove, cause and effect ... all were sifted and weighed to reach an acceptable end result.

One night, after one bottle of wine too many, Conrad let down his guard and explained his simple philosophy of life. "As I see it, everything I do is for the common good of Germany. Who else could you name as a better representative of the common citizen? I work hard and follow my superiors' orders. Is it my fault that my position sometimes presents me the opportunity for lucrative business deals? It's just the nature of the beast, and I can argue that it helps the economy. I am an important source of certain rare commodities that cannot be obtained through normal channels. So you see, what is good for Conrad is really good for all. Now that I think about it, I probably should be awarded some kind of medal."

Conrad's abject lack of conscience allowed him to not only rationalize his black-market dealings, but also to soak up and memorize all manner of odd information. Carl recalled an art history lecture they had attended at the university. Conrad would nudge him and whisper whenever a certain *objet d'art* came up as part of the discussion, who the current owner was, where it was currently located – things of that nature.

This information would serve him well after he was appointed to Air Marshal Goering's staff. He would use this intel to locate and liberate any art objects deemed Aryan in nature. Rumors spiraled about the air marshal's private collection, and where and how it was being accumulated. But as long as Conrad could satisfy Goering's appetite for his burgeoning collection, innuendo was quashed, indiscretions overlooked and scandal averted.

This cloak of protection from above gave Conrad free reign, and opened the door to many new and lucrative money-making avenues. Truckloads of liquor, cigarettes and canned food items were sold with a mere handshake. When staff officers or visiting dignitaries needed a male or female escort for the evening, Conrad was known as the man who could produce.

However, as impressive as these business dealings had become, they paled in comparison to the side bet Conrad wagered: If Germany didn't come out on top, he wanted to have things – unique things for which the Allies would pay dearly.

"I'm taking the family to stay in the countryside near Milan," Carl said casually, "just until things are safer here."

"It might be a long stay, if what my people say is true," Conrad replied as he stepped into the office. "They're not letting on how badly the Messerschmidt and Fokker assembly lines have been damaged – but that is not why I dropped by." He was already quite aware of Carl's travel plans.

"There's a security shutdown on my floor and I can't get back into my office to put this in the safe," Conrad stated as he held out a two-inch-thick leather satchel embossed with a German eagle. "Would you mind locking this away for me for a few days?"

"My office doesn't have a safe," Carl answered with a hint of irritation in his voice. "I only have a lightweight lock on my door – and besides, I'm leaving this afternoon for three days."

Conrad walked over to the window, looked down at Carl's awaiting staff car and exhaled sharply. He already knew there was no safe in this office. In fact, this entire floor had not even been considered a high-level security area.

"I have to go somewhere now and I don't wish to be seen walking around with official-looking documents," Conrad lamented. "Not only wouldn't it be safe, it just wouldn't give the right impression, now would it? The least you could do is lock them in the trunk of your staff car. I'll come by and get them before you leave." He was still looking out the window with his back to Carl, at the two men smoking off to the side of the front entryway.

Conrad knew that because of his position on the air marshal's staff that Carl, a mere captain, was hardly in a position to turn down his request. After all, Conrad did have the ear of the third most powerful man in all of Germany. His main power rested with those for whom he worked, not himself personally. He was all smoke and mirrors, but still it served his purpose if people thought a quick phone call from him could get them a train ride to Dachau or Buchenwald.

Spiriting these valuable documents out of Germany was now worth risking of all his political capital. He could reclaim his prize in Milan and be free to make a deal to the highest bidder.

"One other thing," Conrad casually mentioned. "I checked about in our office to determine if there was any information concerning your wife's parents."

Carl's head snapped sharply upward. He wondered how Conrad could possibly be aware of his family's tragedy. But then he thought, it's not that much of a surprise. He obviously knew about the staff car as well.

"My condolences," Conrad offered. "Their bodies were found in the rubble outside the front of their flat and identified the next day."

This unexpected comment, so casually dropped, caught Carl off guard. He suspected as much, but still, hearing it from someone else had a sobering effect. Carl felt that same old nauseating feeling well up in the pit of his stomach – the very same as when he had first been informed of his parents' car accident.

"I pulled strings and checked every source I could find," Carl said. "Where did you find this out?"

"The air marshal's office, and especially Herr Goebbels's group, are very touchy when it comes to civilian casualties," Conrad explained. "In their eyes, there are acceptable and unacceptable numbers to be released to the public. Numbers – it's always about the numbers. You know, the whole morale and invincibility thing. Anyway, I'm sorry to have to be the one to give you the bad news."

If Carl's wife thought there was even a remote possibility that her parents were still alive, she might be reluctant to leave, Conrad thought. They were probably dead anyway. More importantly, he needed his package delivered.

Conrad placed the leather folder on the desk and walked out of the office. A few moments later, Carl saw him strolling leisurely down the boulevard away from the chancellery, followed closely by the two shadows that trailed him everywhere.

A high-level staff car, with its special privileges, was like having diplomatic immunity in wartime Germany. With the British bombing by night and the Americans by day, there was no absolutely safe time to travel. Who knew what delays and detours Carl might encounter with this incessant, around-the-clock barrage?

Even though Milan was more than 1,100 kilometers away, the drive would still be quite pleasant because the benefits of riding in a Mercedes 302 were more than obvious – being waved through traffic and around bottlenecks, no endless checks for proper papers, and immediate access to more fuel. The general was no fool – he knew this vehicle would ensure that Carl would be back in three days or there would be hell to pay. But neither Carl nor the general were even remotely aware of the events that Conrad was about to set in motion.

Chapter 31. March 11, 1944 – Berlin, Germany

Carl called home to inform his wife that they would be going to the country until things became safer. He felt guilty and weak for not breaking the news in person. Dealing with this bundle of emotions was something he just couldn't handle at the moment. But instead of hearing his wife's voice, the phone was answered by her best friend Enga. She bubbled with excitement.

"They're alive!" Enga blurted out. "They are with her sister in Dresden!"

"Who is alive?" Carl puzzled.

"Elaine's parents!" Enga replied. "They were visiting the grandchildren when the raid took place. They're safe. She was able to talk to them earlier today. It's a miracle!"

Carl's mind was spinning. Conrad could have been mistaken – or did this all have something to do with the satchel in the trunk?

"Enga, where is Elaine right now?" Carl asked anxiously.

"She will be home within the hour," Enga answered. "You know how long it takes to find enough food at all the different shops. She has to …"

"Enga, I need you to do something for me," Carl interrupted. "I need you to pack some things together for the children. I am taking them and Elaine to a place in the country where they will be safe. They will be gone for a month or more. Can you do this?"

"Yes, but I also some very sad news," Enga said somberly. Carl clenched his jaw and braced himself for what seemed to be a never-ending wave of grief. Enga started to cry as she whispered, "Ernst and Helga were taken away today."

Carl's body went limp as Helga's warning not to return echoed in his ears. At that moment, his mind focused on the toughest decision of his life. Up to that point, he had planned to put Elaine and the children on the ship in Willie's care. He would return to Berlin and fulfill his obligations as an officer and a patriot. But if German citizens – good, honorable people who served their country – were being cast aside, then Carl knew that even if Germany was victorious, peace could be far worse than war.

"Get the children packed and ready," he urged, "and I will be there in about one hour. We will leave this evening."

The cool air of the late afternoon helped filter Carl's thoughts as he sorted out the events of the day. His thoughts and emotions had ranged from one extreme to another this morning. He dreaded facing Elaine, but now here she was, bubbling with excitement and relief.

"I talked to my sister Frieda in Dresden and my parents are safe," she exhaled, her face flushed with joy. "They've been there for a week and couldn't get back home because the bridges were out. I was just so scared because we didn't know where they were. In all that rubble, I thought we'd lost them." With that, she put her arms around his neck and started to cry.

If Carl had ever considered playing poker professionally, the lack of emotion on his face would have served him well. Not having to be the villain and deliver the bad news was a great relief to him.

"Are you sure they're alive?" he asked. "I mean, are you really certain?"

"I talked to them today," she affirmed, "and they sounded great. Papa was clearing a spot for a new garden and Mutti was reading to Frieda's children to keep their minds off the bombing. It's less than a two-minute walk to the shelters in the underground subways. They should be fine as long as my father doesn't try to be a hero and refuse to go to with them. You know how the grandchildren can wrap those two around their finger. Anyway, as soon as an alarm sounds, Frieda has each of the children take their hands so they can bring the little ones quickly to safety." She very nearly ran out of breath from talking so fast.

For Elaine, knowing about her parents and the thought of getting her children to safety had reinvigorated her. When she returned from shopping, Elaine showed Enga the traveling bags she kept packed in case of an emergency. By the time Carl arrived, she had sliced bread and cheese for a light dinner as they traveled.

When Carl drove up, Elaine and the children were waiting by the front door. A group of friends and neighbors had gathered outside Ernst's and Helga's house, and conversation dropped to a whisper as the Mercedes pulled to a stop. Loading the bags into the trunk, Carl looked across the street and mouthed the words, "I had nothing to do with this."

It was nearly dusk and the light had begun to fade. Carl just wanted to hit the road and leave all of this nonsense behind. Except for a few minor questions, Elaine was completely composed and relaxed. Tonight there would be a full moon, and if the skies remained clear, he might even be able to drive using only his parking lights. Yes, the big staff car had its benefits, but it might also be a tempting target for a British night-fighter returning from escort duty – or for any number of partisan groups, for that matter. They would travel south and toward the war. They would not run away from it.

Gazing at the rising moon, Carl thought back to a book he had read as a boy – a story about the Plains Indians in America. He had always been intrigued by their adaptability and skill in traveling long distances with no landmarks to guide them on the open plains. Then he remembered a phrase: "Comanche moon."

Attacking at night under the light of a full moon, the Comanche Indians had brought terror to the settlers each month at this time. Carl could only hope that this full moon would be his ally, not his downfall. He looked at his watch – it was time to leave. Conrad or no Conrad, the satchel in the trunk would have to find its own way to its destination.

Before pulling away from the curb, Carl took one last look at his home. This may be the last time I ever see where my children were born, he reflected. So many thoughts pulled him in so many directions: Conrad not showing up to retrieve his package, the looks of distrust from his friends and neighbors, the sound of laughter from his children in the back seat. At this moment, when many things he knew and loved had been tossed aside, Elaine seemed so very calm as she laid her hand on his. This same woman who earlier that day was an emotional basket case now appeared as solid and unyielding as a block of granite.

Chapter 32. March 11, 1944 – Berlin, Germany

By the time Carl pulled away from his home, Conrad had already been on the road for almost two hours. He knew that Carl would have to travel through the Brenner Pass on his way to Milan. All he had to do was simply follow him and wait for an opportune moment.

Conrad had been alerted by an *unterfeldwebel*, or sergeant, in the motor pool that a car being readied for travel was headed for northern Italy – Milan, to be precise. Having used such vehicles in the past to move his "merchandise," Conrad knew that the contents were rarely, if ever, examined.

The sergeant proved to be a reliable source of information. It always amazed Conrad how some people were willing to sell their souls for so very little. A few bottles of schnapps and a weekly visit from a street prostitute, and a loyal informant was his for life – or until he deemed it necessary to terminate the relationship.

Of course, the real trick was setting the hook. He had learned of the sergeant's affair with a Polish girl across the border in Zielona. Conrad knew of an upcoming security sweep in eastern Poland, so he alerted the sergeant in time for the woman and her family to escape. The informant was now his on two levels: Conrad had saved the woman and also showed that he knew of the sergeant's secret life. A mere enlisted man with a Polish girlfriend in occupied German territory – not to mention that he had been assigned to a position of responsibility at the Berlin offices of the National Socialist Party? This was completely unacceptable. The proverbial hook was now set.

Sorting through prized art collections, Conrad might pass over a Renoir or Monet before settling on objects far more valuable than the rest of the trove. His devotion to his superior, Air Marshal Hermann Goering, was the leverage that allowed him free reign. Oh yes, he thought – the German National Museum of Aryan Art and Culture would be more than happy with what was left after he perused its gallery, and still possess the second-greatest art collection in the world. Air Marshal Goering's collection would eventually outshine even the Louvre and might even be viewed as one of the greatest in history. Now Conrad was going to steal it – but he wasn't greedy. He wouldn't take the entire collection – only the finest pieces. In exchange for a new life, Conrad Dimpler would offer the Allies priceless works of such historical and cultural significance that they could not possibly say no.

When the sergeant informed him of the staff car, Conrad realized that this was his opportunity. The plan was carefully formulated over several years. Many of the world's great art treasures and valuables that the Germans had looted from occupied Europe were not put on display, but instead hidden. Conrad, under the authority of Air Marshal Goering, organized and arranged many of these clandestine locations. He had carefully compartmentalized this information while leaving confusing and misleading maps as disinformation. That way, only he knew where everything was hidden.

These locales ranged anywhere from deep caverns and abandoned mines to alpine lake beds – and all had been locked away in Conrad's mind. He knew he was being followed, but not by whom. If injured or taken captive, would it be to his advantage to have written descriptions to trade for his life? Should he draft it in code as a further bargaining chip? These were certainly tough questions with limited options. Eventually, Conrad reluctantly decided to put his insurance policy on paper.

Walking out of Carl's office earlier that day, Conrad had felt the overwhelming uncertainty of his future as it rode in the trunk of that Mercedes. Sweating profusely as he left the building, he nevertheless was convinced by his two uninvited escorts that he had made the right move.

Now, as he drove through the mountains, Conrad felt more relaxed and actually smiled to himself. He held the extra set of keys the sergeant had given him, so once in Italy he would regain his satchel and make a quick getaway to Genoa. With money, contacts and especially what he offered, Conrad would simply disappear. Now the only questions remaining were simple: What would he choose as his new name and where would he decide to spend the rest of his days?

The only messy detail could be the Friedrick family. If Carl's curiosity got the better of him and he looked inside the satchel, then Conrad's secret might not be so safe.

Conrad knew in the dark recesses of his mind that he was many things. Perhaps some considered him a thief, a liar or even a traitor. But until that moment, the one thing he never realized was that he possessed the ability to take another human being's life. It was altogether different to make a phone call than to kill someone with your own hands.

And it would also be most inconvenient if Carl Friedrick and his family should reappear at some point in the near future – for they well knew of Conrad's sordid past.

Chapter 33. May 27, 2008 – Fairfax, Virginia

"You said you found a fourth reference to the plane," Ryan reminded Alex.

"Several months ago, I got a call from a buddy of mine who works in immigration," Alex responded. "Seems something interesting popped up on his screen and he thought I might want to take a look at it."

"I've worked with, and for, a number of agencies in the past," he went on, "and I still have close friends and contacts in most of them – but you can forget about all that camaraderie and information-sharing crap that supposedly went on after 9/11. The general atmosphere is better, I suppose, but the same suspicions and turf wars still exist. The more power you have, or that Congress thinks you have, the bigger your slice of the budget pie. More power means more money, and more money turns into even more power. It's a vicious cycle.

"But nobody likes to share information with each other. Everything stays within a particular intelligence circle or agency. That, in a nutshell, is the economic reality in Washington. Here, the measure of your success is power, not efficiency."

Alex then noticed Ryan's body language as he shifted impatiently. "Sorry," Alex offered, "I'll get off my soapbox. Anyway, it seems there's this woman in Decatur, Georgia who hadn't received any child support payments for the last four years. All of a sudden, monthly checks started coming in from Washington state. They said it was from garnished wages. After a few of these, her curiosity got the better of her, so she called the number on the back of the check stub to see where the money was coming from. She was told that a federal program to locate deadbeat dads matched her case file to her ex-husband's Social Security number. Boeing Aircraft in Seattle was notified and so began the garnishment process. She found this explanation 'very mysterious.'

"On an interesting note, the husband never once complained about the healthy chunk taken from his checks. It would appear that he may not have even known the money was being deducted. His pay went into a direct-deposit account, so he never touched the funds."

"And this story is related to the plane because ... ?" Ryan let the question hang awkwardly to emphasize his confusion.

Alex raised his index finger to signal that he was close to making his point. "Because Boeing is a major defense contractor. Any discrepancies associated with employees' Social Security numbers are looked into very closely.

"Besides his bank records, we also gained access to his cell-phone history. Our mystery man used several phones and was very careful. On one of them, we traced three calls to the same number in Vienna, Austria over an eighteen-month period. In fact, until that time, those were the only calls ever made on that phone.

"I'm not especially proud of this," Alex continued, "but we usually get better cooperation from Interpol than some of our own sister agencies down the street. When I spoke to their liaison officer, he immediately became very interested. That number in Vienna belonged to a person of interest, and because of my inquiry, the liaison would see what he could do for me.

"Six days later, I received a fax describing what we call a 'sneak and peak' they had conducted the night before. The idea was to gain access, search the premises, take pictures and make copies of computer files, while leaving no trace of ever having been inside. After the files were copied, they inserted a virus into a laptop which, as far as we could tell, was not connected to any Internet service provider. The bug we planted would locate a wireless connection and transmit updates of all files on the laptop in short, encrypted bursts whenever changes were made. The virus gave us a real-time window into the laptop and another computer in the house that was linked to it."

"Wow, that's impressive and intimidating at the same time," Ryan said with more than a little dismay.

"That's not all," McCormick continued. "By matching files in the laptop against a time-correlation program, we located an Internet cafe in Salzburg, Austria about three-and-a-half hours away. Once the files were accessed at the cafe, they were downloaded to the laptop within twenty-four hours.

"So the obvious question is this: Why would you drive three-and-a-half hours each way to do this so many times? The most plausible explanation is that you probably have something to hide.

"Our European friends installed a camera to monitor the cafe, so the next time a correlation on the laptop and cafe computer occurred, they could review the camera logs. Our computer jockey didn't appear on any recognition software, so for now we're still trying to put a name to the face."

"Well, that's really an interesting story," Ryan observed, "but how does that relate to the airplane?"

"Our mystery group was looking for information on the location of our German 'bat' aircraft, so they used the Freedom of Information Act as a search vehicle. At the same time, they also tried to hack into the Russian archives – and for the exact same reason. There's something about The Bat that these people just find extremely interesting."

As this new tidbit sank in, Ryan jumped to a previous topic. "Not to change the subject, but why did the wife find the garnishment process so mysterious – that is the word you said she used – if she had received child support in the past?"

Alex leaned against the plane, smiled and answered, "That one is simple: Her ex-husband died four years before the new checks started coming in."

Chapter 34. March 11, 1944 – Berlin, Germany

As he pulled away from his home for the last time, Carl calculated that, depending on the weather and inconveniences of war, they could reach Genoa in twelve to eighteen hours.

He knew the route quite well. He had driven it many times before on skiing vacations to Innsbruck in Austria and farther south in the Tyrolean Alps. He reminisced of his boyhood as they traveled, and the feeling of being in the high country for the very first time came back to him quite clearly. His mind drifted to youthful memories of the light dusting of snow in the foothills, and the majestic grandeur of the higher passes and bowls with their deep, white winter coats.

He then remembered the proud day that his father and uncle allowed him to ride the gondola to the top of the mountain on their very first ski trip together. During this rite of passage into manhood, the two men he loved and admired the most had then let him lead the way as he cut a path down fresh and uncarved trails. He still recalled how his youthful frame had not needed his thoughts to give it direction. The pure and natural state of being at one with his skis and the mountain itself simply flowed through him. This was pure instinct and reaction.

Shortly after he met the challenge of the mountain, he would have to face an even greater obstacle: polio. But that cruel affliction never diminished the awe and reverence he held for this place. It seemed an almost magical and holy experience.

For the last three hours, Carl's thoughts had been trapped in the past. Now he returned to what this area had come to mean for him over these last four years: munitions and aircraft factories with their railheads sending materials and supplies south to Italy, and west to France and the low countries. Carl didn't even want to think of the future that awaited the human cargo on those ill-fated rail lines.

Driving South, Carl could see the absolute devastation at the manufacturing facilities Conrad had mentioned. In some places, the Junkers factories and test sites looked more like barren fields of wheat after the chaff had been burned away. Others had remained virtually untouched. Conrad had been correct in his initial assessment – there was much more damage here than the party machine was willing to acknowledge.

Even in the rural areas, away from industrial targets, stretches of forest had completely vanished. Original reports had said British and American bomb sights were not that accurate, but the sheer volume of explosives dropped in what seemed a random pattern brought back an old adage. He whispered it under his breath as he surveyed the desolate wasteland: "Even a blind pig finds an acorn once in a while."

As they reached the outskirts of Munich, he thought of the beer hall, the *Bürgerbräukeller*, where it had all symbolically begun back in 1933 – or was it 1934? Carl couldn't quite remember for sure – especially now, when it was all he could do just to keep his eyes open.

It was now 1:30 in the morning. He felt that they were making good time. He heard distant sirens, saw searchlights sweeping the skies and even passed through areas that had been recently bombed. Luckily, the roads were still clear and his fortunate timing had placed them between attacks.

Carl wondered if the famous drinking hall where the *Führer* had first tried to overthrow the Austrian and eventually the German Weimar Republic governments had withstood the Allied air raids. Located on Rosenheimer Street, this edifice to the Nazi Party should best end up as ten square blocks of smoking ruins. He thought if he were the Allied bomber commander and had tried to break the German people's spirit, he would make sure of this. In fact, not only Rosenheimer Street, but the whole damned Haidhausen district should be obliterated. His mourning for the probable fate of Ernst and Helga had finally boiled over. Germany, this mighty beast surrounded by so many enemies, was now devouring its own.

To the northwest of Munich stretched the rail spurs and facilities of the first – and one of the largest – detention camps: Dachau. Carl could name those rail lines in his sleep. He knew which ones skirted the camp and headed south through Switzerland and into Italy, and those now bringing their human cargo to this final destination at an ever-quickening pace.

As it raced through the valley under cover of darkness, Carl could barely make out the silhouette of a locomotive. The only other telltale clue of its existence was the occasional puff of steam. He wondered if Ernst and Helga might be on that train. If they were, he hoped some kind of miracle would save them.

Even in the darkness, Carl could feel the road changing. His headlights illuminated the rock formations and plant life. They were different now as well. Long, sweeping turns on the sides of the ridges had changed to what seemed an endless series of hairpin switchback turns as the steepness of the mountain drive became even more extreme. Tall, thick stands of pine and juniper reached skyward to grab a splinter of sunlight, while lush fiddlehead ferns, sheltered amid fallen trees, grew unchecked along the roadside. The hypnotic hum of the engine, the day's roller-coaster events and his not having slept for almost twenty-four hours had left Carl with little more than the urge to just close his eyes and grab some much-needed rest.

Only another hour-and-a-half and they would be in Bolzano – on the Italian side of the Brenner Pass. There he would ask for Father Giuseppe Pardemo at the Holy Mary Cathedral on the main *piazza*, or plaza. They would be safe there and could rest before continuing to Genoa. But for now, he needed to stop, stretch his legs and let the cold mountain air reinvigorate him.

As the Mercedes pulled off of the pavement, the sound of its tires sliding onto the gravel caused Elaine to suddenly open her eyes. She started to sit up, but he quietly motioned for her to go back to sleep. He was only getting out to stretch.

At lower elevations, the scattered clouds caused just enough drizzle to smear the windshield when the wipers made their pass. As they climbed higher, the mist became a combination of rain and sleet, which streaked and blurred his visibility as the wipers labored to scrape away the slushy mess. When they neared the summit, the light sprinkle transformed to a fine white dusting of powder which threatened to hide the curving mountain road.

The way through the Brenner Pass was a vital artery from Austria to Italy. Snow-removal crews made regular runs over the highway and the residue of their efforts lay in uniform piles heaped along the sides of the road. Breathing deeply while relieving himself on a snowbank, Carl glanced up between the towering trees and thought of how much he had missed the simple pleasure of the evening sky in the high country. Framed between open patches in the clouds, the moisture in the air caused the stars to twinkle and dance in the night sky.

As he walked around to the front of the car, he brushed away the accumulated snow on the road with his foot. The heavy Mercedes, with its wide tires and deep tread, had been designed to travel under conditions such as this. However, Carl still knew that no matter how carefully he drove, if he were to hit an unexpected patch of ice, he could easily slide into a snowbank – or worse. Below the dusting of powdered snow, the road was quite dry. This night was not cold enough to freeze the day's melt into a hidden layer of deadly "black ice." As he slid into the driver's seat, Carl shivered and was now wide awake. He pulled back onto the road and headed toward the Italian border. When they reached the summit at over 4,500 feet, the sky suddenly cleared, leaving the clouds and snow below them – stranded on the other side of the mountain.

This was the last checkpoint before leaving Germany, but unlike the others it was manned by German Army regulars. Judging by their age and decorations, these men were hardened veterans. The lieutenant in charge seemed more suspicious of a captain with his family in a general's staff car than at the other checkpoints. Since the American invasion of Sicily, Germany's southern border had become considerably more dangerous.

The lieutenant examined the letter of transit closely, handed it back and said, "Wait one moment." Carl became quite nervous as the guard walked into the kiosk and picked up the phone. Talking while gesturing toward a large map on the wall, the lieutenant nodded his head as he answered several times, "*Ja, ja.*" He returned the phone to its cradle and walked back outside.

"I am sorry to inconvenience you, sir, but there has been some partisan activity in the area, and since you have your family with you, I wanted to be absolutely certain of the latest reports."

Carl swallowed hard. Even though the cold night air flowed through the partially open window, a small trickle of perspiration appeared on his brow. He was about to answer when Elaine softly replied, "Thank you, *herr leutnant*. It is certainly reassuring for us to know there are men like you guarding our borders. We will personally speak to your commander about your attentiveness."

Stepping back from the window, the young lieutenant saluted and raised the checkpoint gate. Ahead stood a welcome sign – it announced the Italian border.

Carl's heart raced uncontrollably. He liked – no, *demanded* – being in control of the situation, and the feeling of being the hunted instead of the hunter was most unsettling. Right now, you must focus – concentrate, he told himself. His logical German mind began tackling the problem, setting up a step-by-step plan of action and analyzing all possible outcomes. First he would go to Bolzano. Once there, he would tell Elaine everything. How and when, he didn't know. He just knew it had to be done – and soon. It was eating him up inside.

Tonight the moon seemed so large and close that it seemed he could almost reach out and touch it. As they rounded a curve, Carl never quite grasped how sometimes the moon could seem so huge, yet other times it was but a tiny sphere in the sky. But now, on the edge of this mountain, it was massive enough to completely fill the windshield. Its soft light cascaded into the vehicle and provided enough illumination to read even the old, faded bible page neatly folded in his breast pocket. But Carl didn't need any heavenly light to read this missive once again. It kept playing over and over in his mind like an endless refrain. Slowly, he mouthed the words, "No one does he command to act unjustly, to none does he give license to sin."

Carl was so engrossed in his thoughts that he didn't even notice the tan Volkswagen pull out onto the road behind him. With its lights extinguished, Conrad Dimpler could simply follow the Friedrick family down the winding road into Bolzano.

Chapter 35. March 12, 1944 – Bolzano, Italy

The soft glow of the approaching dawn painted the sky above the mountains to the east with its early morning alpine halo. In most Italian cities, towns and villages, the church or cathedral was considered the cultural center of the main *piazza* – and Bolzano was no exception. Located next to the church, a rundown turn-of-the-century hotel was to be their sanctuary for the evening.

Driving around to the rear of the hotel, Carl noticed the faint glow of a candle radiating from a small window next to what appeared to be the back entrance to the church. Wondering if anyone would be up at this early hour, he was surprised when the door opened almost immediately after one soft knock.

"Father Pardemo?" Carl inquired.

"We've been expecting you," the priest answered. "You made very good time. I gather you must be tired. Your room is ready next door. We assumed you would have small children, so we arranged for a ground-floor room because we knew they would probably already be asleep. Your room is at the bottom right corner. If you go in through the side entrance, it is the first door on your right. It is unlocked and everything has been arranged. You will find a change of clothes for you and your family. They are old and worn, but will serve your needs until you reach Genoa."

"Thank you for staying up and waiting for us, Father," Carl said gratefully.

"I would be up soon, anyway," the priest replied. He pointed to the bell tower three stories above the *piazza* and continued, "In a short while, the bells will be calling the faithful to morning prayers. Peace be with you, my son."

Their small room contained two single beds pushed together and a third one in the corner that made the living space seem even more cramped. On one bed sat four sets of clothes, neatly folded. Clean but threadbare, these were their new traveling outfits.

On Carl's and Elaine's clothing lay a sterling silver St. Christopher medal and chain. Elaine picked up one of the medallions and examined it closely. This particular angel was the patron saint of travelers, and these specific religious symbols were inlaid with mother-of-pearl around the edges. The front of the medal featured the traditional saint carrying the Christ child on his shoulder. On the back was engraved, in German, "Church of the Most Holy Mary, Bolzano, Italy 1944."

As she fastened the medal around her neck, Elaine's attention turned once again back to the room. An older building from the late 1800s, it featured ten-foot-high ceilings with a faded and cracked plaster cornice. A single wooden sash window that had been painted shut years before looked out over the open space where Carl had parked the car. A bathroom at the end of the hall served the entire floor, while a small boiler in the basement made the room only bearably warm. But still, the prospect of sleeping in a bed made the room look like heaven. Elaine spread a blanket over the children and walked over to the window.

On his way back outside to retrieve their traveling bags, Carl was surprised to see a short-statured man in a black leather coat standing at the back of the car and looking into the trunk.

"Hey, what are you doing?" Carl yelled. The man turned and pointed the flashlight directly into his face. Instinctively, Carl raised his hand to shield his eyes. He then heard a familiar refrain.

"Why Carl, is that any way to greet an old friend?" Conrad's smug, smirking voice once again answered with the catchphrase he always used.

"Conrad, what are you doing here – and why weren't you at my house as we discussed?" Carl said as he took a step forward. Conrad lowered the flashlight to reveal a small-bore Mauser pistol pointed directly at Carl.

"What I am doing here is simply retrieving my property," Conrad responded with a detached air. "And as for why I didn't meet you at your house – well, let's just say you were a more convenient courier for the safe delivery of my package. But I had no idea how resourceful you were," he said while holding up Carl's travel papers. "Letters of transit, death notifications, Red Cross refugee documents, Argentine travel visas … my, but you have been a busy boy. Very impressive, I must say."

Carl stammered as he sought to find a bargaining chip in all this mess. He finally blurted, "I can get you papers, Conrad – I can probably get them for you by morning."

The pompous art dealer grinned and replied, "I don't need papers, Carl – I have plenty of papers." He once again held up Carl's documents. "As you can see, we have another problem: You know about my package – you know when I gave it to you and probably what it contains as well."

"How could I know what's inside?" Carl stammered, the sense of desperation beginning to creep into his voice. "It was locked!"

"There, you see? No sense of trust," Conrad glared while shaking his head. "You wouldn't have known it was locked unless you had tried to open it. What am I going to do with you, Carl? If you would lie over a simple detail such as this … don't you see that you have put me in an extremely awkward position?"

The bells in the tower above pealed their morning call to prayer, causing Carl to flinch at their sudden, harmonious cacophony. At the second striking of the large brass hammers, Conrad opened his mouth to speak, then suddenly jerked forward as his eyes bulged with a look of abject surprise. Two red splotches bloomed on the tunic under his open leather coat. The flashlight and pistol slipped from his hands as he dropped to his knees and fell face-down onto the gravel.

There in the early-morning light stood Elaine. She brandished Carl's service revolver and held a pillow she had used to help muffle the report. Goose down and feathers floated all around her as what remained of the pillow smoldered from the pistol blast. Her eyes burned with the look of a mother lion protecting her cubs.

"We can't stay here – it's much too dangerous now," she said without emotion. "Someone may have seen or heard us."

Carl, still stunned, answered, "There may not be anyone in Milan to meet us yet." He immediately became angry at himself for not having the courage to tell her that there was no Milan.

As Elaine and Carl stuffed Conrad into the back seat of the Mercedes, she whispered, "We must leave for Genoa – *now*."

Chapter 36. March 12, 1944 – Bolzano, Italy

Two German *SS* officers sat in an unmarked black Opel and watched the tan Volkswagen across the square. They patiently awaited Conrad Dimpler's return. Individually, the two made an odd pair, but as a team they meshed like a zipper. The older of the two by twelve years was Erhard Mauer. Tall even by German standards, he stood well over six feet and held the chiseled facial features of a hawk. With dark, piercing eyes set deep in their sockets behind high cheekbones, he rarely showed any emotion.

Early in life, he had been a high-school mathematics teacher, but lost his position because he had turned his classroom into a propaganda forum for the National Socialist Party and its somewhat controversial doctrine. One of the original Brownshirt street thugs of Hitler's private army, the *Sturmabteilung* or SA, he escaped what history referred to as "The Night of the Long Knives," when more than eighty people whom Hitler viewed as political rivals were summarily executed. Mauer avoided that massacre partly because of his blind loyalty, but mostly due to his complete lack of any political aspirations.

Now, nine years later, he sat alongside his partner, Kurt Drescher, intently watching the vehicle across the square.

The younger officer was shorter in stature, built more like a bull, with features more Slavic than German. Close-cropped blond hair revealed a four-inch scar running up the right side of his forehead and into the hairline of his round face. He had originally claimed it was the result of an accident during a childhood game of stickball, but he actually received it while jumping from a second-story window when a comely neighbor's husband unexpectedly returned home from work.

Impulsive and violent, Drescher was a common street thug until Mauer saw something more suited to a higher calling and pulled him off the urban trash heap. His mentor, to whom he would refer as Herr Mauer, offered him the two things he had always lacked: direction and discipline. Kurt Drescher thus became his partner's alter-ego – the quiet man in the shadows who, when directed, could explode at a moment's notice.

Conrad Dimpler successfully ditched the two men tailing him in Berlin by changing clothes in a public toilet and slipping out through the restaurant's side entrance. The backup team of Mauer and Drescher waited outside the eatery and the new duo followed Conrad for the remainder of that day and throughout the night.

On a specific request from Air Marshal Hermann Goering, Conrad would be followed and closely watched twenty-four hours a day. Heinrich Himmler, the chief of Germany's dreaded secret police, sent his two best undercover teams to keep track of and report on Conrad's every move. One mile after the checkpoint at the Italian border, Conrad suddenly pulled off the main highway and onto a secluded, heavily wooded side road.

The two German officers drove past and acted in similar fashion at the next bend when they backed into a clearing lined by young saplings. They cut down some of the small trees and stacked them in front of their vehicle to avoid detection from the road, then waited for Conrad to pass. Two hours later, at exactly 3:37 a.m., a large black Mercedes 320 staff car roared past their location, followed less than a minute later by a tan Volkswagen with its headlights extinguished. It was now clear: Conrad Dimpler had waited for someone and was now pursuing him.

Presently, the unmarked car with the two SS officers pulled back onto the main road. The glow of the lead car's headlights allowed the two chase vehicles to follow at a safe distance so as not to be discovered. If the black Mercedes didn't leave the main road, all three vehicles would eventually end up in Bolzano. Erhard Mauer hoped that Conrad Dimpler would be so intent on whoever was in the car ahead of him that he wouldn't realize that, once again, that the hunter had become the hunted.

Sitting across the *piazza*, the two German officers could make out the faint glow of a cigarette in the front seat of the Volkswagen. Two minutes later, Conrad climbed out of the car and crushed the smoke into the brick pavement with his boot. He wore a long black leather topcoat and carried what appeared to be a flashlight as he made his way around the back of a church.

That trademark leather coat, so very emblematic of the SS, was one thing Conrad relished wearing. To him, it was just part of a costume – a stage prop meant to leave the impression that he could make you disappear, or worse, with a single phone call.

The terror that the coat represented was carefully cultivated for use as a tactic by and for the *SS*, not something to be used by some peddler of pretty pictures from the past. These men despised Conrad Dimpler – not only for who he was, but for what he represented. But this mutual loathing was more than a professional point of view. Their hatred was personal.

Ten minutes later, a man appeared from behind the church. As he strolled past several cars, he seemed to be examining them as he slid his hand across their hoods. Approaching the rear of the Volkswagen, he placed his hand on the engine cover and quickly pulled it away while rubbing his fingers together. He pulled a key from his pocket, climbed into the vehicle, started the engine and drove behind a building next to the church – a building that advertised itself as a hotel.

The two officers jumped from their car and melted into the shadows near the buildings that ringed the *piazza*. Moving quickly but carefully, they rounded the rear corner of the hotel, only to find an empty gravel parking lot. Erhard Mauer pulled a flashlight from his coat pocket and examined an area where the gravel had been washed away by the rains. Two fresh sets of tire tracks led away from the building.

The two had turned to hustle back to their car when Mauer's flashlight beam caught a glint of something metallic on the ground. Two spent cartridge casings lay between the stones. Erhard picked one up and held it close to his nose. He fancied himself quite the expert in a wide array of German firearms. The familiar smell of cordite told him that it had been recently fired and, given its compact size, it probably came from a .32-caliber Mauser HSc – standard issue for members of the *Waffen-SS*. They would have to be much more careful from now on. Conrad Dimpler, it would seem, was more dangerous than they had originally calculated.

Chapter 37. March 12, 1944 – Bolzano, Italy

An awkward and uneasy silence filled the tan Volkswagen as it sped down the dark mountain road. Earlier, back at the church, Carl and Elaine had worked quickly to put her plan in motion. Conrad's blood-soaked leather coat and tunic were removed and tossed into the hotel's basement furnace. A blanket covered the body in the back seat and Elaine sent Carl out to find Conrad's car.

When he returned with the Volkswagen, Elaine stood at the back entrance with three travel bags and two dozing children. Even as he brought the car to a halt, Elaine began to wedge one bag into the back seat. Carl popped the hood, topped off the fuel in the Volkswagen and replaced the petrol can on the Mercedes trunk's bracket. He then shoved the two remaining bags into the front trunk and quietly closed the lid. As the children jostled to gain some measure of comfort in the tight space that remained, Alex asked before drifting back to sleep, "Why can't we ride in the nice car, Mommy?"

Elaine led the way in the Volkswagen, with Carl following in the Mercedes. As the sun crept over the mountaintops to the east, they realized that they must dispose of the Mercedes – and its unwelcome passenger – as quickly as possible.

Five minutes later, Elaine found the perfect spot. Due to the steepness of the hillside over the last two miles, the road had narrowed to one lane – with an occasional turnout only where the mountain permitted. A decades-old fallen tree lay on the opposite side above the road. Elaine flashed her lights twice in quick succession. Carl understood the signal and immediately pulled over. With the children now fast asleep, she pulled around the corner and off to the side of the road as far as possible, then hurried back to help.

By the time she reached the Mercedes, Carl had already pulled his captain's jacket onto Conrad's body and placed him in the driver's seat. As they doused the interior with gasoline, he made sure to apply a substantial portion of the fuel to the corpse.

Elaine tore two lengths of cloth from the lower hem of her skirt and soaked them with gasoline from the remaining petrol can. She stuffed the first rag down into the can itself. The other she snaked into the sedan's fuel tank. Then they rolled the felled tree trunk down the hillside to block the road.

Carl put the car into neutral and went to release the brake when Elaine said, "One more thing: We may need the extra fuel. Get the other can and put it in the back seat of the Volkswagen."

She walked to the driver's side and pulled Conrad's Mauser from her pocket. In quick succession, Elaine fired three rounds through the door into Conrad's lifeless body. She hoped that this would be the final act of their performance. What took place here appeared to be no more than a partisan attack on a German military vehicle.

Elaine pulled Conrad's lighter from her other pocket. It was the very same one he had used a mere twenty-five minutes earlier to light his last cigarette. A fitting torch for his funeral pyre, she thought. As she thumbed the flint on the lighter, the yellow-white flame shot up, illuminating the eagle and swastika on its stainless-steel case. She stared into the dancing firelight for just a moment and imagined what its previous owner was prepared to do to her family – and then finally what she was about to do to him.

Carl had wedged a rock ahead of the left rear tire so the car wouldn't roll when he released the emergency brake. Now he was ready to kick the stone free. Elaine touched the flickering light to the corpse's left sleeve and the blue-white flame advanced like a miniature tidal wave across the front seat. She then walked to the rear of the vehicle and ignited the wicks dangling from the fuel tank, and finally she lit the remaining canister. Elaine tossed the lighter into the back seat as the entire interior burst into flames. She and Carl gave the Mercedes a unified shove and the sleek sedan slowly slid over the edge of the ravine.

The flaming machine bounced down the hillside and crashed through thick brush that left long scratches on its polished black exterior. It picked up speed as it rolled down the hill while the stiff breeze in front of the moving vehicle fanned the flames. When it finally hit a ledge and went airborne, it looked like a falling star coming to Earth.

Its initial landing was quite violent and sent chunks of the car flying in all directions. The vehicle flipped on its side. This dislodged the flaming gas canister. The vehicle rolled twice and slid another sixty feet, then came to rest at the edge of a river that sliced its way through the valley. Moments later, the dislodged canister exploded, sending burning gasoline over the hillside and igniting the scrub brush and smaller trees. A few seconds after that, the blaze made its way to the heap's main gas tank. A second explosion echoed through the valley and sent burning debris raining down in a wide area, leaving the car now fully engulfed in flames.

* * *

In the town of Trento below, Ricardo Contorie awoke with a start. He ran to his bedroom window and looked north up the narrow valley that ran through the heart of their small community. Less than three miles away, the glow on the hillside told him that their old adversary – another deadly fire – would soon be on its way. Steep, natural ridges on either side of the river funneled the winds to the south. Once a fire started, it would create its own wind and drive the flames through their valley. Twice in the last 150 years, fires had roared through their settlement and completely destroyed the village – and twice they had rebuilt.

During a prolonged drought, lightning strikes could set the tinder-dry grasses and brush ablaze. He heard the two explosions and wondered if an aircraft returning from war in the south had crashed in their peaceful valley. Whether it was an act of nature or man-made, the source was irrelevant – their only hope was to contain the fire before it burned out of control.

The war was inching ever closer. Ricardo heard large formations of airplanes high above them, and he feared that sooner or later the war would be at their peaceful valley's doorstep.

Ricardo woke his two sons and told them to quickly gather the rest of the volunteer fire brigade. He went out behind his barn and removed a tarp from the only piece of firefighting equipment in town. The old engine was well-maintained and in good running order, but Ricardo knew it would need to warm up a bit before she started her climb out of the valley. At seven hundred gallons, the old truck carried a heavy load, but if they could get to the fire quickly it might be enough. Time was of the essence. Temperatures would rise quickly at daybreak and the winds would begin to whip – then the real trouble would arrive.

Ten minutes later, the fire brigade was assembled. Two pickups, one delivery van, a rusty Peugeot and Ricardo's fire engine started to snake their way out of the valley toward the fire.

Descending on the curving mountain road, Carl and Elaine could see the five sets of lights making their way up the mountain. At the first opportunity, they pulled off the road and waited for the parade to pass. In the darkness, Carl finally asked, "How long have you known?"

"Not until yesterday, after I talked to my parents in Dresden," Elaine replied while looking straight ahead. "It took what seemed like hours for the phone call to get through. When we finally made the connection, I talked until I lost the connection. I hate this war.

"After the line went dead, there was a knock at the door," she continued. "A young man – some kind of courier on a bicycle – arrived and said he had a letter for me. I took it and thanked him, and as I began to shut the door, he said he was instructed to tell me he could not leave until I read it in his presence. I didn't recognize the markings on the uniform and was about to protest about such demands as I opened the envelope. The opening sentence took my breath away, but I quickly read the rest. I looked up and he was still standing in the doorway. I then read it a second time. He asked if I understood, and as I nodded my head, he stretched out his hand and took the letter and envelope back from me."

"What exactly did it say?" Carl inquired.

"It began by telling me that it was from Wilhelm," she answered, "and then it said his death notice was a fabrication. It was the only way for him to stay safe while in hiding. He wrote that he would see us soon, but for now the most important thing was to get us and the children to safety. I was not to question you and do whatever you requested or needed to bring the family to Genoa."

"Did he say anything else," Carl inquired further, "or do you know anything else about Genoa?"

"No," she whispered, "only that we are to be extremely discrete and trust no one – including the German authorities."

Chapter 38. March 12, 1944 – South of Bolzano, Italy

When the first of the firefighters arrived, the two *SS* officers in their black leather coats stood at the edge of the road and watched the burning wreckage. Like an army of ants, the town's people slid down the embankment *en masse* and beat back the blaze. It almost appeared as if they had drilled for this type of conflagration each and every day of their lives.

A rock ledge blocked their view of the crash site at the bottom of the ravine. As Ricardo Contorie began to work the hand pumps on the old fire engine to build water pressure, he yelled to one of his sons, "Go down to the crash site and tell me what you see!" A few minutes later, a breathless thirteen-year-old boy scrambled back up over the ledge. The two strangers moved closer to hear the townsfolk discuss their findings.

"We are lucky," his son panted as he gasped for air. "The river is on one side and there is no wind yet. So far, the fire hasn't jumped to the other side of the river. With the water from the pumper, we have a good chance to knock it down before it spreads."

"Was the airplane large or small?" Ricardo asked with concern. "After all, there might be unexploded bombs or munitions lying about the wreckage."

His son answered, "I don't think it was an airplane. It looks more like an automobile."

One of the *SS* officers in the black coats stepped forward and asked, "Could you tell if there was anyone in the Volkswagen?"

"The car was too big for a Volkswagen," the boy replied. "It was more like a large sedan. There might have been at least one person inside, but I couldn't tell for sure."

Looking back at his father, he continued, "On my way back up the hill, I found these." He held up a soot-covered cigarette lighter and license plate. The number read *IZ 5631477*. Ricardo took the lighter and rubbed the metal case with his thumb to reveal a German swastika and eagle. Before he could turn it over, the stranger to his right grabbed it and rubbed the back of the lighter against his jacket. Two soot-filled engraved initials stood out: *C.D.* This was Conrad Dimpler's lighter.

The older of the two Germans, Erhard Mauer, recognized the license plate for what it was. The prefix *IZ* was a designation for a German motor pool staff car, not a common Opel like the one they were assigned. A person of some significance rode in this vehicle.

In Ricardo's eyes, a cigarette lighter, license plate or even the rudeness of strangers were not his main concern. Now, with the big picture in mind, he went back to directing the firefighting effort.

The two Germans stood to the side while trying to sort out this new predicament. "If that corpse is Dimpler, then who is in the Volkswagen? And if it is not Dimpler, he must still be in the Volkswagen. Either way, the key here is to find the Volkswagen – and find it quickly."

Erhard walked over to Ricardo, who was not nearly as tall as the officer, and ordered him to move his vehicles so they could pass. The German enjoyed using his height to intimidate others. "If this fire burns out of control, it will sweep through the valley and destroy our town," Ricardo protested.

He started to turn away and a hand grabbed his coat. Erhard spun him around. "Listen to me, old man. I am only going to tell you this once. If you don't do as I say, and do it quickly, a burnt village will be the least of your worries." As Erhard seized Ricardo, the German's coat sleeve slid up his wrist to expose the twin-lightning-bolt tattoo of the German secret police.

As he turned his head, Ricardo's eyes quickly moved from the tattoo to Mauer's burning stare. He hesitated for only a second, weighing a possible disaster from the fire against certain retribution from the Germans. He made the obvious choice.

Ricardo barked his orders, first at the men manning the pumps on the fire engine. He cried for them to stop fighting the blaze and begin moving the cars back down the hill to clear the road. He heard shouts of dismay from the men below as their water pressure fell. Without water, their only hope of containing the fire had evaporated. Keys had been left in all of the vehicles except the rusty old Peugeot, so four of the townspeople and the two Germans pushed it into a ditch. This cleared the final obstacle from the road.

Rushing back to their waiting vehicle, the two Germans stepped over the log that blocked the road as the firemen struggled to push it down the embankment. Kurt Drescher stopped to examine three more spent cartridge casings on the ground. Like the previous two found behind the church, these also had been recently fired, but were of a smaller caliber. This would be the kind of gun a man like Conrad Dimpler would carry, Drescher thought.

Ricardo looked down into the canyon at the raging fire. The morning breeze had begun to pick up and a light layer of ash could be seen through the splinters of sunlight creeping over the craggy rock formations to the east. Even in the springtime, the wind would build as the sun rose and start blowing through the valley. This would cause the fire to grow and generate an even denser plume of smoke. That in turn would generate more wind and cause the cycle to perpetuate itself.

Only fifteen men had been available to battle the blaze to begin with. Ten were already heading back down to the village to try to save their families and what few meager possessions they could gather together. The remaining five now climbed out of the gorge and headed for their vehicles. Ricardo knew that unless the wind changed or it started raining that this fire might not stop until it reached the other end of the valley. It was now out of control.

They had missed a golden opportunity to gain the upper hand. Now the fire was its own master. The town's structures might be lost, but the people were still alive and, as their ancestors had done twice before, they could rebuild their tiny village. The tattoo on the wrist of the mystery man in the leather coat had convinced Ricardo that he made the right decision.

Chapter 39. March 11, 1944 – Trento, Italy

As Carl and Elaine reached the outskirts of Trento, the town was a beehive of activity. Residents streamed from their homes while frantically loading their most important and irreplaceable possessions onto every kind of vehicle, from hand- and horse-drawn carts to even a hearse.

Up the valley, the first tongues of flame leaped from tree to tree and advanced toward the town as burning embers blew in their direction – not a solid wall of flame, but separate blazing fingers pushed by the wind. That very same wind would cause the fire to consume everything in its path and at times spare an entire area in the same way as one would blow out a candle. This was the random disaster pattern spawned by a wind-driven fire.

Carl had not told Elaine of the two figures seated inside the dark sedan across the square silhouetted by the light of a street lamp in Bolzano. He wasn't even sure if there was one man or two, but he knew one thing for certain: The grill of that car in the shadows belonged to a German-made Opel, a mainstay of their military's motor pools. With that in mind, he convinced himself that this was probably as good a time as any to be a little paranoid. He didn't know why they were there. Maybe they had come with Conrad – or *for* Conrad. But no matter. Whoever it was had seen him drive away in the tan Volkswagen.

Carl drove up to the front of a house where a man in his mid-fifties was helping an older woman load furniture onto a flatbed truck. An empty bakery delivery van with its rear doors open had backed up to the front of the house. The woman wore a long floral-print dress and a scarf around her head. She placed the last box in the back of the truck and had just begun climbing into the front seat.

Carl jumped out and yelled, "How much do you want for the van?"

"This town will be a pile of ashes in thirty minutes and you're shopping for a car!" she exclaimed as she shook her head in disbelief and finished her ascent into the vehicle. "You should be praying for a miracle!"

"So you're waiting on another offer, is that it?" Carl inquired loudly.

The younger man in the driver's seat motioned with his head and shoulders for her to see how much Carl was willing to pay. She then answered the question with another question. "So what will you give me?"

"How does it run?" Carl further inquired.

"So now you want to negotiate with the fire already on our doorstep?" the woman queried as she looked up the valley. The smoke had gotten much thicker.

"No, I'm not trying to beat the price down," Carl insisted. "There is not enough time to test it. I just want to know how it runs."

"My son is the mechanic and takes care of the van for the bakery," the old woman stated. "It's ten years old, the meter shows about 120,000 kilometers and it runs really smooth. Do you want it or not? We need to get out of here."

"First let me see if it starts and what it sounds like," Carl said as he held out his hand for the key.

She pulled a handful of keys from her pocket, sorted through them and pulled one out for him. Carl slid the key into the ignition, put his left foot on the clutch and pumping the accelerator pedal with his right. The engine coughed twice, turned over and started. She was right, he thought. Her son was a mechanic – and a damned good one. The engine hummed like a racehorse at the starting gate.

Carl slid out of the driver's seat and walked over to the truck. "You were right," he affirmed. "It sounds really good."

He reached into his pocket and pulled out a wad of Italian *lira*. Handing about half the bills to the woman, Carl hesitatingly asked, "Is that enough?"

The stunned woman looked at the bills in her hand and muttered, "That seems fair." She turned to her son and whispered, "I only paid 200,000 lira four years ago and he gave me 800,000."

Elaine had already transferred the bags to the new vehicle when the old woman noticed the two drowsy children in the back seat.

"Wait one minute," she said as she walked up the stairs and went back into her home. A moment later, she returned with two folded sleeping cushions. She handed Elaine a package wrapped in newspaper and said, "These are for the children. We baked them this morning. They may be the last things ever to come out of my ovens." Looking at the flames now clearly visible in the distance, she wiped a tear from her cheek, took one last look at her home and climbed back into the truck.

Carl checked to make sure they had left nothing in the Volkswagen, then drove around the corner behind the bakery. He intended to abandon the vehicle there, but as he turned into the alley, he spotted an old couple pulling a hand cart loaded with their belongings. Suddenly, Carl was struck with an idea. He got out of the car, walked toward them and asked, "Do you know how to drive?"

The old man, clearly annoyed by this presumptuous lout, snapped, "Of course I can drive! But as you've probably guessed, we do not have our own vehicle. Do you think we are doing this for the exercise?" The bitter old man wondered to himself: Why are Germans such arrogant bastards?

Carl tossed him the key and said, "Good, then I suggest you drive in that direction as fast as you can." He then pointed to the tan Volkswagen behind him.

This was not so much a crisis of conscience as an opportunity for Carl to rid his family of this conspicuous clue. No, he wasn't the least bit concerned about these two strangers escaping the approaching blaze. He merely wished to provide another fox for those German hounds to hunt.

The old man looked at the key and back at Carl, then nodded in a gesture of gratitude. He began to load his new ride. Bags and sacks and books and pictures were quickly stowed in the back seat. These were the few meager belongings the old couple had been able to grab at a moment's notice – an entire lifetime condensed into the rear of one small vehicle.

The woman looked at him, wiped a grateful tear from her cheek and mouthed the words, "God bless you."

As Carl walked away, something inside him was touched by this small, unexpected gesture from a complete stranger.

For the second time in two days, Carl had allowed his emotions to take hold of him, but right now he simply could not allow himself the luxury of thinking or grieving about the probable fate of Ernst and Helga. The precious commodity of time had become scarce. Then it struck him: Yes, he actually did care if these two strangers survived.

One more thing needed to be done – one final detail. Carl turned and walked back to the old woman. He reached into his pocket and removed a small silver medallion on a chain, placed it into her hand and gently closed her fingers around it.

Before leaving, Carlo, the bakery woman's son, took the last remaining fuel canister from his truck. It was only half-full, but he was able to top off the tank in the van with it. This left only a small amount of petrol in the last canister from the Mercedes. Carl put it in the back of the van and wedged the bags around it to keep it from moving around. Then he closed the doors. The old-fashioned needle-and-float gas gauge indicated that the tank was full. Now, with the reserve can, they should have more than enough fuel to make it to Genoa.

Carl climbed in and was about to drive off when a stone-faced Elaine glared at him and demanded, "What the hell was all that about? I kept quiet because of Willie's letter, but you …" Just then, she was distracted by a black sedan speeding down the street. It swerved violently, narrowly missing a man riding a bicycle. "I wonder why they're in such a hurry?" she asked.

"Probably because they're looking for a tan Volkswagen," Carl commented. "You know – *us!*" He then told her of a black sedan in the town square at Bolzano, when a tan Volkswagen didn't quite make the turn at the corner, careened up a dirt path that served as a sidewalk, bounced off a rock and partially dislodged the running board.

The driver pulled out onto the main road heading south. He obviously struggled with the clutch, but managed to finally get it into gear and head off in the same direction as the black Opel sedan. Carl finished his story and allowed the old couple to put some distance between themselves and the van. Pulling out onto the street, Carl found a wool hat in the front seat and stretched it down over his ears. It wasn't much of a disguise, but somehow it seemed to lift his spirits.

Most people, especially trained engineers, would compare a rattle in an automobile to an itch that can't be scratched – a source of irritation that just could not be reached. The metal can resting on a metal floor and lodged against the metal side of the van had begun to make quite the metallic clunking sound. It was really beginning to get on his nerves.

Carl began to make mental calculations about how much fuel they would need to burn to make room for the extra gas in the spare can.

Then he happened to glance down at the gauge. This can't be right, he thought. We couldn't have gone through half the tank already!

Then he remembered that the van had been parked on an incline. Those old float-type gauges were only accurate if the vehicle was on level ground. Damn the sorry luck!

Now, running out of gas is more than just a possibility, he thought. But the good news is at least I can get rid of that damned noisy can. Carl pulled over, drained every last drop from the spare canister into the fuel tank and tossed the empty container into the bushes at the side of the road.

If we have to walk part of the way, we may arrive in Genoa looking more like refugees than the Friedrick family had original planned, Carl thought.

Chapter 40. March 12, 1944 – Verona, Italy

The road from Trento to Verona rolled through the foothills of the Dolomite Mountains. As they traversed the valleys and switchback turns, Erhard Mauer realized they were also burning valuable fuel – and something even more precious: time. To make matters worse, those cheap tires the German motor pools supplied for their lower-echelon vehicles slid like butter on the treacherous black ice. Neither of the two German officers wished to end their careers at the bottom of a ravine. Even though the driver concentrated all of his attention on the wet, curving road, the same question festered in both of their minds: Who exactly *was* in that tan Volkswagen?

Verona, the setting for Shakespeare's *Romeo and Juliet*, was just now awakening. Except for the early rush of workers up before the morning sun, the rest of the town took its own sweet time coming to life. Just as Shakespeare had described it five hundred years earlier, Verona took pride in playing the part in its own sleepy, bucolic way.

It wasn't until the Opel passed through Verona and once again entered the rolling hills that the *SS* officers came upon a construction crew repairing a bridge. Stopping next to a man in his sixties wearing baggy, threadbare pants, Erhard yelled, "You there, have you seen a tan Volkswagen pass by?" As in Germany, Erhard had noticed that many of the men performing manual labor were older, and seemed relieved and anxious for any excuse to lean on their shovels to rest for just a moment.

Dark, weary eyes studied the men in the car. "What is a Volkswagen?" the workman answered, even though he knew perfectly well what Erhard referred to. A lesson quickly learned in wartime Italy and Germany was that any information offered could lead to a long – and often intense – interrogation. State security had established a wide net with no clear or defined limitations. Security protocols and interrogation techniques were defined as whatever the authorities wanted them to mean. A question simply answered could turn into a long and drawn-out session with men of a somewhat shady past. But it was also not wise to appear unwilling to help. The man quickly added, "Only a few automobiles have passed since we started two hours ago, and they were all Italian."

The two Germans spoke for a few seconds and tried to determine whether the man was lying, then decided to head back toward Verona. On their return trip and just before entering town, a tan Volkswagen came around the curve and headed toward them. Kurt Drescher turned the steering wheel hard to the left and slid across the lane to block the Volkswagen's path.

As they leaped from their vehicle with pistols drawn, Erhard screamed, "You two, out – *schnell!* Where did you get this car?" The old couple whimpered their way to the front of the Volkswagen and told their tale, while the German repeatedly prodded them for more details.

"So, he just gave you this car and told you to drive that way as fast as you can?" Erhard asked incredulously. "Old man, people just don't give their cars to strangers! If you are not telling me the truth, we can make you disappear right now – and no one will ever find you. I swear if you are lying, you will not leave this spot alive."

While Erhard Mauer conducted his interrogation, Kurt pulled their belongings out of the back seat and tossing them into the street. Suddenly, everyone looked up as they heard the sound of an approaching vehicle.

When Carl first realized what was taking place down the road, he grabbed Elaine's arm and pulled her down in the seat below the window and out of sight. He slid down in his own seat so as to appear shorter and kept driving like any good citizen who did not want to get involved. "Quiet," he cautioned as they rolled past the other two vehicles.

As soon as Carl's delivery van passed by, the elderly couple renewed their frantic attempt to convince the Germans that they were telling the truth.

"Sir, I swear on the eyes of my children that what I am telling you is true. We thought the car was a gift from God – to save us from the fire! I have never seen the man before or since – really! He was not very tall, spoke with a German accent, and his Italian was not very good. Oh yes, and he walked with a slight limp."

"Was he alone, or were there any others with him?" Erhard grilled.

"As I said, he drove up, handed me the key and said to drive in this direction," the old man insisted. "Then he just walked away."

"Did you see which direction he walked?" Erhard pressed.

"He just went back down the street and around the corner, probably back into town," the old man described. "More than that, we really don't know. We were just trying to get everything loaded into the car. By this time, we could clearly see the flames, so all we really wanted to do was escape. That's the absolute truth. You have to believe us."

"I have a hard time believing that a complete stranger would just walk up and hand you the keys to an automobile," Erhard observed, "and you barely even watched him walk away."

Kurt, having already emptied the back seat, reported, "Nothing back here."

"Check under the front hood in the storage compartment," Erhard muttered as he stared absentmindedly at the rust-stained outlines on the back seat. He returned to the elderly couple and warned, "You can go now, but if anyone asks, this event did not take place. Do you understand? We were never here!"

Chapter 41. May 27, 2008 – Fairfax, Virginia

"I'm still trying to figure out why you brought me here," Ryan wondered. "You have the actual aircraft available to test, the radar footprint readout should be straightforward, and you yourself said that your best and brightest are trying to crack the formula for that black goo. You also have a window to the inside with your friends in Vienna. So why exactly am I here?"

"We want you to go to Colonia and get some answers," Alex replied. "Just take a little trip down to South America, talk to some people and come back home. That's all."

"So I just walk up to their door, introduce myself and say some 'spook' in Washington would like me to ask a few questions," Ryan mocked. "I'm sure they're just going to fall all over themselves to tell me what they know after that approach."

"Actually, you're going to tell them that you are with the Smithsonian Institution and you're putting together an exhibit of World War Two aircraft. You would like to know, depending on their background, whether they were in Germany at the end of the war and if they had any information that might be useful."

"That's a great way to start off the conversation," Ryan countered. "I'll gain their confidence right off the bat by lying to them."

"Right off 'The Bat'. That's a good one," Alex chuckled as he pointed out the plane's unofficial nickname. "But you know, 'lying' is such a nasty word. Personally, I prefer 'fabrication' or 'manipulation of reality.'"

Alex unfolded a sheet of paper he had just pulled from his inside coat pocket and said, "Actually, Ryan, this bank statement says that you *do* work for the Smithsonian. It reads – and I quote – 'For the past three years, Mr. Ryan Lessley has been on retainer as a consultant with the Smithsonian Institution concerning rare and experimental aircraft' … unquote."

Ryan grabbed the paper from Alex and looked at the monthly brokerage statement with his name and account number at the top. He still could not believe his own eyes.

"The Smithsonian has been very generous with your $42,500 yearly retainer," Alex stated, "and as we say in Texas, 'it's time to get on your horse and earn your pay' – that is, unless you're one of those 'big belt buckle but no cattle' kind of guys."

"Now, I have to ask myself," Ryan pondered, "why would you put …" he paused for a moment to perform some quick mental arithmetic … "$127,500 into an account to make this cover look so convincing unless you thought maybe someone – like perhaps your Israeli friends – might do a little more in-depth snooping? But I can certainly see where this is going."

"Well, it's really closer to $132,000 and change with the interest," Alex countered with a smile, "but who's going to quibble over a little petty cash at the agency? This really is a classic example of a large, prestigious institution hiring the best and most-renowned authorities in the field and then compensating them at the going rate on the open market. This could be viewed as a textbook definition of capitalism." Alex was obviously pleased with his explanation.

"Wow, that was an especially heavy load of crap – even for you," Ryan observed. "I'd like to offer a little different interpretation if you wouldn't mind: First of all, with this cover you arranged, you have your plausible deniability. I'm a civilian, a private contractor, and technically not working for the government. If and when things get sticky, you'll just throw me under the bus – as you say – 'in a Texas heartbeat.'"

"I suppose you could look at it that way," Alex returned, "although I would much prefer you look at it as fulfilling your contract. You know, Mr. Lessley, a reputation can be such a difficult thing to repair. Whether you like it or not, this is not fiction – it is very real. These people think that whatever they're after not only does exist, but will serve their purpose as well. They view The Bat as the last piece of a puzzle."

Ryan Lessley was not accustomed to being backed into a corner. "And what is it exactly that you think they believe?" he asked.

"We think they are convinced that, as you say, this 'mysterious black goo' renders whatever it coats invisible to radar," Alex answered, "and by tinkering with the chemistry, they may also enable it to shield objects from other areas of the visible spectrum. For example, who knows what contraband could pass through detection machines at airports around the world, were it smeared with this curious crud?

"In theory, you could move a nuclear device anywhere you choose," he went on. "From our window in Vienna, we have surmised that they believe they are very close. In their minds, this is the perfect piece – the missing link, as it were. Perfect because we partially supply the delivery service."

With his jaw clenched, Ryan glared at Alex, but he knew he was outmatched. Then Alex flashed him that big Texas grin and said, "Good, I'm glad that's settled. Now we won't have to discuss it again. Back to your previous question: No, I don't expect them to tell you anything. The reason you are going to Colonia is to ask just one question."

* * *

During the hour-long drive from the airport, Ryan rehearsed a hundred times what he was going to say. He imagined a grizzled old man answering the door and slamming it shut before he could utter his first words. His concentration was broken by the vibration of the secure satellite phone McCormick had given him.

"Lessley, are you at the farmhouse yet?" Alex asked. His query came across as concerned.

"This thing's got a GPS chip in it," Ryan answered tersely. "You already know my location." He was stressed out enough without having to explain how the damned phone worked.

"Pull off to the side of the road if you're not there yet," Alex urged. "I need your undivided attention. I'm sending you a picture and I need to know if you recognize him."

Ryan pulled over and left the engine running. He stared at the picture and replied, "Looks familiar, but I can't quite place him. Where would I know him from?"

"He was on your flight yesterday." Alex sounded really tense.

"Oh yeah, he was the guy in the next aisle who moved when we traded seats," Ryan remembered. "That young pregnant woman seemed so uncomfortable. I guess we both felt badly for her. I gave up my seat in first class for hers in coach and the other guy had even more space on his side, so he switched to give her the extra room."

"The first-class seating configuration is back-to-back on that plane," Alex said. "He changed seats so he could turn around and keep an eye on you."

"Keep an eye on me?" Ryan blurted. "Who is this guy – and why would he want to do that?"

"'Who *was* this guy' is a more appropriate way of putting it," Alex corrected. "His cover was as an air marshal, but yesterday he was your babysitter. We found him dead in his hotel room this morning when he didn't show up for his flight to Los Angeles."

A long pause ensued, during which time Ryan could only hear heavy breathing. When Alex spoke again, his words came out slowly and deliberately – almost as if he was having trouble organizing his thoughts. Ryan could almost hear the wheels turning in Alex's head. "He was sitting in your spot and now he's dead," Alex toned. "Did you make any special meal requests during the flight?"

"Yeah, I always order special," Ryan replied. "I'm allergic to peanuts and I'm lactose-intolerant."

"Peanuts and lactose – holy crap, what a delicate doily. Jeez, can't you rough it for even a few hours?" Now Alex really sounded agitated.

"Listen, I don't know what you're getting at, but I've been declared clinically dead on the operating table – *twice*," Ryan defended, "and one of those times they had to open my trachea and insert a breathing tube. So, no, I pretty much can't just 'rough it.'"

"Okay, sorry – that was out of line," Alex apologized. "It's just that now I've got a dead agent and I'm scrambling to get someone down there to watch your back. So when you get to the farmhouse, don't leave. I'll send the cavalry as fast as I can. Understood?"

"I have no desire to be one of your heroes," Ryan assured him. "So, how did he die?"

"We didn't catch it at first," Alex replied, "but we kept screening for toxins that caused the same symptoms as a heart attack. Athletic, healthy men at age forty-one don't usually drop dead of heart disease. No history of that in his family whatsoever – and he was a soccer player. Doesn't mean it couldn't happen. It just seemed too much of a coincidence to accept.

"We finally came across traces of a toxin found in shellfish that accumulates when a certain kind of plankton is present in high concentrations in the ocean. This phenomenon is referred to as a 'red tide,' because the water reflects a red fluorescence at night. It literally looks like there are millions of tiny lights in the water. When this happens, the shellfish are quarantined and not allowed to be shipped to market."

"So you're telling me your man died from a bad bowl of clam chowder?" Ryan asked halfheartedly.

"I can see this hasn't sunk in, so I'll give you a few points to think about," Alex admonished. "One, global satellite-scanning photos show no red-tide blooms occurring anywhere in the world at this time. Two, there was enough of the toxin in his body to kill fifteen men. And three, he would have needed to eat close to thirty pounds of shellfish for this much poison to accumulate in his system. Mr. Lessley, the only conclusion that can be drawn is that this 'bad bowl of clam chowder' was meant for you."

Chapter 42. March 12, 1944 – Verona, Italy

"Dimpler – or someone – sent the couple as a diversion," Erhard Mauer said. "He knew we would chase the Volkswagen. Perhaps he is planning on doubling back across the Swiss border in a different car, or at least hiding in Verona until the trail goes cold." He tried to convince himself that one choice made more sense than the other. A coin toss should decide this one: They could continue on the road to Genoa, not knowing what they were looking for, or head back to Verona. Finally, after determining that this method of decision-making was juvenile, they decided to use common sense and pick up the trail where Dimpler had last been seen. They turned the Opel around and drove back to Verona.

As they headed back along the winding incline, Erhard caught sight of something on the opposite side that looked out of place. "Stop!" he barked. Kurt Drescher backed up the car and braked to a halt. Erhard got out and walked to the edge of the road on the downhill side. There, lying in the sparse scrub brush, was a shape that simply did not belong.

The dull, flat surface of the fuel canister contrasted sharply with the surrounding vegetation. This is what caught his discerning eye. Erhard didn't know what it was at first, but instinctively he knew that it was just out of place. It was of German design and manufacture. Of that he was certain. A container identical to this was attached to the exterior of their Opel. As he touched the bottom of the vessel, a slight trace of rust rubbed off on his fingers. He lifted the can to his nose. Near the spout, he could smell a strong aroma of petrol. This told him that some still remained inside. His thoughts turned immediately to the stains in the back of the tan Volkswagen. This can had been in that car!

Tire tracks leading back to the road were different in size from their vehicle. Furthermore, that car would be easy to identify, for the two rear tires showed different tread patterns. He raced back across the road, jumped into the Opel and instructed Kurt that they were now looking for a vehicle with two rear tires from different manufacturers.

Carl had tried to maintain his speed at a rate which would maximize his mileage per liter of petrol. But now, after seeing the two officers at the side of the road with the old couple, he pushed the accelerator pedal to the floor of the delivery van as soon as they were out of sight. If that black sedan ever caught up with them, running out of fuel would be the least of their problems.

Busalla, at an elevation of about thirteen hundred feet, signaled a gradual and gentle drop through the coastal valleys to Genoa. The sharp turns and switchbacks of the Dolomite Mountains to the north now gave way to long, straight downhill stretches and occasional slight inclines of the coastal foothills.

Here, the delivery van's carburetor sucked its last bit of nourishment from the tank. Carl coasted as far as he could and pulled to the side of the road. As he weighed his options, his heart began to race as a small speck appeared in his rear-view mirror. As it approached, he was relieved to see that it was merely an old truck. He jumped out of the van and waved his arms to flag it down. And as the truck slowed to a stop beside him, the smell of chicken manure filled the air and assailed his nostrils. The old flatbed was loaded to overflowing with cages filled with fowl.

"We've run out of gas and I must get my family to Genoa by this afternoon," Carl implored. "If you have a can of petrol, I will gladly buy it from you – or I can pay you to give us a ride." Just then, Elaine and the two children peered out the window.

Sensing the opportunity for an easy windfall, and since he was heading in that direction anyway, the driver said, "I can give you a ride, but you will have to pay in advance – nine thousand lira."

"If you take us to the waterfront district, I will give you twelve," Carl offered.

"Done," the driver agreed, "but there is only room for the lady and children in front. You will have to ride in the back with the *gallinas*. Here is an old tarp you can sit on. I'm sorry it will smell, but that is the best I can do." His smile displayed a mouth that was a stranger to any form of dental care.

Carl shot a worried glance at Elaine, but she smiled and patted her coat pocket where Conrad's Mauser pistol still rested. Carl climbed into the back of the truck and wedged himself between the crates. He thought of how his upwardly mobile Elaine had gone from traveling in a top-of-the-line Mercedes to a tan Volkswagen, then a faded green bakery delivery truck and now an antique rattletrap that hauled chickens to market. At this rate, if they were lucky, the high point of their day would turn out to be boarding a rusty tramp steamer.

Then a thought caused a smile to creep across his face: Carl Friedrick and his family had been pursued by a pair of German SS officers. Their superior, Heinrich Himmler himself, was a poultry farmer before his rise to power. Now, here they were, running for their lives while hiding in a truck filled with chickens.

Chapter 43. March 12, 1944 – Genoa, Italy

After dropping off his passengers three blocks from the waterfront, Vincente made his delivery to the butcher shop. The chickens – hens mostly past their egg-laying prime – were tough and scrawny. But if a cook knew what he was doing and slowly stewed them in a good wine broth, they would be more than tasty. Besides, meat of any sort was a luxury these days.

To celebrate his good fortune, Vincente decided to treat himself to a hearty dish of pasta primavera and a glass of chianti at his favorite waterfront *ristorante*. As he sipped his drink, his mind raced with thoughts of his recent passengers. What did the little boy say about bathing in the hot springs? The only mineral springs he knew of were north of here, near Milan. And why did she keep her hand in her coat pocket for nearly the entire trip? One of the children rode in her lap, and as they moved about to situate themselves, he thought he saw what could have been the handle of a pistol protruding from her coat. Also, they were all dressed as refugees, yet they rode in a vehicle – and the man carried a large quantity of cash.

Yes, he decided – when he finished his meal, he would report this to the authorities. One could not be too careful. If they were up to something suspicious, he wanted the *Carabinieri*, Italy's national military police, to have no doubt as to whose side he was on. Then he smiled. Perhaps there was also a reward for these "fugitives". Now that would be something. He had not only been paid to save them – he could also be paid again to turn them in!

* * *

The Opel pulled up behind the delivery van and the two Germans emerged with weapons drawn. They approached from opposite sides and, seeing it empty, quickly searched the interior. They found nothing but sleeping pads, blankets and a newspaper from Trento, dated the day before. Kurt placed his hand on the hood cowling. The engine was still warm. Erhard knelt down behind the vehicle and looked at the rear tires. The tread patterns did not match. "Hello, my old friends," he muttered. Then he saw the footprints. They were now looking for two adults and two children.

* * *

Carl and Elaine, with their children in tow, stood before the steps of the old Renaissance-style steamship terminal. He had requested that the truck driver drop them off several blocks away from their actual destination, but the driver knew there were only a very few places where people with so much luggage would go. They walked in an indirect route, doubling back to confuse anyone who might be following them. Now, finally, they were here.

At some point in the past, this had been quite a beautiful structure, but chips were now visible in the columns where bomb shrapnel had torn chunks from the walls. Even before the Allied air raids, the effects of the sea air on the marble facade had taken their toll. British and American shells had only hastened a process begun by corrosion, fungus and various types of bird droppings. Carl and Elaine realized that walking through these doors was the symbolic final step in leaving their old life behind. After a few seconds, they squeezed each other's hands and started up the steps.

Here, people from all parts of Europe gathered to look for the answer to their prayers. Those without the proper papers approached strangers and, in hushed tones, bartered for their ticket to freedom. Spies, informants and Italian security agents hid everywhere – sometimes in plain sight. Occasionally, the *Carabinieri* would come into the station and drag someone away. Buying and selling could be dangerous in these hallowed halls.

Elaine and the children found a bench along a side foyer where she could watch the entryway and still keep Carl in view as he stood in line. He surveyed the crowd to see if anyone was paying him more than the usual amount of attention. Presently, he moved to the second line from the right as he was instructed.

* * *

At the local *Carabinieri* precinct, Captain Giuseppe Pescatore tapped his fingers impatiently and asked a second time, "Now, why is it again that you, a truck driver, are suspicious of these people?"

The police captain had just spent forty-five minutes with not one, but two, German security officers who were looking for a man named Dimpler. Certain that he was in Genoa, they assumed the captain and his office would give their full and immediate cooperation. After what seemed an eternity, the two left to consult with some of his local patrol officers.

As the two Germans left his office, the truck driver poked his head through the doorway and removed his hat. "*Mi scusi, signor,*" he implored, "if I could have a moment of the captain's time." Completely exhausted from the Germans' interrogation-like chat, Captain Pescatore leaned back in his chair and listened to the truck driver's story. It was already well past the time of day when the middle-aged captain allowed himself a single glass of afternoon wine. Today, he needed it more than ever. As soon as he could rid himself of this driver and his wild tale, the captain could get back to his normal routine. But Vincente would not stop talking. In fact, the more he talked, the less interested the captain became.

The man rambled on about his passengers running out of gas, a hot spring somewhere up north, a gun, a lot of money and, finally, in exasperation, he blurted to the captain, "I tell you, there was something suspicious about those people. They weren't even Italian – they were German."

Just then, Erhard Mauer walked back into the captain's office and overheard the end of the conversation. "You say you gave them a ride?" he asked. "Where did you pick them up – and what kind of vehicle were they driving?"

"About twelve miles north of Genoa," Vincente answered reluctantly. Suddenly, he was not so happy to have these people so interested in his story.

"And the type of vehicle?" Erhard inquired further.

"A faded green delivery van," Vincente answered. "It was pulled off to the side of the road where they said they ran out of gas."

"Show me on the map where you let them off," Erhard invited.

"Here, about three blocks from the immigration and departure offices at the waterfront," Vincente pointed. "Wherever they were going, they seemed to be in a hurry."

* * *

The two German *SS* officers slowly moved through the marble hall and watched for any telltale signs of nervousness from anyone standing in line. Elaine saw them as soon as they entered and watched in stark terror as they walked past her husband. Her hand firmly gripped the handle of the Mauser, but Elaine could feel the perspiration building in her palm and the anxiety of wondering whether they would be caught.

Carl had been quite startled when the two marched past him, but he still strained to hear what they were saying. Flashing identification papers, they requested to talk to the supervisor in charge. An overweight man in his late forties emerged and quickly pulled sheets from clipboards. Carl thought he heard them say Dimpler, but he couldn't be sure.

Suddenly, Carl felt an overwhelming urge to leave the line and melt back into the crowd. Just then, he felt a hand on his shoulder. "This is a good line to be in," a low voice said. "It moves quickly. It is the best line for you – and you should also take off that hat." The voice was deep, with a cadence and rhythm he hadn't heard in years. He took a deep breath and slipped the hat into his pocket.

As the two Germans walked back toward the entrance, Erhard stopped momentarily and made eye contact with Carl. He searched for a name or place to match with the face. When none materialized, he continued walking toward the entryway to join his partner out on the docks. Stopping at the doorway, Erhard glanced back at Carl one last time.

When he reached the front of the line, Elaine and the children joined him. The clerk stamped their exit visa papers without question. He then directed the family toward a door to the side of the main hall for passport and luggage inspection. As Carl bent down to pick up his suitcase, he cast a quick glance behind him. The only other people in line were two elderly women.

Chapter 44. May 11, 2008 – Colonia del Sacramento, Uruguay

As he bounced along the dirt road on the outskirts of Montevideo, Edwardo couldn't keep from smiling at the thought of the cold beer that awaited him. Once a month, he made his trip out to the foreigner's hacienda with his load of coal, just as his father had done for fifty years. A rare commodity in this part of the world, coal had been mined in open pits in only a few places in the foothills. Even though it was not good enough for industrial use, it was still burned in open fires for cooking, even though United Nations health workers had repeatedly warned of the hazards – in fact, they claimed that coal produces many of the known air pollutants identified by the Environmental Protection Agency as being harmful to human health and the environment.

The smiling faces that would greet him with the tall, frosty mug simply said that coal helped power the hacienda. They would wink, smile and whisper that they actually used it in their family recipe. Who could argue that there was not something special about a brew this good? The hearty and nutty flavor left no bitter aftertaste, and on a hot day it would really quench a powerful thirst.

The stone ranch house peered out of the mist as Edwardo drove through the courtyard gates and past the outbuildings on the perimeter. An old woman in a Panama hat leaned on a cane and stood waiting for them in her usual spot on the front porch. His father had told him when he started delivering many years ago that there was an old man in America who used to dress the same way. He always chuckled to himself when he thought of the old woman who looked like the man who sold chicken on TV.

Miguel, the foreman in charge of all workers at the ranch, waved as Edwardo pulled in and walked over to the large building that housed the coal chute. Edwardo always wondered why they needed coal to brew beer. His brother, Timataeo, concocted a fine local beverage, which he bottled in large plastic jugs stored in an outbuilding near their chicken house – but it was no match for the German gringo's excellent brew.

Edwardo was always curious as to why the building had no smokestacks and emitted no soot from the coal. Also, he never got to smell that wonderful earthy aroma that Timataeo's creations always produced. Yet he always came back to that same burning question: Why did they need the coal? That is why they're called secrets. Anyway, the ranch hands were always more than generous with a mug or three of their product. For two generations, these questions had been asked around his kitchen table, but as long as the beer flowed and they paid their bills, no one really seemed to care.

Edwardo carefully backed up his brightly painted truck to the coal chute and got out to open its rear doors. His payload slid effortlessly into a shallow bin at the bottom of the chute, after which he closed the double doors on the back of the truck and reattached the makeshift lock. From the outside, the building looked like all the others: weatherworn and in dire need of a coat of paint. But when he looked down into the coal chute, the glint of metal below revealed a different – and quite modern – world within.

* * *

Two days later, inside the low building, two figures slid between the shadows cast by the maze of tubes and vats. Edwardo and Timateo studied the layout of the room. Like the time they had visited their first brothel in Montevedeo, the experience of a new and magical place nearly overwhelmed them.

At first glance, it resembled an oversized backyard still – with one glaring exception: Instead of the sweet, heady aroma of hops, barley and yeast, it smelled more like a fuel depot.

The building was surprisingly clean and modern for such an old structure. Large ventilation fans and ducts extended from the ceiling and led to the exterior walls. These ducts had been built into the side of a sloping embankment. They disappeared into the hillside and emerged some one hundred fifty feet away near a swiftly flowing stream. Here, the jungle's dense foliage had been cleared away – but not by chopping as with conventional brush-trimming techniques. It was as if an invisible hand had simply swept away all vegetation. Nothing grew within a twenty-foot radius of the opening – not even the strangler vines indigenous to so much of this tangled woodland.

Outside, the ground crunched like eggshells beneath their feet as the brothers pried open the ventilation duct cover. Deathly afraid of snakes, Edwardo made his brother go first. When they were youngsters, Timetaeo had regularly caught the more harmless of these reptiles and hidden them around the house to torment his brother. But this was not the time for joking. A *fer-de-lance* or any number of other venomous snakes could be lurking in the dark, three-foot-wide tunnel, and by the time they could reach a hospital, its bite might have proved fatal.

Shining his flashlight into the opening, Edwardo was relieved to see that the shaft had been cleared of all obstacles. Except for a small trickle of water, nothing else was visible in the old galvanized pipe. A few roots from the vegetation above fingered their way through the distressed metal and hung like strands of spaghetti from the top of the duct.

Edwardo pushed his brother into the opening. "You keep all the snakes and spiders away from me," he warned, "or I swear you know what I'll do with this flashlight." Timataeo just smiled and said, "Don't worry, big brother. I promise you'll be the first to know if I see anything."

Both men were relieved to find only a few pebbles in the slick, slimy coating that lined the bottom of the pipe. At the end of the tunnel, they saw a large fan mounted on a hinge – presumably so it could be pushed aside for cleaning. They swung it open and dropped into the brewing chamber.

Once inside, they looked for the finished product. Two weeks earlier, after his coal delivery, Edwardo came across three cases of beer stacked behind this very building. After making sure no one was watching, he slid the brews into the back of the truck and covered his prize with an old tarp. Even though it had initially been intended for their own enjoyment, it soon became evident that it was worth much more if they sold it to tourists at the local flea market. A cousin who attended the university in Montevideo designed and printed some brightly colored labels for Timataeo's home brew. That is how "Papagayo Pilsner" was born.

They encountered one obvious problem, though, midway through their initial inventory: Since everyone in their family thought they were the *braumeisters*, they needed to find a way to tap into the source so they could maintain a constant supply for their customers.

As soon as they climbed down into the room, Timateo nudged his brother and pointed out the size of the vats. Containers this large could hold so much beer that surely their petty thefts would go unnoticed. A room with containers this large would also need a large storage area to hold the product, and with the coal deliveries scheduled monthly, they reasoned that the brewery must be running around the clock.

The next thing they noticed after entering the brewing chamber was the soot. Its inky blackness literally covered the walls. A complex sprinkler system, fire-suppression equipment and numerous *No Smoking* signs were scattered throughout the room. Edwardo and Timateo joked that the high alcohol content of the beer might actually be a potential fire hazard!

Suddenly, the chute doors opened and a large load of coal slid down from the storage area above. Edwardo had delivered this very payload just two days earlier. The two men froze in the shadows. When the coal settled into its bin, the door slammed shut and the silence of the room washed over them. After their eyes readjusted to the darkness after the sudden flash of sunlight, they began to investigate their surroundings more closely.

As they explored, they made another observation: Where was the storage area with its brewed treasure for them to pilfer? The room off to the side only contained fifty-gallon metal drums, and judging by their weight, they were much too heavy to be filled with beer. And another oddity – they saw no lizards or insects scurrying about this old building. What chemicals had been used to discourage them from occupying this space?

They moved into the splinters of light to more closely inspect the room. The print on the containers, vats and barrels was not Spanish or Portuguese, but German. Although clean, the equipment displayed streaks down its sides that told a different story: older equipment in dire need of maintenance. Liquids escaping from small pinholes in the various containers collected over time into dried, multi-colored puddles on the concrete floor.

The gurgling of liquids flowing through tubes could be heard as the brew flowed into the vats, and large gas-fired burners flared up under the soot-blackened bottoms of these containers. Suddenly, fans energized and an acrid odor started to fill the room.

Timetaeo told his brother to hold his breath as he stood on Edwardo's shoulders and climbed into the ventilation shaft. He then reached down and pulled Edwardo up after him. Crawling and sliding as fast as they could through the rusty pipe, the two brothers hastily made their way back to the entrance. Blasts of air from the fans blew past them, after which they felt a slight tingling on their skin. The hanging roots brushed against their eyes and faces, and the slimy accumulation at the bottom of the vent splashed up as they hurriedly crawled to escape. The burning in their eyes and lungs had now become even more intense. Just a little further and they would be outside.

Timataeo made it out first and pulled himself up on an old log. The rush of fresh air only briefly relieved the searing pain he felt in his eyes and on his arms. Edwardo was still ten feet behind him, but finally pulled himself free of the shaft. He crawled to the water's edge and thrust his entire head into the flowing stream. He gulped down mouthfuls of water, but nothing could stop the searing fire in his lungs. It was already too late.

Chapter 45. May 28, 2008 – Colonia del Sacramento, Uruguay

The phone call from Alex McCormick now made Ryan Lessley feel even more apprehensive as he walked up the steps of the hacienda. Even so, he still made mental notes of the various sights that greeted him. The exterior needed a new coat of paint and general maintenance, but he could still feel the tropical charm of a once-elegant home. When Ryan knocked, he was surprised when greeted by an attractive woman in her late twenties with smoky blue eyes. Her hair was straight, she wore no make-up and her jeans were not the designer type, but merely off-the-rack work apparel.

Ryan stammered and tried to speak, all the while not taking his eyes from hers. Once, many years before on a summer vacation, he dated and fell head-over-heels for a girl with eyes just like those. Unfortunately, she showed up a week later with emerald green eyes and claimed that she had mislaid her contacts. A lot of the magic of their first encounter dissolved as a result of that charade, but he never forgot those eyes.

"Good afternoon," he began. "My name is Ryan Lessley and I work for the Smithsonian Institution in Washington, D.C. Your name came up through our research and if I could have a few moments of your time, I'd like to ask you a few questions. Maybe you can help with some loose ends regarding one of our upcoming World War Two exhibits, and some recent events around here."

Her eyes fixed on his until he finished speaking. However, it appeared to him that she did not believe a word he said. She turned and directed her voice to the next room. "*Mutti*, someone is at the door and wants to speak to you. I think it's about the two men at the river."

A few moments passed and an older woman emerged into the foyer. She was still quite spry and very agile for her age. Dressed all in white, she carried herself with a sense of strength and dignity.

"I've already told the police everything I know," the older woman said. "A real tragedy, to be certain – and both men with families and small children." Sharp, twinkling eyes behind wire-rimmed glasses now evaluated and sized him up.

"Mr. Lessley, I learned many years ago out of necessity to read people quickly," she went on. "I would guess that you did not come all this way to ask about the deaths of two of our local inhabitants. Also, you have something else you wish to ask. I'm sure you are a busy man and I have very little desire to be bothered by fishing expeditions, so I'll make this simple. Ask your question and then you can leave."

This very scene had played out on their porch so many times before: The young woman answered the front door, called for the older lady and listened as the identical words were spoken. It always ended with the same results: Strangers asking questions eventually left believing this stubborn old woman knew nothing and told them even less. Was this American different? she would ask herself each and every time someone appeared on her doorstep. Was he going to fish or cut bait?

"Do you know a Conrad Dimpler?" Ryan asked.

Her eyes hardened as he finished his request. As she answered, she chose her words very carefully. "There was a Conrad Dimpler. He was an associate of my late husband in Germany, and ..."

But before she could finish her answer, Ryan asked, "Did he work at the Chancellery?"

"Yes, at the Chancellery," she muttered. "But I only met him once and I have not seen him since we left the continent." This was actually a half-truth. He came to her every time she went to sleep. Her nightmares were filled with his visitations as a grim reminder of that terrible morning.

"Why do you ask?" she inquired.

Sensing a softening in her voice, Ryan gave an answer that he hoped would open the door. "He's part of a puzzle and, like you, I also pride myself on reading people. So here's my read: I believe that you are also part of that puzzle."

While Ryan talked, he noticed the old woman's eyes as they kept returning to the medallion hanging from his neck. "That is a rather unique St. Christopher medal," she observed. "Would you mind if I asked where you got it?"

"It was my great-grandmother's," Ryan replied. "It held a special meaning for her. The only time she ever took it off was to have the chain repaired. To honor her memory, I also never remove it."

"What exactly made it so special?" Elaine Friedrick asked. She was now clearly very interested.

"The story she told was of a stranger," Ryan answered, "and this was a gift from him. The real gift, though, was that he saved them from a firestorm many years ago in Italy. She always said this was from their guardian angel, and as long as she wore the medallion no harm would come to her. She was ninety-seven and was having the silver chain replaced when she suffered a fatal heart attack."

"Back to the stranger – what exactly did he do?" Elaine asked.

"With the fire bearing down on them, the stranger miraculously appeared and gave them the keys to a car so they could escape," Ryan said as he held the medallion between his thumb and forefinger. He gave it a kiss as if remembering a loved one. "It was a Volkswagen, I think. He then gave this medallion to my great-grandmother before he walked away. She never tired of telling the story of their escape from the fire and the stranger who saved them. They were eventually able to come to America after the war."

Elaine held her hand over her mouth. She stared at the medallion as her eyes welled with tears. She then reached inside her collar, pulled out an identical medallion and likewise kissed it gently.

"Sixty-four years ago, my husband was the stranger who gave that medal to your great-grandmother," she said in a trembling tone. "The last time these two medallions were together was the morning I shot Conrad Dimpler."

She looked as if a great weight had been lifted from her shoulders as she said, "If it's not too early, would you care to share a drink with an old woman and listen to her story?" Then she ushered Ryan into the hacienda to sit and reminisce.

"When we entered the room for our luggage and passports to be checked, Wilhelm was waiting there for us," Elaine explained. "He hugged both of the children, kissed them on the forehead and commented on how big they had grown. Of course, having never seen him before, they were naturally quite nervous about being hugged by a stranger, since Carl and I had warned them of such things. He then hugged Carl and me for what seemed a bit longer than proper.

"Then, as we all dried our eyes, Willie said, 'Something strange is going on here. There are many more security people than normal on the streets – not just Italian police and military, but the Germans are here also. They seem to be very preoccupied with finding just one man.'

"Carl then asked, 'Would you happen to know who he is?' As he asked, the joy suddenly drained from his face.

"'I couldn't hear exactly, but I thought I heard them say the name Conrad,' Willie said as he patted the children on the head. After that, I couldn't catch anything more." Elaine looked truly shaken as she regaled this tale from her past.

"Then I asked Willie, 'Could it have been Conrad Dimpler?' I couldn't keep myself from asking him about that horrible man."

Elaine explained further. "'Was Mr. Dimpler traveling with you?' Willie asked me. He acted like he really needed to know."

"I told him, 'Mr. Dimpler caught up to us in Bolzano. Unfortunately, he had a tragic automobile accident.' I replied with no more emotion than if someone had asked for directions or a newspaper."

"'I see,' Willie replied. 'This could complicate matters, but does not make it impossible. It seems they are still looking for Dimpler, not you, so we will proceed just as we planned. Here, give me your coat and hat,' he said to Carl.

"'They will have people watching the docks, especially the departing ships, and I saw how that SS officer looked at you,' Willie told him. 'I will walk out on the dock, light a cigarette and move to the edge of the water. I will look lost in my thoughts, then casually glance to my left and right. If I turn my collar up, it means I will have gotten someone's attention and I will start walking. Wait five minutes and go directly to the ship. There will be a man at the top of the entry plank. You will know him by a crooked finger on his left hand. He can be trusted. I will meet you back at the ship, or in Argentina if the ship sails on the tide before I can return. Above all, do not leave your cabin until we are out of port. I or someone else will be waiting for you in Buenos Aires when you dock.'

"He then hugged Carl, myself and the children, then stepped out onto the dock," the old woman said wistfully. "After turning up his collar, he walked off and that was the last time we ever saw him. I don't know if it was harder to lose him the first time or the second."

Chapter 46. March 12, 1944 – Genoa, Italy

Willie casually strolled away from the docks, occasionally checking reflections in nearby windows and passing cars to make sure that the man following him was still there. He didn't know the man, but he knew the type: not dirty enough for the docks, yet too muscular to be an office type. He didn't carry himself like a businessman, anyway. It was in the eyes – always it was the eyes that gave them away. He had seen men just like this one at the German embassy in Buenos Aires. They were always out there, watching.

As he turned the corner and strolled out of view, Wilhelm quickly shed his coat and hat and handed them to an associate, who quickly donned them. With his new look, Willie then continued down the street at the same meandering pace.

Sidling into a doorway of a small cafe, he took a seat at a table in the rear with a view of the sidewalk and square in front. The stranger rounded the corner and quickly turned his head until he caught sight of the hat and coat, then continued at a relaxed pace with his hands in his pockets and his eyes trained on his target.

In another two minutes, Willie thought, they would be out of sight and he could double back to the docks. Just then, a chill ran down his spine as two men entered the cafe. They each wore the distinctive leather topcoat of a German *SS* officer. Willie picked up a newspaper from the table next to him and raised it as if to be absorbed in an article. The short, stout man stood near the front door, while the taller of the two, Erhard Mauer, took a seat at the table next to Willie.

As he sat, Erhard slowly turning his head to make sure no one was close enough to overhear him. He leaned toward Willie and said, "Congratulations, your plan was flawless – almost. If it hadn't been for Dimpler, we would never have stumbled upon you."

Reaching into a satchel, Erhard pulled out a flat piece of metal, laid it on the table in front of Willie and pushed it under his newspaper. Erhard then reached over with one finger and pulled a corner of the newspaper down so their eyes met.

"This license plate was attached to a Mercedes staff car that a Captain Carl Friedrick checked out from the motor pool in Berlin two days ago," Erhard explained. "Unfortunately, it was involved in a serious accident and a single body was found inside the wreckage – burned beyond recognition. I called Berlin and official records show that the good captain and his family perished in an automobile crash – tomorrow morning.

"The papers Captain Friedrick carried from the Red Cross, the Argentine visas and the letters of transit ... all his documentation is legitimate. There is not a forgery among them. I even received a call from Heinrich Himmler's private secretary. She informed me that this was a matter of state security and to be concerned only with Conrad Dimpler."

Erhard Mauer stared hard into Willie's eyes and said, "I asked myself, who are you and why is it so important that this Captain Friedrick and his family not only leave Europe, but also disappear completely? This is quite the smuggling operation you've put together."

Willie finally spoke. "I'm not doing this for money."

"No, I will accept that if you say so," Erhard said. "In fact, technically you're not a smuggler because you do have all the proper papers. What you have is a unique export business. I don't suppose you've thought what this service of yours might be worth on the open market. It could be priceless – or it could be your final bargaining chip."

Erhard leaned back and casually pointed to the man standing at the door. "His name is Kurt Drescher," he went on. "He can become exceptionally violent, so I want you to listen carefully to what I am about to say. You offer a service to a select clientele. Since you claim you're not doing this for money, I propose a simple trade. I have an elderly mother, a wife and daughter in Munich. I would very much like to grow old with my wife and watch our children and grandchildren grow to be adults, but I know this is not possible. I realize I have become something that can't easily be stripped away. The uniform I wear is not only on the outside, it is also in here." Erhard Mauer lightly tapped his chest with his fist. "This uniform has become my life, and to walk away from it would be like trying to live without breathing. I have come to accept that what I have become is the only way I could live. For better or worse, I will stand with Germany until the end.

"The trade I propose is simple," he said. "My family for yours. For arranging the 'export' papers and subsequent delivery of my family, I will allow Captain Friedrick and his family not only to leave, but also to live."

Willie's mind raced as he considered all the possibilities. He opened his mouth to speak, yet no words came out.

"Let me help you make your decision," Erhard said. "You should realize that you and Captain Friedrick have been linked to the death of a high-ranking German official – not to mention the possible theft and destruction of valuable state property. The other matter involves the only two ways you will leave this café: either walk out with us or be carried out under a sheet."

"This could take some time," Willie said in desperation. "I have to speak with my contacts in Buenos Aires. It could take weeks to make all the arrangements – and I'll need a way of contacting you when everything is ready."

"That is not a problem," Erhard replied. "You will just turn to me and say 'it's done.' I don't plan on letting you out of my sight. Certainly you, more than anyone else, can understand why I couldn't let a man with your contacts and resources take a little side trip to South America."

"What does your partner think about this arrangement of yours?" Willie asked.

"He doesn't know about our agreement," Erhard countered, "and I take it we do have an agreement – yes?"

In the last few moments, Willie had learned two important details: Leaving with these men didn't necessarily insure Carl's and his family's safety, but it did signal the fact that he was a dead man. A senior *SS* officer would see no benefit in Willie being left alive to implicate him after his family was safe. Willie would simply disappear. His only real choice at this point was when and how he would die. But more importantly, Willie now realized that the man at the door knew nothing of Erhard Mauer's plan to get his family out of Germany. The lone threat to Carl and his family sat a mere two feet away. The clear simplicity of this logic suddenly put him at ease. He was now at peace with himself and what needed to be done.

While in Genoa, Willie had taken to carrying a .32-caliber Beretta M1935 pistol for protection. It was rugged and reliable, and its small frame made it easy to conceal. While it chambered too small a round for military use, it was deadly at close range. He could probably get one shot off at the man seated next to him and have a chance to get a second round off at the man by the door before anyone realized what had happened. But he had to be certain that Erhard Mauer would not survive.

Wilhelm nodded to indicate his agreement, and as the two men rose from their chairs, Willie quickly pulled the gun from his pocket. Erhard's eyes grew large and he lunged for the pistol. Willie fired two quick rounds into Mauer's chest, then spun the pistol toward the door. However, white puffs of smoke already floated from the muzzle of the gun in Kurt Drescher's hand. Now everything seemed to evolve in slow motion.

The first round hit Willie in his right shoulder, shattering bone and slamming him back against the wall. The next two shots struck him high on the left side of his chest, bounced off his ribs and tore through his heart and lungs. As his legs buckled and he slowly slid to the floor, red trails of blood traced his path down the back wall of the cafe. Willie's eyes began to glaze, but not before he saw Erhard Mauer's heart pump the last of his life through the two holes in his chest. Slumping to the floor, Willie closed his eyes for the last time.

Chapter 47. May 28, 2008 – Hacienda outside Colonia,

Uruguay

In a moment of clarity, Ryan looked into Elaine's eyes and asked, "Did you ever tell Carl that Willie was the father of your children?"

A sorrowful smile came to Elaine's face as she replied, "No, but I think there were times he may have suspected. I believe he wanted to ask, but he was too much of a gentleman. Even though Willie, as you have guessed, was their biological father, my husband was their *papa*. No man could ever have fulfilled that duty more honorably than my Carl."

Elaine paused for a moment to collect her thoughts, then continued. "You didn't ask, but I want to tell you why anyway: While Carl was away on an inspection tour to the Eastern Front in Czechoslovakia in the spring of 1938, we received word that he was missing. We were frantic to receive any information, but could get none. A soldier dying in war for his country is just another form letter or a number on the wall – that is, until it happens to you. Then it is very personal, very real. Looking back now, it was a terrible way to find comfort, but back then it was all we had."

Elaine's eyes settled on the wrinkled hands folded in her lap. "You know the rest of the story. We made our life here and raised our children. Then four years ago, Carl passed away from pneumonia."

"Did you ever go back to look for friends or family?" Ryan asked.

"Those who were not killed ended up in the Eastern Sector with the Russians. That part of our life was over. We returned once in late 1947 – or maybe it was 1948. It was so long ago I can't even remember. We were able to get into the area that the Russians controlled, but nothing had been rebuilt. Whole city blocks were still just piles of rubble, while the Western Sector had started to rise from its ashes.

"We tried to find my parents, neighbors and friends, but most were displaced or missing. We received word that my sister and parents had died in a fire-bomb attack on Dresden just three months after we left. We could find no records to verify it, but where they used to live looked like the end of the world, and we never heard from them again. We sifted through what records we could find in West Berlin, but we never found what happened to Ernst and Helga. We could only assume the worst." She rubbed her aged hands together, obviously deep in thought. Then she arose and said, "Wait here – I have something I want to give you."

Returning a few minutes later, she held an aging, cracked leather folder embossed with the German eagle. "When we returned to Germany, Carl was deeply troubled that so many awful people who were responsible for these horrible crimes still walked freely about. Because of their administrative skills, many were now even a part of the new government." She handed the folder to Ryan and he a noticed a dark, smudged handprint that once long ago could have been blood.

Ryan opened the top of the folder and started to thumb through the papers. "Do you know what is in here?" he asked.

Elaine nodded and said, "Carl told me if he should die first, I was to open the satchel and treat it like a safety deposit box. I would find instructions inside. He said we were only the caretakers of its contents, not its owners. The rightful owners of what was inside would need to be found. If I was not able to find the right person, I should pass it on to our children with the same charge and instructions. You see, Carl had a very insightful understanding of human nature and the greed that goes along with it. He said I should look for a man or woman who would have the strong moral convictions to do what was correct – even in the face of such a temptation from all of the hidden wealth.

"There is an additional file in the satchel with a wax seal and the emblem of this ring." She handed a gold band to him. "Claus von Duckworth was given these documents by two close family friends when he fled Germany in 1923. He was told that the knowledge within could do a great deal of good or harm, depending on who had the files. I think you are the kind of person who could find its rightful and best home.

"There is a man in town who has information you might find important," Elaine continued. "You hid your interest in an airplane, but your eyes betray you. He lives above the *Restaurant Caracol* in Colonia, but he does not talk to strangers.

"These days, his only passion is playing cards. We play every Tuesday and I beat him badly almost every time, but he will tell you that he lets me win. Tell him the *Senora Blanca* will forgive all of his gambling debts if he will speak with you."

Ryan looked at her in disbelief. However, he decided to call her bluff. "Why would you think I am interested in an airplane – and how would he know anything about it?"

"Because that is what the others always asked about," she explained. "Eventually, all their conversations led to the airplane. His name is Jan Reisling. He was a very famous and highly decorated pilot. My granddaughter Kristen will show you the way to the restaurant. She needs to get out more often, anyway …" Elaine winked as she finished "… and be around people her own age."

Chapter 48. May 28, 2008 – Colonia del Sacramento, Uruguay

The twenty-minute ride into Colonia was mostly silent. Kristen only occasionally spoke to mention local points of interest. As they entered town, she pointed to a two-story building to the right that bore a sign with a large snail's shell – it read *El Restaurante Caracol*. As Ryan pulled to the side of the building, she stepped from the car and went directly inside without waiting for him. That went well, he thought.

She sat at a table in the corner and was kissing an old man on the cheek as Ryan entered the establishment. She straightened up as Ryan approached and said, "Jan, this is Mr. Ryan Lessley. He is a friend of grandmama and has come a long way from America to ask you a few questions about the war. You can talk openly with him. For that, *mutti* said that she will forgive all of your gambling debts that you were not going to pay anyway."

The man put both hands on his silver-handled cane and leaned forward to speak. "The woman is a witch with cards, I tell you. She almost never loses. I think the only reason she lets me occasionally win is so I'll continue playing. But what's a man to do at my age? There are only limited options anymore. She even torments me with a new game called 'farkle.' She makes up the rules as she goes!" He laughed loudly and said, "Such a wonderful woman – still with a zest for life."

"I am trying to get information about an experimental aircraft that looked like and was called The Bat," Ryan said.

The old man blurted out, "What do you know about *Fledermaus*?"

"What do *you* know about the plane?" Ryan countered. "Did you ever see it?"

"See it?" Jan said. "I flew it against a Messerschmidt Me262 in a test flight!" He sounded very much like a proud father.

"That's why your name sounded so familiar," Ryan remembered. "You were the pilot who was supposedly lost over the North Sea on a flight in 1943."

"The day before the British experiment, our guards and staff were challenged to a soccer match by the *SS* guards at Buchenwald," Jan recounted. "I was taken down by an especially vicious tackle. I tore two knee ligaments and suffered a dislocated shoulder. Since I was the senior test pilot, my back-up flew the mission in my place the next day. I felt I was the unluckiest man on Earth – that is, until he didn't return. It has been almost sixty-five years, but I can still remember my disappointment like it was yesterday. What is it you wish to know?"

"The black coating," Ryan replied. "We're trying to get information on how it was manufactured and its composition."

"How do you know about the membrane?" the old man asked as his eyes grew sharper.

Ryan sensed that Jan was being careful with the information he revealed. He seemed reluctant to tell everything he knew. So Ryan tried one more time to coax just a little more out of the old man. "Well, we're studying it to find out exactly what it's composed of, where it came from, and how stable or dangerous it might be."

Jan cocked his head and asked, "Where did you get your sample?"

Now it was Ryan's turn to catch Jan off-guard. "We took a small section from behind the cockpit."

"You have the third plane?" Jan gasped as he clasped his hands together.

"Yes," Ryan replied firmly. Now he would let the old pilot fill in the blanks.

"For all these years, I thought it was lost," Jan said wistfully, "and here you have it. Is it still complete and intact?"

"I'm sure it's exactly as you remember it," Ryan said.

"Oh, you have quite a treasure, my friend," Jan said as he yearned to once again sit in the old aircraft. Leaning forward, he spoke in almost a whisper now, "Tell me, did you look into the cockpit? Did you sit inside it? What did you see?"

"Yes, I sat in it," Ryan replied. "It seemed really tight and cramped, with almost no room for any movement at all. Once you were fastened in, you felt more like a component than a pilot."

"Was there any kind of a cable present?" Jan inquired.

"There was a flat one which resembled a modern ribbon cable with some kind of fitting on the end," Ryan responded. "We stretched it in every direction, but couldn't find any corresponding fitting for it anywhere in the cockpit."

A smile crept across the old man's face. Ryan knew that the old man was hiding something, so he just asked the question. "But you know what it's for, don't you?"

"I have something in my room upstairs that you will find very interesting," he said while rising with some difficulty. "Ugh, to this day, when I sit too long, the old soccer injury that saved my life …" with that, he let the sentence just trail off.

Ryan arose to follow him and looked around to see where Kristen had gone. Jan noticed him glancing over his shoulder around the restaurant and said, "She was talking with a man outside and they left together."

At the top of the stairs, Jan turned the key and opened the door to his one-room world. A few flying mementos adorned the walls, including a picture of a dashing young German pilot standing beside a Messerschmidt Bf-109 fighter plane parked on a grassy field that also served as a runway. Painted on the fuselage just below the cockpit were eight small flags – three American and five British. Around the picture hung a German Iron Cross First Class on a faded red, white and black ribbon. Besides being a test pilot, this man had also been an aerial warrior in the Luftwaffe.

Jan stooped and pulled a scratched, dusty box from underneath his bed. Setting it on the table, he sat down beside it and looked at Ryan. "Without what is in this box, you do not have a complete *Fledermaus*." Lifting the lid, he revealed a cracked leather pilot's flying cap with goggles neatly folded inside. He rolled the cap over to reveal a gold fitting on the back.

"I know nothing about whether the membrane is volatile or explosive," Jan said, "but I can tell you what was to be tested that day over Britain. That coating was being tested against their radar and whether the plane would be invisible to their electronics – but we never found out. Another test had been conducted, but because the plane never returned, we thought we would never know the answer to that, either.

"We called the coating a membrane because it was to be the material that attempted to fuse man and machine into one." He stared directly into Ryan's eyes and exclaimed, "That test was to see if the aircraft could be controlled by the pilot's thoughts alone!" The old man paused for a moment to let this sink in. Jan placed the leather cap back into the box, closed the lid and handed it to Ryan. "I give this to you to see if what we dreamed is really possible."

* * *

Ryan sat behind the wheel and waited for Kristen, all the while staring at the wooden box in the passenger seat. Hesitantly, he reached over and lifted the lid. The sixty-five-year-old leather was a little stiff and a series of fine hairline cracks ran through it. Lifting it out of the box, Ryan turned it over to examine the fitting and, without thinking, slid it onto his head. Unlike what a modern pilot would wear, this piece of gear seemed more designed for warmth. He felt rather uncomfortable with the fit, so he carefully removed the pilot's cap and returned it to the box. Whether from excitement or maybe something else, he had felt a slight tingle run down his spine as he removed the headgear. Before he closed the lid, he wondered what secrets this piece of leather might conceal.

He then turned his attention to the leather satchel Elaine Friedrick had given him. There was so much to see: Swiss bank account numbers, detailed maps and lists of hidden art treasures, volumes of technical files on paper yellowed with age – including one on coal-to-oil conversion … and one labeled "Fledermaus." At the very back of the folder, a black envelope with an unbroken wax seal caught his eye. The seal matched the signet on the ring perfectly.

He was about to open it when a tap at his window caused him to say, "Your side is open." He looked out to see Kristen, a large man and what appeared to be an even larger pistol pointed at his head. Her arm was pinned behind her back and the man motioned for Ryan to leave the vehicle.

"Get out and start walking, Mr. Lessley," the man ordered, "and please do not do anything rash. It would be a pity if I were to accidentally shoot the young lady."

As the three walked toward the thick brush behind the restaurant, Ryan blurted out, "You sat next to me on the flight to Washington, didn't you?"

"Very good," the man complimented. "You have an extremely sharp memory. I'm sorry you didn't get the meal you ordered. I do imagine that the other gentleman lodged a strong formal complaint about the quality of his dinner. I'm sure it wasn't what he ordered."

Glancing around, he said, "You know, this really is an extremely dangerous part of the world. People wander off in this jungle and are never seen again. Who would think that working for a museum could be so dangerous?"

Ryan turned around and walked backwards, deliberately facing the two as they came toward him. "You'll never get away with it," he said. "Someone will hear the shots and come looking."

"I don't think so," the gunman returned. "Gunfire is a common occurrence around here, and with all the drug traffic, the locals have learned not to be too curious. So you see, no one is going to come to your rescue, and in a few days, after the animals and insects have had their way with the two of you, no one will really be able to tell what happened. Oh, and one last thing: It would be extremely rude of me not to thank you for all of the reading material you have collected for us."

He raised the gun, then hesitated for just a moment. "Pardon me for asking, but we've been trying to gain that old woman's trust for more than ten years. Some of our best people slipped in and went through the house, but found nothing. And yet you walk in and she tells you everything like a long-lost relative. What exactly did you say to her? I promise that, as a professional courtesy, I will make your deaths quick and painless if you let me in on your little secret."

As Ryan stalled for time with a rambling tale of cloak and dagger, Kristen motioned to the right with her eyes. Her captor may have been a large and powerful man, but he was not a professional killer. He had made a fatal mistake in the way he grasped her arm, so she bided her time for that one opportunity. They did not have to wait very long.

Kristen suddenly acted as if she had stumbled and lost her balance, which caused him to loosen his grasp. In one fluid motion, she grabbed his arm and her right leg flew up over her head, catching the gunman squarely in the nose. Blood exploded from the flattened cartilage and the intense pain temporarily blinded him. As his grip on her arm relaxed even further, Kristen spun and drove her fist hard above his right breast, then followed immediately with a kick just above his heart.

Bones cracked and his eyes rolled back as the thug fell to the ground with a sickening thud. His forearms and hands twitched uncontrollably. Kristen knelt down, placed two fingers on his carotid artery and checked for a pulse. Then she started to go through his pockets. "It would appear that your friend from the flight has just had a heart attack."

Ryan was still in shock from the sudden counterattack. "How long until he regains his senses?"

"I should have been more precise," Kristen replied. "It seems that your friend has had a *terminal* heart attack." She concluded her search with frustration. "Damn, he has no identification on him." Then she took his pistol and tucked it into her waistband.

"Does your grandmother know you do things like this?" Ryan inquired.

"She's not my grandmother," came the quick response.

"So what does that make you?" he countered.

"I'm her bodyguard." She then gave him a look that reminded him of a bouncer at a bar. He was convinced immediately.

"After all these years, is she still in danger from the Israelis?" Ryan asked.

"By the very nature of that question," Kristen answered, "I can only guess that grandmama did not trust you enough to reveal the complete story. I *am* Israeli." Alex McCormick's analogy of The Bat resembling an onion now made even more sense to Ryan.

"So, if you're her bodyguard," Ryan countered, "it's probably safe to assume that grandmama, as you call her, wasn't just playing matchmaker when she sent you into town with me. Correct?"

"Men are so predictable," she said as she shook her head.

Suddenly, Ryan had an epiphany. He pulled out the cell phone Alex had given him, snapped a picture of the man on the ground, pressed the dial button, and in a matter of seconds he heard a familiar voice. It was Alex.

"Lessley, where the hell are you – and where did you get that picture?"

"I need you to try and identify this guy with your facial-recognition software," Ryan said. "He sat next to me on the Washington flight. He's also the man who killed your air marshal – and just now he tried to kill us."

"Well, I can tell you right now who he is," Alex came back. "He's our boy at the Internet cafe in Austria – and by the way, who is the 'us' you're talking about?"

Kristen pulled to a stop in front of the old hacienda, turned to Ryan and grasped his forearm. "You never asked why *mutti* needed a bodyguard," she said. "She told you more than she has ever told anyone else, but still held back part of the story to protect her children and grandchildren. Her son is an architect in Buenos Aires and her daughter lives in America – Kansas City, I believe she said. She also has a daughter she bore out of wedlock when she was fifteen in Montreal, Canada. They are the only family she has left. To this day, we have what we call our 'shadows' watching over them twenty-four hours a day."

"I understand being protective, but who is she in danger from now?" Ryan asked.

"In 1957, Elaine and her husband Carl witnessed a private celebration at an Oktoberfest in Buenos Aires, then reported it to us," Kristen replied. "With this information, we began an investigation. Three years later, we captured and smuggled Adolph Eichmann – the man in charge of Germany's 'Final Solution' and responsible for six million deaths in the internment camps – out of Argentina to stand trial at an international war crimes tribunal in Israel.

"They also provided the intel that helped us track down Joseph Mengele, the 'Angel of Death'. Unfortunately, he died of natural causes before he could be brought to justice. These are only the highest-profile criminals. Numerous others were brought to our attention with their help. We take care of our own. However, so does the other side. You see, it is important that they be protected not only for who they are, but for what they represent. They might look to be part of the silent majority, but they chose not to remain silent."

Kristen stepped from the car, closed the door and leaned through the window. She extended her left forearm and rolled up her sleeve to reveal a small, crude tattoo consisting of six numbers with eleven small Stars of David surrounding it.

"Just as you wear that medallion in memory of your great-grandmother, I wear this mark for mine," she declared. "This identification number was tattooed on my grandmother's forearm at Auschwitz. She survived and was liberated by the advancing Soviet troops in January of 1945. The eleven stars represent the members of my family who perished in those death camps. They are the one part of my family and life who I never got the chance to know."

Kristen pulled her sleeve back down and continued. "If you do ever make it to Israel, Mr. Lessley, I have another grandmother in Tel Aviv who *does* like to play matchmaker. *Shalom*, my friend."

As he watched her walk up the stairs, Ryan couldn't help but think, now there's someone I would change religions for.

Chapter 49. May 28, 2008 – Colonia del Sacramento, Uruguay

The Rio de la Plata is a silt-laden stretch of water that flows east to the Atlantic Ocean. As it feeds into the sea, the deposits slowly settle and the visibility begins to clear. From a distance, the differences become more discernible. Ryan thought about the last forty-eight hours and how the waters had begun to clear for him. Alex's phone buzzed and Ryan pressed the answer button.

"We've had a change of plans," Alex stated. "Your flight leaves in forty-five minutes."

"I'm still a good hour-and-a-half from the airport," Ryan replied. "I won't be there in time." He was hoping that this delay would cause his flight to be rescheduled. That way, he could at least travel at a normal hour and catch some much-needed sleep before leaving.

"I know," Alex answered. "We've made other arrangements. You will be flying from a private airfield. We have you on GPS and a white Toyota should be pulling out from a frontage road ahead of you right about … *now*. In approximately 2.6 miles – no, make that *exactly* 2.6 miles – the car will slow down and you will make a left turn up a side road, where you will drive for 1.3 miles. You will come to a security gate and a guard will direct you from there. This time, you will be on a private jet, not one of those pesky commercial flights."

"What a shame," Ryan mocked. "You mean I'm not going to get one of your special travel packages? I love the layovers in, say, beautiful downtown Albuquerque – or maybe even Dayton at 0-dark-thirty. You haven't had a chance to see me at my best so early in the morning."

Alex calmly responded, "Nope, we sent a company jet for you and your flight is priority – that means non-stop." After a slight pause, he added, "Oh yeah – you need to know something else: We've had a break-in at the warehouse. I just wanted you to hear it from me."

This one caught Ryan completely off-guard. "How could anyone get in there? That place had more guards and surveillance cameras than Fort Knox! Was anything taken from The Bat?"

"Unfortunately, a portion of the burned second test plane is missing," Alex grumbled. "We're reviewing the tapes as we speak, but it seems that they were able to shut down the system."

"They shut down the system and there wasn't a back-up in place?" Ryan fumed. "Pardon me for asking, but you seem – what's the phrase I'm grasping for – oh yeah, strangely calm. If I were a betting man, it would seem like you're not the least bit concerned about that stolen piece. And another thing: Why *that* piece and not something off the undamaged plane?"

Ryan listened to dead air for a few seconds, then Alex continued, "I may not have been completely candid with you on a number of details."

"Well, I certainly am shocked and surprised to hear that!" Ryan exclaimed facetiously.

Alex continued as he attempted to ignore Ryan's lament. "Our technicians made a great deal more headway with the formula than I originally let on. In fact, we cracked the code. We solved it so completely that we were able to reformulate it so it didn't work as efficiently as the original. Then we added a chemical marker to it and replaced the original coating on the damaged parts with the new formulation. If and when they figure out how to make it and try to use it as a masking agent, we will be able to detect it and track it. Oh, and as for why nothing was taken from The Bat ... well, it was no longer there, anyway."

"So that was the plan all along?" Ryan asked as the subtlety of the ploy began to sink in. "This whole thing was just an elaborate scheme to trick them into stealing something that's really a fake?"

"Well, except for the air marshal and whatever is in the papers you were given by the Friedrick woman, that's pretty much been the program all along."

"The car is slowing down and we're turning left," Ryan announced. "You said that the plane was no longer there, so where exactly is it?"

"It's at the McDonnell Douglas test site in the Mojave Desert," Alex replied. "That is where you're headed right now. You'll be wheels-down at 6:15 tomorrow morning and the test is scheduled for 8 a.m. tomorrow. Don't be late." Then the phone went dead.

When Ryan's vehicle pulled up to the guard shack, he handed the sentry his identification and looked out toward the runway. Men in uniform scurried about as they positioned temporary lights to illuminate its outline.

Noticing his interest, the guard said, "We don't get many arrivals or departures after dark. It's a pretty short runway, and because of the steep terrain and vegetation at the end, it can be dangerous. This must be something pretty special. You can leave your car at the side of the hangar over there. That's where you'll catch your ride."

As he made his way toward the hangar, the sun had already slipped behind the low hills and trees. This made the runway lights appear even more vivid. Suddenly, a black blur flashed past the vehicle and touched down on the tarmac. The aircraft's drag chute opened and the plane slowed as it neared the end of the runway.

But it didn't roll into the hangar, as most planes do when they make a landing – it turned completely around with its engines still burning as if to prepare for an immediate departure. The canopy opened and Ryan immediately recognized the familiar form silhouetted in the twilight: an F-117 stealth fighter! Alex really had sent the company jet. Ryan stared at the military's latest miracle of modern technology as he stepped out of the vehicle – but not before checking for the wooden box and leather satchel.

* * *

More than five thousand miles to the north, just off the Georgetown Pike in Langley, Virginia, rests an inconspicuous industrial park consisting of one-story concrete tilt-up buildings. The quarter-inch-thick copper mesh embedded within their walls effectively prevents any electronic signal from escaping to the outside world or even to an adjacent room. It is essentially an electronic safe house.

Gerald Woods – assistant director of the CIA – and Alex McCormick stared intently at a laptop computer's screen. The image beamed up as an encrypted signal from a private airfield in Uruguay, bounced off three military communications satellites and unscrambled on their laptop in almost real time with only a six-second delay. An open bottle of Glenfiddich single-malt Scotch whisky sat on the nearby table. Although alcohol was not allowed in the complex, since Alex was accompanied by the assistant director, an after-hours cocktail could be overlooked.

Woods swirled the amber liquid in his glass and watched as a thin, streaky layer clung to the sides. "Ah do love the way that some *likkahs* embrace the interior of their containers, don't you?" he drawled. "You see these narrow markers creepin' down the glass? They're called 'legs'. Only the best labels can boast them – and this one definitely walks." He peered at Alex through the potent nectar and asked, "Do you think Mistah Lessley is still pissed that you weren't giving him the straight scoop on that black substance?" His Southern articulation had already begun to thicken, this being his second scotch of the day.

Alex took a sip, rolled it around in his mouth to savor it fully, and remained silent as he stared at the screen. Discretion, after all, was the better part of keeping your job in this business.

The assistant director finally said, "Yeah, that's kinda what I thought, too – but is he enough of a team playah to keep working on the project?"

"Oh, he'll keep working – and he'll keep digging, too," Alex answered. "He's got his teeth sunk into this one. You can count on that. He may not like us, but this is in his blood and he just can't stop. There is no chance he could walk away and never be sure that that old German pilot wasn't telling him the absolute truth."

Woods brought his glass up for another sip, but first felt the need to respond. "Ah think it's probably bettah that you don't tell Lessley we've been after that satchel and wooden box from the get-go. Just let him play explorer and see what else he might come up with." Then, after taking a long pull from his Glencairn crystal, Woods added, "You kinda like the guy, don't you?"

"Yeah, he's got an edge to him," Alex replied. "He's a real pain in the ass, too, but he's a bottom-line guy. He doesn't care about the politics. He's only interested in results."

"The reason ah asked," Woods explained, "is despite what a lot of people think, ah believe deep down that you are basically a decent human being. And because of that, ah wonder if there will come a time when you might think Lessley deserves to be told why he was really chosen for this project." After another slow swallow, he continued. "Ah also wonder if you might think he should be told about the Friedrick woman."

"Let me correct you on that one," Alex returned as he downed the last of his scotch. "You mean what we *think* we know about the Friedrick woman."

Woods reached into his coat pocket and pulled out an envelope. "Well, we do know this much for sure," he said as he tossed it onto the table.

"What's that?" Alex inquired.

Just then, the two were distracted by a message flashing across the monitor: "Bears in August."

"Well, well – they took the bait," Woods declared. "How about that? Looks like the package is on the move in Iran toward the Turkish border."

He then hit a key on the laptop and turned to Alex. "Your journalist did a fine job and smoked those bastards out. Now just make sure you get *him* out."

Chapter 50. May 28, 2008 – Colonia del Sacramento, Uruguay

As a fighter plane, the F-117 came with very few amenities. First in a series of groundbreaking designs, the pioneer aircraft in America's stealth arsenal would be retired this year as the new models were introduced. Even though their usage had run its course, these old warriors would be stored not in some desert boneyard, but maintained in a state of constant readiness should their service be required once again. Though no longer top-of-the-line, they were still more advanced than ninety percent of the world's military aircraft.

For training purposes and ferrying VIPs, two of the planes had been fitted with a jump seat directly behind the pilot. Ryan Lessley was about to be treated to a ride that very few outside a select military elite would ever experience.

Even though Ryan brought only the folder and wooden box, lack of storage space meant they would ride in his lap. A ten-inch flat-panel monitor with a light on either side built into the back of the pilot's headrest provided his instructions. The aviator, a boyish-looking major with a big toothy grin, explained the pre-flight checklist with military precision. As he spoke, the left light on the panel illuminated. Ryan let the major continue until he came to the panel. "The screen is encrypted, sir," the major explained, "so communications and images can be sent securely while in flight."

"What do the two indicator lights represent?" Ryan asked.

"The one on the left means we have an incoming or outgoing high-priority message," the pilot answered. "When that happens, the plane automatically shifts to high-security mode."

"While you were going over your checklist, were you just checking the light or did we actually receive a message?" Ryan inquired.

"There was a transmission, sir," the pilot toned flatly, "but I am not authorized to discuss it."

"I see." Ryan accepted this cryptic reply as military gospel. "And the one on the right?"

"When that one flashes, it indicates an imminent threat," the pilot warned. "In that case, you have three seconds to prepare for ejection. You would lean back, make sure your helmet is tightly strapped and just relax. The aircraft will do all the work. Once we're airborne, I'll point out a few of the constellations here in the Southern Hemisphere. Things look a lot different in the sky on this side of the equator."

The short airfield, full throttle and quick ascent of this multifaceted piece of machinery slammed Ryan back into his seat. However, as soon as the landing gear retracted, the smoothness and silence of the remainder of their flight reminded him of a glider. It was like skiing on new powder or surfing on an absolutely wind-free day.

As they climbed to cruising altitude above the cloud layer, he was suddenly reminded why it had been worth the cost and effort to send the Hubble telescope into space. Above the ambient light of Earth, the stars practically screamed "look at me" in the clear night sky.

The profound mystery of that black void had always intrigued him. As a young boy, Ryan would stare at the stars and wonder how far away they were – and whether they really existed. His high school physics teacher once explained it this way. "You might see the stars, but they may no longer be there. They are so far away that the light we see today may have left them hundreds, if not thousands, of years earlier. The light from that star is just now reaching your eyes, yet it could have been its last dying flicker. In that way, our sense of time really is affected by distance."

Now Ryan gazed into the vast swirl of the Milky Way. When he used to view the heavens back home in the Mojave Desert, the skies certainly were different. Above the equator, the North Star, or Polaris, kept its constant vigil over the North Pole. Absolute north could be found directly under Polaris, but here, below the equator, there was no single star positioned above the South Pole – rather, various beacons of light to point the mariner's way home.

Once again, Ryan scanned the myriad of heavenly bodies comprising the Milky Way and looked for the two brightest, known as The Pointers. He only needed a few moments of stargazing and there they were – Alpha and Beta Centauri. A straight line drawn between them and extended a bit to the right brought him to the constellation Crux, or the fabled Southern Cross. The same line extended to the left and slightly downward would point to a third constellation. Lines drawn perpendicular to the earth from these three clusters of stars would intersect above the true South Pole.

"Damn, what was the name of that third constellation?" Ryan asked aloud.

Just then, the pilot turned on the intercom. "Up above and to our left are the three groups of stars that not only ancient, but also our modern-day, mariners use for navigation. The two bright pointer stars in the center, the Southern Triangle or Atria to the left, and finally The Southern Cross on the right. Here in the Southern Hemisphere, the four stars of the Southern Cross are woven into our history and folklore."

Ryan seemed at once confused and curious. "Excuse me, major, but did you say *our* history?"

"My mother's side of the family is from Brazil," the pilot responded. "In our family room, we had flags from Brazil and Ireland – my dad's side – framed on the wall. Above them was a larger flag of the United States. My parents were proud of their cultural heritages, but wanted everyone, including their children, to know who was the top dog in our house.

"When I was little, I remember asking my mother why the American flag had so many stars and her flag only had four. She told me there were so many stars because there were so many different people who came to America, and that the four stars on her flag symbolized looking to the heavens for guidance. That simple answer satisfied the curiosity of a small child, but I've never forgotten what she said. Off the top of my head, I know that Brazil, Australia and New Zealand are three countries that have the four stars symbolizing the Southern Cross on their flag." As the pilot rambled on, Ryan's mind began to wander.

"Atria," Ryan said. "That's the one I couldn't remember."

There it was, just off to the left. Then he thought, if we were heading north, they should be more to the right. Ryan remembered his little finger was the width of about one and one half degrees when measured off the horizon.

As the pilot described the different constellations, and their legends and history of how they received their names, Ryan glanced at his watch and started. "Excuse me, major – we've been in the air almost twelve minutes. Would you please be so kind as to tell me where we are going?"

"I'm not sure what you mean, sir," the pilot replied almost cryptically.

"Boy, when you retire, I'm sure you'll have a bright future as a tour guide," Ryan complimented. "You really know your stuff about the constellations, but we have a small problem: Your stars are in the wrong spot in the sky. Since we took off, we've been traveling at about a forty-degree angle to the south, but we're supposed to be flying north. By my rough estimate, using your stars, we are headed toward North Africa or the Middle East, not North America." The intercom went silent and the light to the left of the monitor flashed. Thirty seconds later, the screen came to life and a familiar face appeared – it was Alex McCormick.

"Ah, Mr. McCormick, what a surprise!" Ryan hailed. "It is indeed a pleasure to see you again so soon. I guess by now you are aware that your jet-jockey has taken a slight detour. At this rate, I'm going to have a really tough time getting to the test site by eight tomorrow morning. You hiring ex-cab drivers for your shuttle flights these days?"

"Put a lid on it, Lessley – we've got bigger problems," Alex toned. "We're not sure what's going on with the stolen parts."

"I thought the whole idea of this little nightmare you dragged me into was so you could keep track of all this interesting hardware," Ryan pointed out. "Now you folks have gone and lost it. Wow, I bet that's really embarrassing."

"You done yet?" Alex asked tersely. "Actually, our problem isn't that we've lost it. Our problem is that now we have *two* 'its' to track. One of the packages is headed south toward the Zagros Mountains in Iran, near the Straits of Hormuz. We suspect the Iranians have one of their nuclear research and refining facilities hidden there. The other is headed north toward the Turkish border. It would appear that they took the same shortcut we did and simply peeled the coating from the part. We think one is being sent to their facility in Zagros for study and duplication, while the other is on its way north to hide something."

"I know I've asked this question before," Ryan said, "but why me? You can obviously track whatever the 'it' turns out to be – so why not just take it out?"

"We don't think they've linked the coating with a bomb yet," Alex explained, "and we also don't know exactly where the bomb is. Another minor problem would exist if we were to be tied to a nuclear event at our Turkish allies' doorstep. At this moment, we only know where the coating is, and that means that we think we know where the bomb eventually will be. We've maintained constant satellite surveillance on the stolen part from the time it left Washington, so we're convinced the hook-up hasn't occurred yet."

"OK, I'll play along," Ryan mused. "Where do you think the bomb is coming from?"

"Our best guess is that it originated at the Zagros facility," Alex answered, "and I'll be truthful – they hid that one really well for a very long time. Those mountains have large, natural caves which they enlarged to house a squadron of fighters to patrol the Straits of Hormuz. It is a huge facility with a series of large metal blast doors that secure the entrance in case of an air raid.

"The Iranians regularly rattle their swords and threaten to close the straits. They do it for political leverage and to pump up the crude oil prices on the world markets. Just remember two things: One, Iran is a major oil producer. And two, almost thirty-five percent of the world's oil supply from other countries flows daily through those straits. If they were to be closed, it would have a crippling effect on the world economy – not to mention it might just kill some of the more moderate oil-producing nations in the region.

"There was a lot of traffic in and out of the air base," Alex went on, "and judging from satellite photos, we thought they were enlarging the caverns for their fighter squadrons. We now believe they were putting together a uranium-enrichment facility inside those caverns.

"Our first two clues became apparent when they built a large hydroelectric facility along the Korun River on the other side of the mountains. Their stated goal was to provide more and cheaper power for the city of Bandar-e Abbas near the Straits of Hormuz on the Persian Gulf. But the site they picked for the dam had our boys scratching their heads. Construction would have been simpler and quicker if they had just started farther down the river and closer to the city, but then we discovered an additional power line under construction leading to the caverns. It far exceeded the airfield's electrical power needs. So, when the Iranian computer systems were hacked and many of the machines that refined the uranium to weapons-grade quality were destroyed, there was a huge upswing in truck traffic at the air base. That's when they moved to the front of the class for satellite and drone observation."

"You can say the word 'centrifuge,'" Ryan said. "I'm aware that's what someone damaged by hacking their computer system. If I were a betting man, I'd guess that you already have a pretty damn good idea who got into their system – and how they did it."

"Yeah, I read about that," Alex remembered. "I think they called it the 'Stuxnet' virus. The papers said once it got into a system, it could lie dormant for months or years and then be called up to cause all sorts of mischief. Imagine people being able to do something like that."

"Son of a gun – imagine that," Ryan agreed. "So I'm also guessing you've also been monitoring the vehicle traffic in and out of the base. What did you find?"

"There is a supply depot north of the city of Bandar," Alex replied, "and from there, convoys head out to the different military bases in the area. Local farmers also deliver fresh produce to the supply depot on a regular schedule, but these vehicles never travel to the facility itself."

"So, you're saying that nothing except the vehicles from the supply depot ever enters the air base, correct?" Ryan asked.

"Nope," Alex responded. "One road in and one road out."

"You are absolutely certain of that?" Ryan pressed.

"The whole area is now under twenty-four-hour surveillance," Alex confirmed.

"You said that you have satellite photos from that area," Ryan reminded him. "Would that include the countryside in and around Bandar?"

"What are you getting at?" Alex queried.

"Well, I'd be curious to see if any of those farm vehicles took, say, an unexpected detour from the supply depot to the city or somewhere else," Ryan surmised, "and then ended up not going straight back to the farm."

He then offered a theory. "Okay, let's play the 'what if' game: What if the people who are smart enough to do the things you say they can do figured out that you let them break into your warehouse and steal the sample? And what if they're also aware that you're tracking them right now? Also, what if they could keep all of your attention focused on one area and do an end run toward another?

"The bad case right now is that the coating is just a decoy and a diversion," Ryan explained, "and you're sending all of your resources in the wrong direction. An even worse scenario is that your bomb might already be in transit – or worst-case, already delivered.

"So now," Ryan continued, "let's take a look at the last three or four weeks on your satellite tapes and cross our fingers that I'm wrong. If we can show a plausible way that they could have moved the bomb – say, three weeks ago, before the break-in at your storage facility – that would be a strong indication that they are using your substance as nothing more than a smokescreen. In that case, it's pretty clear that you've been played."

"I'll get back to you," Alex ended the conversation abruptly – and with that, the screen and light went dark.

* * *

Mark Arroyo hit the last key of the last letter to the last word in his last paragraph, then leaned back and smiled. The Horton brothers had linked the substance from the coal-to-oil formula with an extract from a tropical orchid growing in Uruguay by coming into contact with the plant in their father's greenhouse. A bloom had accidentally fallen into an open container of coal-based oil. This is what changed the black residue's properties just enough to disrupt radar signals.

Mark relaxed with a beer to let that storyline ferment in his mind for a few minutes. There were still a few loose ends to clean up, but he felt confident that McCormick would find this scenario more than plausible.

Mark reached for the bedroom door, but it suddenly slid shut. He heard the sound of sliding metal as three deadbolts hidden inside the door extended into the adjacent wall.

He spun around to look at the monitor and noticed that Alfred's face had already begun to smolder as the "TIME TO LEAVE" message started flashing. Mark rushed to the closet and pushed the box to one side. Peering into the inky black tunnel, he expected the escape chute to descend at an easy angle. Instead, since it faded into darkness and banked steeply around two huge boulders, he had no idea how wild his ride would be. He shoved his feet into the hiking boots McCormick had left for him. By now, the monitor's message displayed Alfred and the front of the cabin in flames. "Oh, crap," he cried, "they're torching the place!"

A small diagram instructed him to lie flat in the chute and cover his face with his hands. Mark had planned on closing his eyes anyway, so this added layer of protection suited him just fine. As he pushed a stray cobweb aside and glanced at the flaming monitor one last time, Mark took a deep breath and let go.

The twisting ride lasted only a few seconds, but it seemed like an eternity as he careened down the steep slide. He came to an abrupt halt in the dark as he sank up to his ankles into the tunnel's sandy floor. As soon as he stood, a series of dim lights along both sides of the five-foot-wide opening suddenly glowed. He took a step, but once again sank deeply into the sand.

Mark then realized that he had left the backup drive for his story in the computer. He looked up above the escape chute just in time to see a rough slab of granite sliding over the opening. He was now locked out of the burning building.

He knew that he must retrieve that flash drive before the house was consumed or none of the work he had put into the project up to now would even matter. "Well," he surmised aloud, "I guess if we can send a man to the moon, we can certainly move a few rocks."

A narrow ledge on the nearest boulder provided a seat as Mark emptied his right shoe. The coarse gravel on the floor had especially sharp edges, and the few stones that had already invaded his tender feet hurt like hell. He laced up his shoe tightly and tied his pant leg over it to keep the sand on the floor where it belonged.

As he fastened the last double knot on one shoe, Mark thought he saw movement on the wall right next to him. He emptied his other shoe and the spot appeared even larger. He reached up to touch it and drew back wet fingers. Soon he noticed water dribbling down the opposite wall as well.

By the time his left shoe was tied, a steady stream of water flowed down both walls. Mark braced himself against the side to keep from sinking, but then realized that he must hurry toward the sloping tunnel entrance before the whole place flooded. He knew he would have to hurry, because the tunnel ran upward and downward like a roller coaster, and contained many exposed boulders.

Numerous motion sensors picked up his activity as lights illuminated the tunnel ahead of him. Mark felt quite fortunate that the security lights behind him had remained lit, because each new bank of lights revealed water pouring through the walls. As the sandy floor absorbed more water, his footing became firmer and he broke into a slow trot. Suddenly, a section of the tunnel collapsed behind him and the water began pouring in.

Only two hundred yards – that's what Alex had said. Now on what seemed almost solid ground, he dashed ahead into the darkness as he outran his lighting. In the pitch blackness, he slammed his left shoulder into the tunnel wall as it made a turn. Thrown off balance, he fell to his knees and felt a sharp pain radiating down his arm, followed by a warm trickle. As the sensors caught up with him and the lights finally came on, Mark looked at his trembling hands and bloody shoulder. At an elevation of over eight thousand feet, he simply couldn't move his sixty-five-year-old frame the way he used to.

He put his hand on the ground to steady himself, then rose and leaned against the wall. Mark saw the water rise above the soles of his shoes, then watched the as imprint of his hand on the floor filled and then disappeared beneath the dark liquid. The tunnel was flooding quickly.

With each hurried step, Mark could feel the water level rising. His heartbeat quickened in anticipation with each turn on the path and his frustration level rose every time the lights exposed another dark chamber. As he forged ahead against the surging torrent, it ascended to his calves, then his knees, and finally, above his waist.

Squeezing around a large, greenish-brown granite boulder, he took a step and sank up to his shoulders. Another step and the weight of his water-logged boots helped pull his head under the water's surface. Even as he struggled to remain calm and not panic, Mark desperately grabbed for any handhold on the side of the tunnel. He clutched and slipped and grasped and fumbled as he advanced slowly toward his salvation. Then, slipping off nearly every smooth, wet surface, he finally felt a metal handle embedded in the rock. He seized it, pulled his head above the water he took a deep, gulping breath. One final step forward and his foot hit solid ground. Three more handles in the tunnel wall and Mark pulled himself completely out of the deluge and onto dry land.

He leaned against the wall to catch his breath for a moment. Could he possibly have made a wrong turn in the dark? Did he miss something? Looking back down the flooded tunnel, he realized that returning to check that option was definitely out of the question. He shivered as his muscles started to cramp in the cold air. It was so much warmer in the water. Mark exhaled and the condensation from his breath hung as a cloud in front of his face. "Got to keep moving," he whispered to himself. "Got to stay warm. Don't want to have to change the book title to *Frozen Bait.*"

Stumbling forward and turning a corner, he triggered yet another motion sensor. Its associated lighting came on in rapid succession, one after another. Ten yards ahead, a dull gray metal door embedded in the rock wall began to open. A hand reached out of the darkness and pulled an exhausted Mark Arroyo into the ski lodge machine shop.

Shaking noticeably and barely able to speak through his chattering teeth, he exclaimed, "McCormick didn't say anything about water! I hate water … I really hate cold water … and I really, *really* hate the dark. I almost drowned in there – I could have died!"

The young management trainee, who only three days earlier had given Mark his walking papers, placed a blanket across his shivering shoulders. "But you did," he smiled. "You are quite dead – and welcome to your new life."

* * *

Ryan Lessley intently watched the window in the lower right-hand corner of the monitor as a clock recorded the time since its last transmission. At seven minutes and twenty-three seconds, the screen once again came alive. This time, instead of Alex McCormick, an older man with a southern accent appeared on the monitor.

"Mistuh Lessley, ah am Gerald Woods – assistant director of Central Intelligence."

Ryan responded with characteristic indignity. "I think it's only fair at this point to ask: *whose* intelligence?"

"Why, ours, of course, suh," Woods replied. "You know, the good guys in the white hats. I'm afraid your time with Mr. McCormick may have tarnished our image just a tad. I'll make sure his personnel file reflects that he attend our next People Skills workshop."

His honey-smooth voice suddenly turned sharp and edgy. "Twenty-three days ago, a group of six trucks left the Zagros facility and headed back to the supply depot. Four two-ton flatbeds were delivering produce from the local farms – cabbages, to be precise."

"How can you be so sure that they were cabbages?" Ryan asked defiantly. "They might have been, oh, say, undercover Brussels sprouts or …"

"I'm beginning to see why Mr. McCormick speaks of you the way he does, suh," Woods interrupted. "Mr. Lessley, our satellites – at an altitude of twenty-two thousand miles – can tell what grade octane of gasoline is being used in those trucks. The infrared sensors on those satellites can tell me not only how many people are in the cabs of those vehicles, but whether the drivers are smoking Turkish or Iranian cigarettes." His voice suddenly rose to a crescendo. "Now, based on our technology, I believe we can damn well say with a high degree of certainty that those are fucking cabbages and *not* Brussels sprouts!"

Woods composed himself before continuing. "Pardon me for going 'blue' on you like that, Mr. Lessley," he apologized. "As I was saying, the Zagros facility is under constant surveillance. It is a strain on our resources, I admit, but we can position a satellite in orbit directly over a certain spot and keep the area under constant surveillance. It is called geostationary or geosynchronous orbit. The satellite stays in one spot because it moves exactly at the same speed as the earth's rotation."

"Yeah, I get the concept," Ryan responded. "Geostationary, parking spot in the sky, my tax dollars at work. What did you find?"

"As I was saying, we already had a satellite positioned directly over the Strait of Hormuz shipping lanes," Woods said. "We merely repositioned some of its cameras to focus on the Zagros area. To alleviate suspicions, we continued to make the normal reconnaissance flights over their air base. It ties up valuable resources and our other assets are spread even thinner over a larger area. These satellite passes can be tracked and timed by the people on the ground. Rail and road traffic can be scheduled between fly-overs, and cargo and personnel can be hidden. It all turns into one big cat-and-mouse game. One of the cabbage trucks left the supply depot with its bed covered. Two days later, as you can see from the picture, the truck is seen returning from the coast empty."

"What's all that white stuff on the truck?" Ryan asked.

"Crap!" Woods exclaimed as he remembered where the trucks had gone.

"What?" Ryan quizzed. "Crap as in you have no idea, or crap as in *feces* crap?"

"Bird crap, Mr. Lessley," Woods replied. "Seagull, probably – and a lot of it, at that."

"Well, hell, you can find seagulls all over the coast," Ryan observed. "Back home, you'll even find them as far inland as Utah at some garbage dumps. In California, they're such a nuisance as scavengers that we call them 'rats with wings.'"

"Rats with wings – that's a good one," Woods complimented. "But there weren't just a few spots. The truck was splattahed with it. Lots of birds would naturally be drawn to a place with lots of food. I didn't think of it before, but along this route near the coast is a seafood-processing plant. The local fishing boats pull directly to the dock and unload.

"Let's just say that the Iranian EPA isn't quite as strict as ours," Woods added, "and as the fish and shrimp are cleaned and processed, they just dump what is left back into the water outside the facility. The outgoing tides flush the guts and whatever else is left out to sea. This makes for a free buffet for the birds. You know, in a funny kind of way, this really keeps the area naturally cleanah and healthiah. The increased fish and bird populations are like nature's own maid service. This processing plant serves the local fisherman who usually travel, say, no more than sixty or seventy miles out to the offshoah fishing grounds. Give me a few minutes to get back to you. I want to check something."

The screen went blank and Ryan shifted into problem-solving mode. The enemy this time was not just a group of fanatic street thugs. This was state-sponsored terrorism with massive resources on a scale the world hadn't seen since 9/11. Plans would have been made to hide the source of the bomb and react to possible consequences. This was not just a terrorist attack brewing in the Middle East, but a full-blown global conflict – and this time all the major players would be drawn in.

Then the monitor came back to life. "As you would expect, the same sixty or so boats from the local fishing fleet keep reappearing on the surveillance photos," Woods began. "But fourteen days ago, a private sixty-five-foot luxury yacht with Saudi registry, the *Al-Jawan*, appeared at the loading dock of the cannery in the dead of night. Its home port is Dammam, three hundred miles to the north on the Saudi coast in the Persian Gulf and the capital of the Eastern Province in Saudi Arabia. As far as we can tell at this time, it is primarily used as a private pleasure boat for day cruising and occasional sport-fishing. It doesn't, as a rule, make long-range trips.

"Nothing was unloaded," he continued, "but several crates were sent below decks and a large box – say, five feet long, three feet high and wide – was lashed to the rear of the vessel. Using infrared sensors, we counted six men on board and it took every last one of them to get that crate loaded. My guess is it weighed eight to nine hundred pounds."

Woods leveled a stern gaze directly at Ryan. "Mistuh Lessley, would you care to take a wild 'guesstimate' at the approximate weight of a seventy- to eighty-kiloton nuclear warhead? Our intelligence analysts have estimated that the Iranians could have produced enough weapons-grade plutonium to build a bomb of about that size.

"There is another other troubling fact," he went on. "The crate on the rear deck gave off a faint heat signature. Infrared cameras detect humans by their body heat, and identify engine locations on a plane or boat by the heat from their exhaust. Radioactive material, either in a bomb or for some benign use such as X-rays, breaks down slowly. This is measured in a time sequence called a half-life. As the material slowly breaks down, it releases a minute amount of heat which is barely detectable. Something that would register at twenty-two thousand miles is more than the glow-in-the-dark face on a wristwatch.

"Everything was loaded at night with no visible lighting, which once again was suspicious, and four days ago, the *Al-Jawan* was spotted moving north in the Red Sea toward the Suez Canal. Once through the canal, it could chart a course to anywhere in the Mediterranean. Unfortunately, because this area is not under constant surveillance, we haven't been able to relocate the vessel since then.

"What we do know is this: The transit fee through the Suez Canal – $4,600 American – was paid from an anonymous account through an electronic wire transfer drawn at the Islamic Commercial and Development Bank in the Saudi capital, Riyadh. And here's the kicker: The ship's name, *Al-Jawan*, means 'The Black Horse,' but in ancient Persian folklore, it was also a famous assassin's dagger.

"In forty-eight hours, the *Al-Jawan* will be in the Mediterranean," Woods concluded. "That's our window before a whole lot of water and sky swallows up that boat."

"If you can detect that much radiation with one flyover, I'm guessing that the crew shouldn't be making long-term plans for extended families," Ryan observed.

Alex McCormick somberly replied from behind Woods, "Oh yeah, I agree, but that's not what's really troubling. I'm guessing that they're not planning on coming back at all. We are relocating our drones and satellites as we speak. If that ship makes it to open water, we'll find it."

"Can you put any of the satellite images on this screen?" Ryan wondered. "I mean, is it too sensitive, or do you have the capability to encrypt and transmit it?"

"Ah'll do better than that," Woods drawled. "Ah'll let you view a live satellite feed. We can have it on-screen in a matter of seconds."

"Wow, that's really cool," Ryan said as the first frames appeared.

"You'll get a still photo about every five seconds," Woods said. "That's the best ah can do with the hardware in the plane and under these circumstances."

"At this altitude, how do you find a single small vessel at sea?" Ryan asked.

"We have software that detects disturbances in the water called anomalies," Woods answered. "Anything that shouldn't be there, other than wind and wave action, will raise a red flag. The closer they hug the coast, the tougher it is to find them, what with all the coastal noise and such. The waves and currents actually produce a low-pitched background noise as they hit shallower water, due to the friction of the sea against the coastline. With sonar, we use filters to separate this noise, but when you're looking for only slight irregularities, then it gets dicey. We also have underwater listening stations planted around the world, primarily to help keep track of submarine traffic. And even with all of this in place, it can still be like looking for a needle in a haystack – but we'll find them."

"Can you get me any close-up pictures of the *Al-Jawan* at the dock?" Ryan inquired.

Images were transferred to Ryan's screen as Woods continued. "The only oceanic anomalies so far have been what you would expect to find in the Red Sea shipping lanes heading to Suez. In the Mediterranean, a large number of small craft are converging on Alexandria and they are receiving a huge amount of coverage from the international press."

"Why mention a group of pleasure boats around Alexandria?" Ryan asked. "Also, what's this thing on the rear deck of the *Al-Jawan* in the second picture? It looks like it has wings."

Woods turned to McCormick and said, "Tell him."

Alex stepped into view and answered, "That, Mr. Lessley, is an underwater sled originally designed as a towed sonar array. It was first developed by the Russians in the late seventies. Since then, the electronics have been refined to the point that the on-board systems do away with any ambient ship noise.

"It is definitely old-school and low-tech, but extremely effective in its simplicity," Alex continued. "Our friends in the DEA say it was occasionally used by drug smugglers, along with a homing device in case they had to dump their cargo. Not the most efficient mule, but it can carry up to fifteen-hundred pounds per load. You do always have the possible problems with water leaks, but with proper camouflage and towing it at, say, forty feet behind the boat and below the surface, it is almost impossible to spot from the air, even in fairly clear water.

"The rear fins make it hydrodynamically stable. It cruises through the water like an airplane. Gas-filled pontoons allow the sled to be towed at any chosen depth. It can be controlled with a joystick like a video game, or programmed from a phone or computer.

"Also, because of its design and materials, it leaves almost no sonar footprint. It does, however, produce the audio anomaly we talked about. The sound is reminiscent of the low hum in your ears when they're plugged with water or wax. So, Lessley, since you pride yourself on building top-notch test models, we need your help to deal with this underwater airplane."

"And just exactly when were you planning on telling me about this underwater sled-thingy?" Ryan inquired.

Alex ignored his question and continued. "As for your other question, the boats are presenting themselves as a humanitarian convoy for Palestinian relief in the Gaza Strip. Supposedly, it's all been organized by the International Red Cross and their sister Islamic organization, the Red Crescent. The media are having a field day with it. They're calling them 'The Cross' and 'The Crescent Flotilla,' and this one's a real knee-slapper: 'The Mercy Armada.'

"Six months ago, a similar convoy tried getting through to Gaza, but the Israelis refused to let them pass. Their position was, and still is, that there are weapons and explosives on those ships bound for the radical group Hamas. It turned out that they were right, but let's just say that our Israeli friends didn't quite handle the situation with finesse. When they boarded the ships in international waters, things got nasty real fast. As a result, seven activists and three Israelis were killed. Even though explosives and arms were actually found, the political fallout from the activists' deaths completely overshadowed the discovery.

"The Israelis still refuse to let them pass without being searched," Alex went on, "but this time they'll handle it differently. Because of international pressure from the media, the plan is to bring them into Israel's main port of Haifa and search the ships with UN observers present. Like last time, there are six large cargo ships, but this time there is also an international flotilla of thirty-eight private boats. Their intention is to act like a human shield and dare the Israelis to try to stop them.

"We think the effort six months ago was staged to provoke and embarrass the Israelis so they'd conduct the search under international scrutiny in an Israeli port. There were reports that the seven activists attacked Israeli Defense personnel as soon as they came aboard and that the soldiers were immediately fighting for their lives."

"So you're saying that those seven men just sacrificed themselves?" Ryan asked incredulously.

"In their eyes, you're a martyr and on your way to paradise just for dying for the cause – now or whenever the bomb is delivered," Alex stated.

"Anything else you might like to tell me?" Ryan inquired.

"Well, there are six private watercraft with transit reservations to travel north through the Suez Canal the day after tomorrow," Alex explained. "The owner of one of the boats has publicly stated that they all plan to join the Gaza flotilla. All mooring fees and insurance in Alexandria have been covered – paid by a money transfer from the same bank that paid the *Al-Jawan*'s transit fees."

"Couldn't you just follow the money and get an account number?" Ryan wondered.

"The money was routed through banks in other countries," Alex replied. "We finally lost the trail in Singapore."

"Can you at least get me a close-up shot of the anchorage in Alexandria?" Ryan requested.

"They're anchored at a private yacht club in the eastern part of the port," Alex answered. "Give me a second to see if I can pull it up … ah, there it is."

Ryan studied the photo carefully and counted the dots anchored in the bay. "With what you just told me, I'm going to make an educated guess, Mr. Woods: In two days, your missing boat is either going to show up with the rest or join up on the way to Gaza. I'm betting there will be more than thirty-eight vessels when the Israeli Defense Forces make contact."

"On that note, you are probably correct," Woods agreed. "They will be sailing past Port Said at the northern end of the Suez when our six private boats emerge from the canal."

"And what makes you so sure of the timing?" Ryan asked.

"Well, Mistuh Lessley, the insurance and fees are only paid up until tomorrow morning," Woods replied. "They won't have a choice in the matter – they will be forced to sail.

"So, if you are going to do anything at all, it had better be before they get loose in the Mediterranean," Ryan concluded. "If they do break out and join up with the others, the next stop for the *Al-Jawan* – and whatever is on that sled – will be Haifa. It's brilliant in its simplicity. The Israeli Defense Forces will literally escort the Trojan horse themselves."

Chapter 51. June 12, 2003 – Moscow, Russia

For Farid Attar, the last ten years had been a nightmare. In 1985, at the age of nineteen, he became the most distinguished and highly decorated pilot in the Iranian Air Force. During the long, drawn-out conflict known as the Iraq-Iran War, he had flown more than two hundred missions and personally destroyed twenty-seven Iraqi aircraft. The victim of a surface-to-air missile (SAM), he was shot down over Basrah near the border and managed to make his way across enemy lines back to Iran. He was a national hero, and appeared on posters and state-controlled television to remind the populace of their holy mission to protect the revolution.

But now, that seemed so long ago. After the deaths of his beautiful wife and daughters, his life consisted of just going through the motions. Because of him, his wife, Zohrek, and two daughters, Farrin and Sadaf, were asked to represent their country on a high-profile diplomatic mission. Now, because of his accomplishments, he carried the burden of their deaths.

When Saddam Hussein, president of Iraq, invaded Kuwait in the summer of 1990, his troops went on a looting rampage. Priceless artifacts in the National Museum of Kuwait – a legacy of a nation's culture – were stolen and shipped back to Baghdad. Among the items taken were pages from a seventh-century copy of the Koran thought to have belonged to the first imam, or religious leader, who served after the death of the prophet Muhammad. Not only were they of great historical significance, but each page was intricately decorated and painted around its borders. Revered not only by Islamists, the art world in general considered them priceless treasures. The only other remaining pages from the text rested in the Topkapi Museum in Istanbul, Turkey.

In the spring of 1998, a member of the ruling Iraqi Ba'ath Party and his family took a short drive across the border from Basrah and asked for political asylum. Having committed the cardinal sin of daring to disagree with Saddam Hussein at a staff meeting, he fled before being shipped home in several trash bags. He brought with him the missing pages stolen eight years earlier in Kuwait. Sold and traded on the Iraqi black market like vacation souvenirs, they were returned by the diplomat to Interior Minister Amir Ghorbani.

As a sign of the Iranian government's desire to support Arab unity, these cherished pages would be returned to their rightful home in Kuwait. Through the Office of Antiquities, the Minister of the Interior had personally asked the three women to be present so as to represent the Iranian people.

At the museum, Farid's wife stood in front of her daughters on the podium when the bomb exploded. As the shrapnel riddled his wife's body, his daughters were shielded by their mother. Though they displayed practically no visible wounds, the concussion from the massive blast still proved deadly. Choking back tears, Farid told himself that his two perfect princesses were only sleeping, but the shock wave from the blast destroyed their internal organs. All three died instantly.

Public outrage swept the nation. The entire country shared in his grief and the whole Islamic world mourned the priceless artifacts lost forever. Iraq, Israel and the United States denied any responsibility, and no radical independent or government group came forward. No direct evidence was ever found, but the whole country was certain who was to blame. Emotions ebbed over time, yet animosity simmered just beneath the surface.

From that day on, Farid buried himself in his career. He would help make the Iranian Air Force the most formidable in the Middle East, even surpassing that of Israel. When his chance arrived, he would collect payment for what had been taken from him.

Strange circumstances sometimes make for strange alliances. With the embargoes imposed by the United States, Iran was forced to turn to Russia for her military hardware. The leaders of Iran, followers of conservative Islamic doctrine, had become joined at the hip with atheist Russia.

While the U.S. supplied Israel with its most advanced equipment, Russia made available only its second-rate aircraft and electronics. Still a vast improvement over the Iranians' present hardware, it was a constant source of friction at negotiations.

In May of 2003, eleven MiG-29 aircraft were to be delivered to the Zagros facility in western Iran as soon as details of the "oil for planes" negotiations could be finalized. Farid was sent to Moscow as a military representative, and to gain insights from Russian pilots and the manufacturer's engineers.

The engineers would prove to be tight-lipped, but a special bond existed in the brotherhood of pilots. At a reception in his honor at the Mikoyan-Gurevich (MiG) factory, Farid was introduced to three Russian Air Force pilots who saw action in the war in Afghanistan. They were cowboys without horses, and the interpreters could hardly keep up once the Russian pilots started in on the vodka. Farid himself did not drink alcohol, but he did drink in every detail of what he saw and heard. He liked these men well enough as fellow pilots, but his memories reminded him of why he was there.

After several hours of stories, Farid had garnered details about the plane that could not be found in any technical manual. The two Russian majors and a captain suddenly decided that the evening would not be complete without a visit to the VIP brothel. They insisted that Farid join them. Excusing himself because of the late hour and explaining that he had recently been widowed, Farid thanked them and said, "Some other time, perhaps."

He was met at the door by Anatoly Karinkov, a colonel in the KGB and a holdover from the old Soviet Union. "Are the women in Iran so beautiful that you have no interest in our Russian girls?" the colonel inquired.

"Yes, they are," Farid replied, "and I have other reasons."

Pausing, Anatoly answered as the tone of his voice softened. "Pardon me for being so insensitive to a husband and father who is still grieving – my sincere apology and condolences."

"Your apology is accepted, colonel," Farid returned.

"Perhaps tomorrow, if you have a few hours, I could show you our Central Museum of the Great Patriotic War – what the western world calls World War Two," Colonel Karinkov offered. "That time frame will not do it justice, but you will get a flavor and feel of what we Russians have endured in our recent history. I can have my driver pick you up at ten."

"I will be ready at eight," Farid said as he accepted the invitation.

"But the museum does not even open until ten," Anatoly countered.

"Colonel, you are an official in the KGB and you are the one who wishes to speak with me," Farid reminded him. "It will be open for you."

After a moment had passed, Anatoly smiled and answered, "Your information is correct. My driver will be there at eight."

* * *

The ornamental iron gates opened and the black, Russian-made ZiL limousine pulled up to the northeast entrance of the museum. Anatoly stood at the top of the stairs as he warmly greeted Farid and led him inside. A monument as well as an archive, it had also become hallowed ground to the Russian people. The two strolled into the large white marble rotunda, where a towering bronze statue with a plaque inscribed with "Soldier of Victory" dominated the room. Around the perimeter, engraved on individual markers, were the names of the more than eleven thousand recipients of the Hero of the Soviet Union Medal, the highest honorary title awarded by the state.

Anatoly strolled behind the statue and placed his hand on a plaque. "Whenever I come here, I need to make this connection," he said. "This is my father. He was a tank commander under General Zhukov at the battle of Kurst and was seriously wounded three times over a five-month period – yet he kept returning to do his duty.

"I brought my father here in 1995 when the memorial first opened," he continued. "He had grown feeble and his eyesight was failing, but he made a point of trying to read each name – even though it took almost five hours. When he came to one he recognized, he would place one hand over the name and the other over his eyes. I had never before seen my father cry.

"After a while, he no longer wept when he read them. As we left the great hall, he muttered, 'What does a man do when he no longer has any tears left for his own comrades?'" Anatoly turned and stared at Farid. "What *does* a man do?" he asked plaintively, as if he were once again listening to his own father. "What, indeed … but enough about my *papa* and of my past.

"The museum took more than twelve years to construct," Anatoly continued. "It is like an iceberg. The archives below extend down for five levels. Under our feet, an attempt is being made to record the name and cause of death for every Russian who died in the Great Patriotic War. Twenty million people perished in Russia alone during World War Two. Just categorizing the seventeen miles of filing cabinets is a daunting task. They are our ghosts – spirits from a lost generation."

"Why did you bring me here?" Farid demanded. "Is this some kind of trick? I would assume you have listening devices. I've been to war, and I've seen death firsthand. I don't need to be reminded or have the pain explained to me like some child."

"No, you don't need to have individual pain explained," Anatoly agreed, "but I wanted you to see and feel what it is like for a complete nation on an unimaginable scale. There are no listening devices here – only the ears of the dead.

"You want to know why I asked you here? Well, I'll tell you: Your own Prime Minister Ghorbani has threatened to destroy Israel. We've heard this rhetoric for fifty years, but this is a man with a hunger for power far beyond your country's borders. He is building a monster in the Zagros facility, and if it is let loose, it will not be easily contained. Entangled interests and alliances will cause the situation to spiral quickly out of control."

"If you are asking me to betray my country," Farid warned, "you are talking to the wrong man."

"Betray your country?" Anatoly repeated. "I would never ask a man such as you to do that. What I would ask is that you be true to yourself."

Opening his briefcase, Anatoly then pulled out a picture and laid it at the marble base of the statue. "I know it is painful for you," he said, "but have you ever looked closely at this picture? As you know, it was taken at Azadi Square in Tehran on the day of the bombing in Kuwait. The image of Prime Minister Ghorbani waving the latest edition of the *Tehran Times* appeared on every evening news telecast around the world. He condemned the United States and Israel for planning such a horrible deed, and called on the entire Arab world to rise up against them. He whipped the crowd into such a frenzy as he reminded them of the cowardly act that not only killed innocent citizens, but destroyed priceless pages from the imam's Koran. That one speech alone spurred a flood of bombings from France to Malaysia. How many wives and daughters died in *those* attacks?"

Anatoly pointed to the front page at a man standing behind the speaker, then asked, "Do you know this man?"

"Yes," Farid replied. "He was the antiquities minister, Roozbeh Esfahmi."

"Well, my friend," Anatoly said, "if not for a faulty fifty-dollar hydraulic valve that kept his plane on the runway in Dubai, he would have been on the same platform as your wife and daughters in Kuwait on that fateful day."

Anatoly pointed to a small column in the newspaper being held in the picture and pulled a second sheet from his briefcase. "On the right is a blow-up of the article in the paper held in the photograph, while the one on the left is a picture of the front page printed that day. My *farsi* is not very good, but I have the translation. You can read it for yourself, if you like. It would seem that the copy being held here in the picture lists the antiquities minister, Mr. Esfahmi, as having been killed in the blast – while the other does not."

Farid stared at the two articles and then at Anatoly. "I realize that games can be played with pictures on a computer," he said. "If these articles are different, it is only because the details were not available at the time."

"Or perhaps one was printed in advance," Anatoly surmised. "Correct me if I am wrong, but wasn't it the interior minister, Mr. Ghorbani, who asked your wife and daughters to be present in the first place? And since he has become *prime* minister, did he not exclude the antiquities minister – a powerful political rival who greatly disagrees with his views – from his new cabinet?"

"This is still no proof," Farid protested. "Just coincidences and suppositions. The prime minister is a friend. He knew my wife and daughters personally." Glancing around at the marble walls, Farid hissed, "This room speaks of death – it is cold, just like your words."

"I know how much your family meant to you," Anatoly said, "and as a man of Allah, surely you realize that the destruction of the Koran's pages was devastating to you and all followers of Islam."

Playing his final card, Anatoly returned the papers to his briefcase and removed a manila envelope. He opened it, took out its contents, and carefully slid them and their plastic case onto the marble base. Then he studied Farid's reaction. The colors were still brilliant, Farid thought, even after fourteen-hundred years. These framed verses were from the holy book he had read to his daughters!

Anatoly spoke first. "You remember that day in the square, and what he called your wife and daughters? He called them martyrs, *not* victims."

Anatoly pushed the plastic case toward Farid and continued. "This is on loan from an anonymous collector in Vienna," he said. "It was made available to him shortly after the bombing." Turning it over, he pointed to a small sheet of formal-looking paper sealed between the layers of plastic. "This is a certificate of authenticity, dated two weeks after their deaths, for items which were reportedly destroyed in the blast.

"Mr. Attar, your government may think it can control events," Anatoly finished, "but if they unleash this kind of attack, believe me when I say this: In the end, you will stand alone."

"Is this the official position of the Russian government?" Farid asked.

"I speak for the twenty million beneath my feet who have no voice, and perhaps the next twenty million as well," Anatoly answered somberly. "I am sure that you have saved copies of those two newspapers packed away somewhere. Compare them for yourself. Think of all the doubts and questions you pushed to the back of your mind for all those years. Late at night, when you ask yourself these questions, whose name and face do you see? A father should not be denied the joy of giving his daughters away on their wedding day."

Anatoly thought he detected a slight misting in Farid's eyes. He had gone for the jugular and was confident that he had succeeded. He offered one last consolation. "Any time you wish to leave, my driver is at your service." Now his work was done.

* * *

The technician walked into the room as a shaken Farid Attar climbed into the back seat of the limousine. Anatoly turned to him. "Did you get it all?" he asked.

"Yes, all of it," the technician replied. "I'll have to clean up a few sections because of all the echoes off the floor and walls, but the quality is more than acceptable. That must have been one hell of a reproduction to fool him that convincingly."

"Oh, it was no reproduction," Anatoly countered. "I called in a favor from a personal friend in Istanbul. This is one of the original manuscripts from the Topkapi Museum. Our Turkish friends understand all too well what is at stake here. Once this begins, they will not be excluded. Now, if you will excuse me, I have a plane to catch. An old friend is waiting on a tarmac in Istanbul."

Chapter 52. May 28, 2008 – Hatzerim Air Base, Southern Israel

Ryan Lessley had just awakened from a much-needed full night's sleep. However, the dry heat of the desert air left him with a pounding headache. Although he was used to arid conditions back home at the Mojave test site, here in Israel he could almost feel the moisture being sucked from his body. He almost felt like a piece of dried fruit. It wouldn't take much imagination to envision a dead body covered by drifting sands and later found as a naturally mummified corpse. Five thousand years ago, an event such as this could have helped shape a completely new culture and belief system in Egypt.

He sat up and stretched, then immediately started massaging his temples to try to at least dissipate some of the throbbing and not have it concentrated in one spot.

"Good morning," a voice behind him greeted. "It will take a while for you to get used to the dryness."

Ryan turned around to see Kristen seated in a corner chair. "You should force yourself to drink as much water and strong Arabic tea as you can," she offered. "It would also be a good idea for you to abstain from coffee and sodas until your system adjusts to our arid clime." She wore her hair pulled back and her military fatigues didn't exactly disguise her feminine appeal. Even from across the room, those piercing blue eyes of hers made his heart beat just a bit faster.

"I must admit that I have had numerous thoughts of you in my bedroom," Ryan confessed. "Just not quite like this."

"I should warn you that I know at least a dozen ways to kill you with my bare hands," she cautioned with an impish grin, "and I wouldn't leave a mark or evidence of any kind."

"Promises, promises," he toned. "I'll try to keep that in mind. So where are we, anyway?"

"We are on an air base in southern Israel," she answered, "about one hundred miles from Gaza."

Kristen rose from her seat and walked to the door. "There is a shower through this doorway and down the hall," she said. "Try to look presentable, Mr. Lessley. We have a meeting over breakfast in forty-five minutes."

As she opened the door, Ryan leaned on his pillow with an elbow and smiled. "You might stay a while," he suggested, "and to conserve water, we could ... 'get presentable' together."

She shot him a glance that communicated without words. "Yeah, yeah, I know," he reminded himself aloud, "'a dozen ways' ..."

* * *

Kristen escorted Ryan a short distance to a one-story reinforced concrete bunker. The warm shower and four aspirin had refreshed his mind and helped sooth his pounding head. Walking beside her, he tried to imagine them strolling on a beach, not some windswept patch of desert sand that generations of peoples had fought over for centuries. Along the way, he noticed a settlement to the south. Its bright green fields stood out in sharp contrast to the desolate landscape. "That is Kibbutz Hatzerim, where I was born," Kristen said. "We are far enough from the ocean that the aquifer is not contaminated by seawater. That is why this area is so lush. So, are you feeling a little better now?"

"Yes, that warm shower sure did the trick," Ryan replied.

She laughed and said, "That is the local joke – the showers and baths are always warm."

When they entered the conference room, Ryan was greeted by Alex McCormick, Gerald Woods and a surly, unshaven man in military fatigues. "So good to finally meet you in person, Mistuh Lessley," Woods said as he held out his hand. "Ah believe you know everyone here except our host, Major Chaikin. You might say he is here to keep us on the path so we don't get sand in our shoes."

Ryan looked at the major and thought, oh great – now I've got another babysitter.

Turning to Kristen, he said, "I thought that Miss ... by the way, I never caught your last name ... had that chore."

"Her last name is Gerstner," Woods answered, "and she has other duties that require her attention elsewhere. The major will be your contact from now on."

An orderly placed an omelet plate in front of Ryan. "A tall glass of water with two lemon wedges, egg whites only, vegetarian, and no dairy," Alex quipped. "Now that's what I call a man's breakfast." Ryan didn't dignify the chauvinist commentary with a response.

Assistant Director Woods handed a sheaf of papers held together with a paper clip across the table. "The *Al-Jawan* has sailed into open water and is headed for the southern end of the Suez," he explained. "It will moor at Port Ibrahim for a day and then overnight in Ismaïlia before a pilot boat leads the group of six vessels north through the canal. While they are in Port Ibrahim is when we plan to make our move. The water there is murky and the daily port activity will be a distraction."

"How do you know they'll stop there?" Ryan asked. "Why wouldn't they just continue straight into the canal and head north?"

"Schedules, Mistuh Lessley," Woods informed him. "Everything here is all about schedules. The Suez Canal operates twenty-four hours a day, so everything must be precisely orchestrated. For most of the canal's length, there is only a single shipping lane. We are talking about one of the busiest shipping channels in the world, yet it is no more than a big ditch cut through the desert. There is a continuous dredging operation going on due to the blowing sands, and the speed limit of eight knots is strictly enforced to keep the wave erosion caused by passing ships under control.

"Along its complete length, there are only three areas wide enough to pass," he continued. "Three convoys a day travel through the canal – two from the north and one from the south. The two southbound convoys leave first, around six, and then the other at eight in the morning to reach the Great Bitter Lake about two-thirds of the way through the passage. They drop anchor there, then wait until the northbound convoy passes and clears the channel. The northbound group leaves around six in the evening, and has a straight shot all the way to Port Said and then on to the Mediterranean. We will know precisely when they break out because we will know exactly when they leave – as well as their true speed."

"I don't even want to know what you've got planned," Ryan said, "but it sounds like you've got it all figured out. Good luck to you. So, once again, why am I here?"

"Because of this," Woods replied as he handed Ryan a four-inch threaded metal bolt. "This crucial piece of hardware is what connects the cable to the underwater sled. Feel how light it is. It's titanium and will not corrode. Now turn it over and look at the top. There you will see a series of nesting cylinders in the center of the bolt head. That is a lock. When the bolt is inserted through the metal cable and into the threaded fitting on the sled, it forms an electrical connection. As it tightens the bolt, a special ratcheting tool activates the pins inside the cylinders. They extend into slots to lock it in place and complete the circuit. If not removed properly, a small charge breaks the watertight seal, and in this case we're not sure what else might happen."

"So how did you come to know all of this up 'til now?" Ryan wondered.

"An ambitious young man from Ukraine – an entrepreneur and engineer in the purest sense of the word – came to us with this information," Woods replied. "When the old Soviet regime crumbled in the early nineties, he bought a dozen or so of these sleds as scrap metal and put his talents to work. He developed the locking bolt, added a camera in front for monitoring, and finally a black-box homing device. Then he simply looked for a niche market.

"One of the Colombian drug cartels used it for a short period until they began employing submersibles," Woods went on. "That would be a submarine to you, Mistuh Lessley. Then, just when he thought his enterprise had dried up, two Middle East businessmen heard of him through the cartel and made contact. He then supplied them with the sled. That is how we got the intel on the bolt. It seems that after final delivery of the product, he got wind of the retirement package they had planned for him, so he decided to come to us for protection. Apparently, his former business associates were trying to clean up loose ends, so to speak."

"So what is it exactly that you are planning to do once they moor at Port Ibrahim?" Ryan asked.

"Well, we would like to make a trade," Woods responded with a smile. "We want to swap their sled – along with its load – for one of ours. But as you can see, this unique little fastener docs present a minor obstacle."

Ryan formed an improbable image in his mind. "So you need me to fabricate some kind of special tool to unlock this thing, but I have no machine shop and no plans to work from – and you need it within twenty-four hours?"

"Well, that's not completely accurate," Woods corrected him. "We do have a machine shop available – and we do have this." He held up an object with a socket head and a two-inch-long metal cylinder on top. "It seems that there are two separate tools – one for insertion and one for removal. The gentleman kept the removal tool as his leverage during our negotiations.

"During that time, we became aware of the fact that he had also kept a few minor disturbing details from us. Seems he rerouted a few of the sleds and skimmed the proceeds from the cartel. I'm afraid that he had lost confidence in our ability to protect him. We think he is somewhere in Ukraine, around Kiev. At least that is where the cartel is looking for him.

"Drug dealers pitted against international thieves and terrorists," Woods concluded. "Sort of makes you feel warm and fuzzy all over, no matter who wins. What is it that you would say, Mr. McCormick – the expression you once used?"

After a moment's consideration, Alex replied, "Back home, we would call it 'culling the herd.'"

"I find it hard to believe that you folks will actually deal with someone who would lie to you," Ryan observed.

Woods clarified their position as he answered succinctly, "Ah believe the proper phrase, suh, is 'that's how we roll'."

Ryan removed the paper clip from the stack of documents and set it on the table. As he did, it moved ever so slightly. He nudged it with his finger and it slowly moved toward the bolt.

"You said this bolt was made from titanium, correct?" Ryan asked as he handed it to Alex. "Put the gizmo on it and see if you can get the pins to pop out." Alex placed the mechanism on top of the bolt, pressed the top, turned it clockwise and all five locking pins came right out.

"Major, do you have any way of erasing hard drives or magnetic tapes?" Ryan inquired.

"Yes," he replied, "we have a portable degaussing wand in the IT office next door."

Ryan saw the opportunity to conduct an experiment. "Would you bring it over here?"

The major hurried out and Ryan reached across the table for the bolt. He held it in his left hand and the paper clip in his right. As he brought them closer together, the metal paper clip jumped out of his hand and stuck to the bolt.

The major returned presently with the instrument. "When you degauss something, it reverses the direction of the magnetic field," Ryan explained as he took the device. "In a hard drive, it reverses the process of magnetic imprinting and wipes the disk clean. The only way a metal paper clip would stick to titanium is if a magnet was present somewhere inside. In this case, a series of magnets moves the pins." Ryan activated the wand, waved it over the bolt and an audible click could be heard as the pins slid back inside.

"Son of a bitch – look at that," Alex marveled.

"There is no second tool," Ryan observed. "He's just a better con man than you two."

"Miss Gerstner, we are back on schedule," Woods declared. "We'll make the switch tomorrow morning while they are still moored in Port Ibrahim. Anything else before you leave?"

"No, I'm cleared," Kristen answered. "I have my documents from the World Health Organization as an observer from the Customs and Quarantine office. All my identification papers list me as an Egyptian national. It's not out of the ordinary for representatives from this office to sometimes board a vessel for an inspection. It won't look the least bit suspicious."

"Just the same, be careful," Woods warned. "You don't know what their state of mind may be."

"Wait a minute," Ryan blurted. "You're sending her alone?"

"Mistuh Lessley, ah believe you've seen firsthand that she is more than capable of taking care of herself," Woods observed.

"Still, you can't just let her go alone!" Ryan exclaimed. "Those people are fanatics. In fact, they're downright dangerous. Who knows what they might do to her?"

Kristen, seated behind Ryan where he couldn't see her, looked at Alex and rolled her eyes.

Woods looked at Alex and then at Ryan. "Well, all right, if that's the way you feel, we'll send you along as well," he said with a sigh. "And as long as you are going, Mistuh Lessley, besides supplying a diversion while our underwater exchange is taking place, there is one other thing I need you to do."

Alex smiled and interjected, "Oh, you do realize that you'll have to ditch those cargo shorts and wear big-boy pants."

On the way back to his quarters, Ryan still waxed defensive. "I can't believe they were actually going to send you by yourself."

Kristen looked at him and smiled. "You really don't have any idea what just happened, do you?"

"About what?" he asked ignorantly.

"They were just baiting you so you would volunteer to go," she replied. "Why do you think they were able to get your documents for Customs and Quarantine so quickly?"

Kristen chuckled at Ryan's apparent naïveté. "You really did knock their socks off when you solved their bolt puzzle. I know for a fact that they would not have let you go unless that happened. I also admit, in a certain schoolgirl kind of way, you wanting to protect me was slightly charming. I might even consider letting you meet my grandmother."

"Oh, so *now* I get to meet the matchmaker in Tel Aviv?" Ryan asked wistfully.

"No, first you have to meet my other grandmother," Kristen returned, "and she'll break your fingers if you even think about touching me!"

Ryan's face went blank as he looked at her. Kristen stood on her toes, kissed him on the cheek and shook her head. "You really don't know a thing about women, do you?"

Chapter 53. May 29, 2008 – Hatzerim Air Base, Southern

Israel

Alex McCormick leaned over the table and placed what looked like a tiny cell phone in front of Ryan and Kristen. "This is what you will be looking for when you board the *Al-Jawan*. Our Ukrainian friend called it 'The Carbon One.' This little piece of hardware is much more than a phone. I don't even know exactly what to call it."

Touching its screen, Alex said, "Keyboard." A hologram of a keypad spread out on the table in front of the phone. Then he said, "Voice." Like a wisp of smoke, the virtual image disappeared back into the phone. He spoke to the phone a third time. "I need the authorization sequence for the *Al-Jawan*. Print." A printer on the other side of the room came to life and a sheet dropped into the output tray. Alex handed it to Ryan.

"Authorization sequence commences upon receiving weather satellite Meteosat-9 imagery Eastern Mediterranean Basin 63557/52*7," Ryan read aloud quizzically. "I don't get it," he stated with bewilderment. "This doesn't make any sense. Weather satellites send streaming pictures and data or the pictures are looped every few minutes. Anyway, those aren't communication birds. They're sending data and pictures, not relaying or receiving. And what's that last sequence of numbers?"

"There is one channel that can be opened," Alex replied, "and that's in the numbered sequence. Orbit adjustments and camera angles can be changed on the Meteosat-9 satellite. These changes can be made manually or programmed in. Our friends at Zagros have inserted a Trojan horse virus into the video feeds from the weather satellite. That same virus gives them access to the steering codes. As you noted, weather satellite pictures are transmitted continuously and most every vessel in the area monitors the weather. There would be nothing unusual about anyone receiving these reports. When a certain combination of orbit adjustments and camera angles occurs, the signal is sent in the video code and this little gizmo starts the countdown.

"On the bottom of the phone is a standard USB port. When you find it on the *Al-Jawan*, we need you to insert this thumb drive. This is the same malware that infected their centrifuges at Zagros. Among other things, it will enable us to disrupt the countdown sequence – when and if it begins."

"Does it give you the ability to detonate that thing on the rear deck?" Ryan asked. "I mean, I'd hate for that possibility to cross your mind while we're on still on board."

"Fond as I am of you, Mr. Lessley, I am afraid that we are not completely sure of the transmission sequence of that code," Alex said. "Once in Haifa, the bug will only allow us to *stop* the countdown, not start it. It also gives us the capability to monitor and mask the on-board cameras that give them a bird's-eye view of exactly what is going on in the harbor. The local security patrols will keep them boxed in near the rear of the flotilla as long as possible."

"Sure seems like an awful lot of cloak-and-dagger nonsense, if you ask me," Ryan lamented. "You'll already have the device at this point, so why is it so important to keep the Iranians out of the loop? There's something else you're not telling me again, isn't there?"

"Well, we're planning on sending the package back to where it came from," Alex replied, "just to let them know that we know. It will be flown to a deserted airfield on the Zagros Plateau, where we have arranged for some, shall we say, politically incorrect citizens to transport it deep into the natural caverns. Since our friends will be handling the live package, in their eyes it has become a rather important issue in the negotiations to make sure that it didn't go 'boom' while they were moving it."

"You know, this cell phone is really sweet," Ryan observed. "Who developed this little baby, anyway?"

"It really is a small world," Alex responded. "The same man who designed the locking bolt came up with this one, too. That's why we know so much about the phone and the scheme with the weather satellite. He hacked the system, designed the software and built the phone – that was the second part of the contract after the sled was delivered. They paid him ten million up front to build and develop the system and he was to pocket another ten upon completion. However, he suspected that they weren't planning for him to be around to collect the final payment. In their eyes, it would be rather inconvenient for him to show up on the evening news. He thought his employers might try something like this, so he built an insurance policy right into the phone. Once he went into hiding, he mailed us the phone with the encryption codes.

"But what is really interesting," he continued, "is that his grandfather is the Russian physicist, Pytor Ufimtsev, the father of stealth technology. When we asked him where he came up with these wild ideas, he said that his sole inspiration came from his grandfather's writings.

"Just look at this," McCormick said as he bent the phone into a ninety-degree angle. "The damned thing is really flexible, and the chips are graphite, not silicone-based. They don't overheat and they're so efficient that the charge on the batteries lasts twenty times longer. The last time we met, he was trying to explain this new battery he was working on that recharged itself with the earth's rotation and changing magnetic fields. His grandfather's notes were his inspiration for that one, too. Pytor Ufimtsev was part of that group of Russian scientists who worked with the Germans between the two world wars.

"Many times, his grandfather told him about two brothers whom he called the German geniuses. He couldn't speak German and they weren't fluent in Russian, but they shared a common bond and communicated through mathematics. They called it the 'universal language.' They shared with him equations and theories he had never seen before.

"Do you know who those two brothers were?" Alex finally asked. "Walter and Reimar Horton, the designers and builders of The Bat. Two brothers with no formal aeronautical training or education, yet they were still able to solve some of the most complicated problems in their field. How did they do that, I ask you? What vast reservoir of knowledge did they draw from?"

Chapter 54. May 30, 2008 – Persian Gulf

As the Iranian interceptor jet cut a lazy, looping path over its designated patrol area, the countdown commenced: three, two, one … at once, the Stuxnet virus came to life. Inserted into the computer system that was directly linked to Iranian Air Defense, the software bug acted much like a real pathogen when it invades its host. It can lay dormant for years and be brought to life with an act as simple as a keystroke – or it may never awaken at all. This same virus that once played havoc with Iran's nuclear centrifuges now targeted the radar screens of the Iranian Air Defense.

A complex program still showed passenger jets cruising overhead at thirty-thousand feet, but the trail that the MiG-29 traced on its assigned patrol over the Persian Gulf was merely a mirage. As the Stuxnet virus took over the screen, the Iranian interceptor dropped below radar-detection level to a mere one hundred feet above the water's surface. The pilot then hit its afterburners and the craft screamed toward the Saudi coast.

The plane made landfall north of the city of Dhahran and touched down at King Abdul-Aziz Military Air Base. As the aircraft rested on the tarmac, engines still burning, crews worked feverishly to change its payload so the pilot could get back in the air for delivery to Zagros. At the same time, a drama quite unknown to the ground crew was unfolding in the skies to the east.

* * *

"Mayday, mayday!" the pilot exclaimed. "Kuwait International air traffic control, this is Emirates Air flight 0876 – repeat, Echo-Kilo-0876, Dubai International, bound for Beirut. We have experienced loss of cabin pressure and smoke in the cockpit. Request immediate emergency landing clearance at nearest available airport. Mayday, mayday – this is not a drill. Repeat, this is not a drill. Mayday!"

"This is Kuwait International air traffic control IATA KWI," the air-traffic controller acknowledged. "We copy, Echo-Kilo-0876. Condition of aircraft?"

"Echo-Kilo-0876, losing altitude," came the pilot's distressed reply. "Flying heavy, slow response, both engines still operating."

"KWI, we have you on our screen," the controller returned. "Specify aircraft, number of passengers, fuel, and if carrying any dangerous cargo."

"Echo-Kilo-0876 Airbus three-three-zero," the pilot came back. "217 passengers. Fuel 24,350 pounds. Zero dangerous cargo."

"KWI, roger that, Echo-Kilo-0876," the controller responded. "Closest available airport large enough is King Abdul-Aziz International in Saudi IATA-JED. Am contacting now. Turn left to two-niner-zero-degrees."

"Echo-Kilo-0876, we have lost instruments," the pilot reported.

"KWI, begin left turn and I'll steer you from there," the controller instructed.

"Echo-Kilo-0876, roger," the pilot said as he accepted his new flight orders.

"KWI, hold her right there, Echo-Kilo-0876," the controller said as the aircraft reached its new heading. "I'll be handing you off to Saudi control. The next voice you hear will be traffic control at King Abdul-Aziz International, designation JED, that's Juliet-Echo-Delta. Good luck."

The next ninety seconds of dead air seemed like an eternity to the Emirates Air crew. Would their new flight plan be accepted, or would they end up as an oil slick in the Persian Gulf?

Finally, the radio came to life. "This is air traffic control, King Abdul-Aziz Military Air Base, temporary India-Alpha-Tango-Alpha, Juliet-Echo-Delta-Mike," the new air-traffic controller announced. "King Abdul-Aziz International has Runway Twenty-Eight jammed, so they handed you off to us. We are twelve miles east of King Abdul-Aziz International at two-niner-five degrees. We have you at thirty-one miles out at approximately two-niner-zero degrees – air speed 208 knots, altitude 11,000 feet. ETA is approximately nine minutes."

"Echo-Kilo-0876, you'll have to line me up for the approach," The pilot cautioned.

"Juliet-Echo-Delta-Mike, turn slowly to the right," the controller said. "That's it. Echo-Kilo-0876, just keep that bird in the air and we'll walk you home. You are clear to start descent to 3,000 feet."

The air-control officer turned to the U.S. Air Force major, who watched his men through binoculars as they scurried around the Iranian MiG-29 interceptor jet still on the tarmac. "We have a developing situation," the controller said. "I have an incoming Emirates airliner with 217 passengers that has to come down right now – and it's going to have to be here. KA International has four jumbos lined up for takeoff and I can't get them cleared in time. We have to get your bandit back into the air."

"We have a problem," the major stated. "I need a few more minutes."

Just then, the radio crackled to life. "This is Iranian Air Defense Control," the voice barked. "We have been monitoring the situation with Echo-Kilo-0876. We have an interceptor on routine patrol in international waters that is experiencing electronic and radio difficulties. We are unable to raise them. They could pass as close as one-quarter mile."

"Juliet-Echo-Delta-Mike, thanks for the heads-up," the controller said.

"They never do anything like that," the major observed. "Something has caught their attention or doesn't seem right. You'd better get that plane back on the Iranians' screen real fast, or this thing could turn into a complete mess – especially if their data shows there should have been a collision."

The major then opened a new communication channel with the disabled aircraft. "Echo-Kilo-0876, we have a visual on the runway." Then, to the ground crew, "All obstacles clear and emergency equipment ready?"

After receiving confirmation that they were in the process of clearing the landing strip, the major continued. "Juliet-Echo-Delta-Mike, emergency equipment on standby. They will follow as you touch down. Last obstacle being removed from runway as we speak. Is your landing gear down and functioning?"

"Echo-Kilo-0876, affirmative as far as we can tell," the pilot replied. "Can you give me a visual?"

Raising his binoculars, the major answered, "Roger, Juliet-Echo-Delta-Mike. They look to be down and locked. You are cleared for landing."

As the Airbus A330 began its final descent, a twin-engine Iranian interceptor just two hundred yards down the runway lifted off and banked to the right at full throttle toward the Persian Gulf.

* * *

Now the final act of the ballet began. Major Farid Attar had to be at the precise coordinates when the Stuxnet program went back into dormancy. The program tracking his plane's flight wouldn't shut down until the two were in exactly the same spot, but he was more concerned that the added weight and instability of his new cargo might cause the aircraft to behave differently on the screen.

The original plan had been to switch the four Russian air-to-air missiles with empty pods in order to offset the additional weight, but it did not go smoothly and was aborted due to the emergency landing. A faulty relay switch wouldn't allow two of the missiles to drop free and be exchanged. Now the plane was seriously overweight on one side, and its balance and center of gravity had shifted. Suddenly, the plane banked to the left as the two air-to-air missiles on his starboard wing fell free. The normal firing sequence would be two missiles fired – one from each side – to maintain proper balance. The two port-side missiles remained firmly in place and Farid struggled to gain control. He repeatedly hit the release switch, but the stuck relay still would not allow a reaction.

In a desperate move, Farid tried to fire the two missiles instead of jettisoning them – still nothing. "This Russian piece of shit!" he screamed. "I'm glad I am not in the middle of a dogfight!" Suddenly, one missile finally broke free from the port wing. Balance was now easier to maintain.

Farid switched fuel consumption completely to the port wing tank and hoped he wouldn't have to tap into the starboard side to get back to base. Presently, a smile crossed his face. Zagros was closer than the distant plateau and this is what he had wanted all along. The Russians had convinced him that this is the way it should be played out, but Farid knew that Prime Minister Ghorbani would be at the Zagros facility to witness the end of his plan directly from the birthplace of his creation. Farid Attar would also be there to witness those consequences firsthand.

The more the port wing auxiliary fuel tank fed the plane, the better the stability and balance became – but soon the problem would occur in reverse. Burning close to one-hundred-ninety gallons of fuel per minute that weighed nearly seven pounds per gallon, Farid's aircraft performed an ever-changing balancing act to maintain its attitude, or relationship to the horizon.

While in the air, it was easier for Farid to make slight adjustments, but landing could present a whole new set of challenges. He adjusted his airspeed to just under 200 knots for maximum fuel economy. Now he needed to call upon all of his training and skill to make this one final landing.

With flaps down and having begun his final descent, he could now clearly see the emergency vehicles assembled to the left of the runway. A line of black limousines had pulled onto the causeway that led to the facility's warehouse and parking area. As always, Prime Minister Ghorbani was prompt. This could only mean one thing: The *Al-Jawan* had been positioned at Haifa and the moment was near.

Struggling to keep the aircraft's attitude level as he descended, Major Attar bounced hard twice on the runway and mumbled a prayer of thanks for the plane's rugged Mikoyan landing gear. As the orange-and-white drag chute popped open and spun like a top, emergency vehicles raced down the tarmac to the disabled jet.

Farid couldn't remember the last time that his heart had beaten this fast after a landing. As he unbuckled his harness and climbed from the cockpit, he realized that this was also the first time he had ever landed an aircraft with a nuclear weapon strapped to its underbelly.

"There is something seriously wrong with the electronics," he informed the ground crew. "Tow it immediately to the maintenance docks and tell the service personnel not to touch it until I return."

"And how long will that take?" the crew chief asked. "The base has just been placed on high alert and we may possibly expect an attack at any time."

"I am going to relieve myself," Farid said, "and I will return before she reaches the dock."

The commanding officer of the Zagros air base feverishly barked orders to subordinates, instructing them to bring his squadron of MiG-29 fighters onto the runway and ready them for takeoff at a moment's notice. Up until now, the unit had enjoyed a high level of protection inside the caverns. However, they had to tolerate the one downside: Only one plane at a time could be moved through the narrow opening, so in the event of a missile or bomb attack they suffered quite a disadvantage. A geological study had shown that widening the entrance would cause the rock to lose its structural integrity, so any alterations had previously been ruled out as too risky.

A wider opening was needed for peak efficiency, but not at the price of turning the fortress into a rocky grave.

As they towed his plane the quarter-mile back to the service docks, Farid watched the ground crew top off fuel tanks and run last-minute checks on the other jets in the cavern. He walked toward his quarters and glanced one last time at the crews swarming around the various aircraft. They are taking this alert very seriously, he thought. I wonder if they truly know why.

At Zagros, the number-one safety rule was to never fuel the planes inside the cavern. Even with the most sophisticated ventilation systems, the heavier-than-air fumes from the jet fuel would accumulate near the ground. This could pose a real problem. A small spark from a tool, machinery or static electricity could easily ignite those fumes. However, extraordinary events warranted taking extraordinary risks, so the order was given.

* * *

The air-control officer poked his head into the commander's office and said, "Sir, there's something I think you need to see."

"Not now," the commander barked. "Maybe later."

"Sir, give me two minutes," the control officer pleaded. "This is something out here that really requires your attention."

As he walked to the controller's desk, the commander looked up and observed two monitors that displayed recordings of various radar screens. The date stamps were the same, but the screens were glaringly different.

"Something didn't seem quite right today on our monitors," the controller said, "so I got a copy of the same time frame from air traffic at Bandar Abbas International." He froze the screens at identical times on both monitors and looked at his commanding officer, "Sir, Major Attar's plane isn't on the screen at Bandar, but it is on ours."

The commanding officer stared at the two screens while trying to absorb the significance of their differences, then picked up a phone. "Security, find Major Attar and bring him to my office immediately. If he resists, arrest him. This is top priority – find him now."

He turned to a junior flight officer and gave another order. "As soon as every plane is on the tarmac, get Major Attar's aircraft out of the maintenance facility and onto Auxiliary Runway Seven – away from the others."

Major Farid Attar would use his status as a national hero one last time. He had visited the research-and-development facility on many occasions. There had been times when he served as a guide and spokesman for touring dignitaries. Other occasions were for private business. He had taken photographs for the Russians and even inserted the virus into the computer system.

But today, he was here for personal reasons. Today, he was not Major Farid Attar – he was here as a grieving husband and father.

Chapter 55. May 29, 2008 – Tel-Aviv, Israel

Ryan and Kristen stood next to Alex and Mr. Woods, and watched the bank of screens in the southern regional intelligence office in Tel Aviv. A series of monitors had captured their undivided attention. On one, a drone's-eye view of the harbor at Haifa filled the screen, while another focused on a single vessel with six men kneeling in prayer on its rear deck. Another group of displays consisted of satellite photos that changed every few seconds. This lent a jerking effect to the images. Three screens showed the runway and facilities at Zagros, while a fourth revealed an empty, deserted area.

Ryan spoke first. "I don't see your Boy Scouts at the landing strip."

"We've had a slight change of plans," Alex replied.

* * *

The plan was simple enough for Ryan's and Kristen's inspection tour of the six pleasure craft moored at Port Ibrahim. They would inspect the *Al-Jawan* third so as not to raise suspicion.

The first craft, a luxurious eighty-five-foot yacht out of Sardinia, was owned by a retired and rather stuffy German industrialist. Being an elderly gentleman, he viewed this voyage as possibly his last chance to effect what he considered change in the world. It was also an opportunity to use other people's money instead of his own.

As Ryan and Kristen inspected and stamped his paperwork, he couldn't resist one final chance to explain – to anyone who would listen – the significance of this trip.

"I'm sure you can appreciate the unreasonable restrictions that Israel has placed on the Palestinian people," the old German explained. "The people of Palestine should have free movement and be able to return to their home country."

Kristen looked up at him and responded, "Sir, technically there are no Palestinian people, because technically there never was a country of Palestine – just an entire region with that name. Arabs and Jews alike lived there. Today, to be completely accurate, most of the people in that region have Egyptian surnames. Where we do agree is that they do need a permanent home. Perhaps a good first step would be to stop randomly killing innocent people."

"Young lady," the old man replied, "I do hope when you say 'they,' you are also including Israel."

"Of course," Kristen returned. "A nation's security and dignity is the very cornerstone of its existence."

She smiled as she finalized his papers. "Have a pleasant voyage and safe passage," she concluded. "Oh, and by the way, the channel is deeper over there and more protected from the wind. You might want to move and set your anchor closer to that vessel – the *Al-Jawan*."

A stiff breeze began to blow and the customs boat was buffeted hard across the whitecaps. Even with the breeze, the sweltering desert heat had made it difficult to breathe. As they neared the second craft, Ryan looked at Kristen. "Why did you have to do that?" he asked.

"Did you see the name of his boat?" She answered his question with another question – again, just as she did back in Uruguay. "In big bold letters, it said *Martzen*."

"So?" Ryan returned. "I don't know what that means."

Staring straight ahead, Kristen sternly said, "Martzen was one of the chemical-manufacturing conglomerates that produced Zyklon-B, the gas used in the German death camps. I thought that if anything unplanned should happen, he would want to be close to his 'final solution.'"

"Ah, so that's why you suggested he might like to moor closer to the *Al-Jawan*," Ryan said. "Pretty slick – my compliments."

As they boarded the second boat, the atmosphere couldn't have been more different. At forty-eight feet in length, the ship and crew seemed less than prepared for sailing on open water. Originating out of Sicily, the young Italian crew seemed more interested in lying in the sun and drinking wine than being part of some historical social experience.

Lounging on deck, the crew welcomed the inspectors with an invitation to join them in a glass of wine. They took videos of their group with the hope of seeing themselves on CNN or BBC, but Ryan politely turned down the invitation, then went below for a quick inspection and to stamp their papers. Unlike the well-organized cabin they had just left, a stack of papers lay in an empty wine box in the galley – which, as it turned out, also served as an office. In the end, they were unable to produce all of the needed documentation, so Ryan stamped what he could find and made his way topside.

One of the partying crew members attempted to pull Kristen over to the group of revelers for a picture, and as she pulled her arm away, the button on the cuff of her long-sleeved blouse popped free. She politely asked him not to touch her and explained that if he wished to have the continued use of his hand, to never do it again. When Ryan arrived on deck, the crew members were laughing hysterically. Kristen was already in the customs craft waiting for him.

"What was so funny?" Ryan asked. "Did I miss something, or is that just the booze talking?"

"He said if he ever made love to a woman as beautiful as me that it would make him cry," she replied. "I told him if he needed to cry during sex, maybe he should look for a less attractive woman who carried pepper spray."

Ryan bit his lip to keep from smiling and looked straight ahead.

On board the *Al-Jawan*, the crew seemed sullen and listless. One of them explained that they had contracted a highly contagious form of avian influenza in Saudi Arabia near their home port. Kristen then explained to him that all members of the crew must be called on deck for a medical inspection. The crewman objected, but she insisted that, as a physician, she could take no chances with this potentially deadly disease.

As the six men lined up, she slowly and methodically checked the vital signs, eyes, ears, noses and throats of the crew. Ryan used this impromptu exam as an opportunity to slip below decks. He had just started to remove his thumb drive from their Carbon One phone when one of the crew entered the cabin.

"What are you doing in here?" the crewman demanded. But before Ryan could come up with an answer, a sudden commotion and loud noise from above distracted the crewman. This gave Ryan a chance to race past him up the stairs to the aft deck. There stood Kristen, face-to-face with one of the crew. He pointed at the partially exposed tattoo on her forearm where the button had torn free.

"Miss Olufemi," Ryan spoke sternly, "I have warned you numerous times about keeping that ink of yours covered. It causes problems whenever this occurs. When we return, you will either get it removed or you will no longer be employed by the Customs and Quarantine Offices. Is that clear?"

"Yes, sir," Kristen responded meekly. "I'm sorry – it won't happen again."

Turning to the crewmen, Ryan rolled up Kristen's sleeve to reveal the complete tattoo. "Her father was a tank commander in the Six Day War with Israel back in 1966," Ryan explained. "That was his serial number. The stars represent the eleven Israeli tanks that his force destroyed. I am sorry if any of you found it offensive."

Fifty yards to the west, a man on a houseboat hung his laundry on a makeshift clothesline. As the wash flapped in the breeze, Ryan noticed the sequence of the colors on the line. It was ominously significant. He was initially concerned that they wouldn't be able to keep the crew distracted long enough, but there was his answer: the exchange was completed. As Bob Dylan had sung, the answer to his question was indeed "blowing in the wind."

As they pulled away from the *Al-Jawan*, Kristen whispered, "That was quick thinking – and by the way, wherever did you get the name 'Olufemi'?"

"It was the first Egyptian-sounding name that popped into my head," he replied. "I think I must have remembered it from one of the museums."

"You do realize that it means 'Beloved of the Gods,' don't you?" she asked. "You might want to keep that in mind."

Kristen then felt the need to mention a common thread between the crewmen. "They truly are a shabby-looking group. I think they really do have the flu – or something like it. Three of them had open sores inside their mouths when I checked their vital signs."

"It's not influenza," Ryan corrected. "More like acute radiation poisoning. Did you notice the hair? The one who almost caught me below decks had two spots the size of quarters missing from the back of his head. The sickness may be farther along than we thought. I just hope they're not too ill to continue."

* * *

Back at the command center, the stop-and-go motion of the satellite pictures showed a sequence of images of an aircraft entering the screen from the left and rolling down the runway as its drag chute deployed. It came to a stop and towing vehicles were shown heading toward it. The chute unhooked and the jet was then towed into the caverns.

Ryan looked at Gerald Woods and asked, "So, exactly how many people are at that facility?"

With a deep breath, Woods answered, "At any time, with both bases, maybe seventeen or eighteen hundred."

"Seventeen or eighteen hundred?" Ryan repeated. "I guess it would be naïve of me to ask if you were planning to give them any kind of warning. Was this what you planned all along?"

"No, this definitely was not what we planned," Woods replied. "But right now, we're up to our ass in alligators and just trying to keep this thing under control."

"Trying to keep this under control," Ryan echoed. "Does that seventeen or eighteen hundred include women and children?"

"Guards, take Mistuh Lessley to Conference Room A," Woods finally said. "If he doesn't behave himself, you have my permission – and my blessing – to have him restrained."

Chapter 56. May 29, 2008 – Zagros, Iran

The operations office at Zagros was the nerve center that controlled banks of centrifuges, which operated twenty-four hours a day. But today, their attention focused on a large monitor trained on a single boat at anchor in Haifa, Israel.

Three men occupied the reinforced concrete control room. Amir Ghorbani, the newly elected president of the Republic of Iran, also carried the titles of Prime Minister, Minister of Defense, and Chief of the Joint Staff of the Armed Forces. Even though he won the presidency through a popular election, he served only at the pleasure of the supreme leader, Imam Khomeini. The real political power in Iran always rested with the clerics.

Iran's government structure had always been complex and confusing, but ultimately, based on Islamic Law, the supreme leader could overturn a decision at any time. His advisers, elected and appointed, were given flexibility with day-to-day affairs, but the final power rested with Khomeini.

Because Ghorbani wore many hats in the government, this gave him great latitude within his powers. But in Iran, the ultimate decision that could affect the fate of any country rested only with the supreme leader. Only he had the power to declare war.

The heads of the two armies of Iran accompanied the president. General Danush Mahdi commanded the Army of the Islamic Republic of Iran. Their marching orders were to protect Iran from all dangers outside its borders. General Iraj Firuz commanded the Army of the Guardians of the Islamic Revolution, or the Pasderan, the internal thought-and-political-correctness police.

The Pasderan had spread its tentacles into all aspects of Iranian culture, from legitimate business to the black market. Control of the state-subsidized gasoline market had proved especially lucrative. By diverting a full ten percent to foreign markets, this alone made the

Pasderan the third-wealthiest and most powerful organization in the country after Iran Oil. That was about to change.

These three men were present as required by Iranian political and military protocols. In case of a national emergency or impending attack, the president and commanders of the two armies must be present and accounted for. Their identification must be verified before the defensive use of a weapon of mass destruction could be deployed. While the details were top secret, this protocol was considered a common necessity in any number of countries as a safeguard. Biological and chemical weapons were on the list as well, but the Iranians were members of a select club that held the nuclear genie in its bottle.

"President Ghorbani," General Mahdi spoke first, "please identify yourself and insert your card."

"I am Amir Ghorbani, President of the Republic of Iran." He slid his identification card into the first slot and placed his hand on the screen to wait for a match. Next, Iraj Firuz followed suit, then Danush Mahdi placed his card in the final slot to verify his own presence.

"Do you two men, as sworn officers of the Republic of Iran, fully accept responsibility for this decision?" General Mahdi asked. "If yes, do so by keying in your identification codes. Before you do, it is my duty to remind you that only our supreme leader, Imam Khomeini, has the power and authority to order an offensive strike."

"This is a defensive measure before our nuclear facilities are attacked," Ghorbani protested. "And who are you to challenge my authority? As Minister of Defense and Chief of the Joint Staffs of all armed forces, I do have this authority. And you, General Mahdi, are relieved from your position as commander of the army. I will now assume that position."

"It seems your title of commander may be more a matter of semantics than substance," General Mahdi observed. "Here, on this base, I am in command. You have moved us to the brink of war with this so-called 'defensive' nuclear strike. This one event will rally the entire world against Iran – and for what?"

"The entire *Islamic* world is looking for a country and a leader to finally remove the stain of Israel from the earth," Ghorbani declared. "Iran is that country – and I am that leader."

"You may find it difficult to lead your crusade from a prison cell at The Hague as you await trial at the hands of an international war-crimes tribunal," Mahdi retorted.

"The Republic of Iran has no extradition treaty with any western nation," Ghorbani pointed out. "And even if you were able to bring charges, who do you think the supreme leader and the people who put me in office would believe – their legally elected president or some disgraced military has-been?"

"You're correct about the lack of an extradition treaty with the West," Mahdi allowed. "It's good to know that you actually learned something in law school." General Mahdi turned, opened the door and Major Farid Attar walked into the room. "We have the pleasure of an unexpected guest."

His lips pressed tightly together, Farid's eyes burned with hatred for Ghorbani, and the president felt it. "I believe you are acquainted with Mr. Attar," Mahdi said. "Some people would even say that your political career began its meteoric rise on that day in Tehran Square. I know, for I was there. I can still remember how I felt during that speech. You could almost taste and feel the passion and emotion in the crowd. At that moment, all I wanted was revenge.

"Since you consider yourself a master at manipulating passion and emotion, you should be able to appreciate this," Mahdi went on. "I mean, as a politician, you must know the intense pressure that would be brought to bear on a government if it was discovered that a nation's leader was directly responsible for the deaths of Kuwaiti citizens on their own soil. And of course, there are also those three innocent Iranian citizens – murdered on a peaceful mission at the behest of their own government. The pressure to turn the guilty parties over for trial would be overpowering, and that pressure would come from Kuwait as well as from Iran. You are absolutely right, Mr. President. It is true that the Republic of Iran has no extradition treaty with any western power – but Iran does have such a treaty with Kuwait."

General Mahdi moved around the table so that he now faced the two other men. "Now, this is the part you should find especially interesting. When Saddam Hussein was expelled from Kuwait in 1990, Kuwait did sign such a treaty with Great Britain, the United States and, more importantly, the Netherlands and The Hague. They did this for the specific purpose of bringing to trial suspected terrorists and those accused of international war crimes in Kuwait.

"Mr. President," Mahdi continued, "I can assure you that after your trial in Kuwait, no matter what the outcome, there will be a private jet waiting at Kuwait City International Airport to take you to

The Hague to stand trial at a war-crimes tribunal. We all know how that went for Saddam Hussein."

"I am not a terrorist or criminal!" Ghorbani screamed. "I am the legally elected president of Iran, and the embarrassment to Iran alone would keep the supreme leader from allowing this to happen."

"You always were a much better politician than you were a lawyer," Mahdi commented. "Perhaps you should think about hiring one now. Here, you may use my phone." General Mahdi pushed the Carbon One phone across the table to Ghorbani. "Remarkable little instrument," Mahdi said. "Are you acquainted with it?" Amir Ghorbani clenched his jaw and stared defiantly back at the general.

Leaning across the table, General Mahdi picked up the phone and slowly mouthed the words, "Today, there will be no nuclear detonation in Haifa. You not only jeopardized, but now have lost the entire stockpile of the fissionable uranium that our country has amassed. For years, we steadfastly guaranteed to the west that the bomb was not our objective. Now you have destroyed, by this one selfish act, what so many have sacrificed and toiled over for their entire lives."

Movement on the monitor caused the three men to look up and watch as uniformed assault squads stormed the *Al-Jawan*. "This is the best – no, the *only* – offer you will receive from the imam on the matter," Mahdi declared. He placed a sheet of paper in front of Ghorbani and General Firuz, then continued. "You will both sign these statements and step down from office. If you do, this will be handled as an internal matter. You will be tried in Iranian courts, with Iranian jurists and under Islamic law."

Minister Firuz looked at General Mahdi and said, "Surely the imam does not believe that I am capable of such things, or even holds me responsible. After all, I am ..."

General Mahdi raised his hand to silence the minister. "Speak no more of culpability or innocence. The supreme leader quoted an ancient Persian proverb when your name was mentioned: 'He has eaten so many snakes that he has become a viper.'" General Mahdi looked hard at General Firuz and, showing his abject disgust, quoted another proverb. 'When you lie down with dogs, you get up with fleas.'"

"And if we choose not to accept?" Ghorbani growled defiantly.

"Ah, I can just imagine what you are thinking," Mahdi replied. "You still believe that all of your political power and wealth can get you out of this one. But I have spoken with the supreme leader and I know this to be his final position. If you choose not to accept and decide to fight, you will be handed over to Kuwait as soon as they serve the extradition papers. We both know that will end badly for all concerned. You will be denounced as a rogue politician and henceforth considered as *persona non grata* by the government and people of Iran. Oh, and then there is the matter of all of that money – more than eight billion dollars, I believe."

"That was *my* money!" Ghorbani hissed with contempt.

"I'm glad you chose to use the past tense, Mr. President," Mahdi said. "Once again, you are quite correct – it *was* your money. However, the Islamic Republic of Iran now holds you personally responsible for any losses incurred during the course of this unfortunate matter. Besides, how you managed to accumulate such a fortune is completely beyond the supreme leader. He also finds it quite troubling that the direction of your most recent investment moves has taken such a sharp turn for the worse. A very high percentage, I believe – more than ninety percent of your assets – was liquidated in the last ten days, and the instruments you purchased were placed as a wager that the world's markets would collapse. You must have felt very confident to purchase the most risky and shortest-term contracts available. Mr. President, you would have to be extremely lucky or know of some upcoming event that would rock virtually every financial center on the planet.

"In an Iranian court, I suppose you could make an argument that this move was planned with the sole purpose of damaging western markets and their economies, and that these proceeds were for the Republic of Iran and would be returned as soon as you were finished with them. If I were your counsel, that might be a viable direction for your defense. With that type of aggressive posture, you might still possibly escape with your life.

"However, I do not believe that possibility exists with your other choice," General Mahdi went on. "You see, I pride myself on being an observer of the outside world. Let's say for discussion's sake that you were extradited to a foreign court – The Hague, for example. From their point of view, it would appear that you were prepared to murder millions of innocent people – but not for political motivations. This was all about personal and financial gain. Anyway, this is how I would paint you if I were a prosecutor at The Hague."

Ghorbani glanced furtively around the room, then looked toward the door.

"If you are wondering about your security detail, they are quite busy at the moment," General Mahdi said. "It is such an honor to be called personally by the imam. He has the ability to become extremely convincing when discussing one's plans for eternity."

General Mahdi pushed the phone toward Ghorbani. "Mr. President, I suggest you cut your losses. Make the call to all of your brokers and financial advisers. A fortune of this magnitude disappearing like a puff of smoke couldn't help but have a negative influence on the courts."

Chapter 57. May 29, 2008 – Tel-Aviv, Israel

Gerald Woods and Alex McCormick watched as the *Al-Jawan* was taken without incident.

"Your journalist's disappearance go smoothly?" Woods asked.

"He's tucked away, safe and sound," Alex replied. "Even accommodated his retirement wishes. Set him up in Sicily. He's living on the coast and working as a deckhand on a tour boat. We should all have it that good."

"Details of his disappearance?" Woods inquired passively.

"We have a sworn statement that his vehicle slid off a road in Idaho into a flooded river," Alex answered. "It was dragged about a half-mile downstream, but no body was ever recovered.

"In about five weeks, even though his body is still missing, the insurance company will settle the claim naming his ex-wife as beneficiary. A surprise check for $350,000 will no doubt soften her outspoken views of Mr. Arroyo. He will be mourned as a brave journalist who suffered a tragic death doing what he loved the most. Funds will be transferred from the agency to cover the insurance settlement and we will all disappear into the sunset."

"Let's just hope she doesn't use some of her newfound fortune on a Mediterranean vacation in Sicily," observed the director. "That, suh, could get a little sticky."

"Between the plastic surgery and not shaving that beard, his own mother wouldn't even recognize him. But damn, I'm sure going to miss that cabin at Big Bear," McCormick pined.

* * *

Ryan Lessley sat with his wrists and ankles tightly zip-tied to a chair in Conference Room A. The resulting lack of circulation had turned his hands a rosy red hue that matched his face. Kristen walked in and laughed, "You must have been a real pain. The only reason they cinch them down that tight is to make a point."

She walked over to the TV and flipped on *BBC World News*. "If you promise to behave yourself, I'll cut you free," she said playfully.

But before he could answer, the news broadcast the day's most important events. "In the top news story of the day …" Ryan braced himself "… the president of Iran has stepped down citing health reasons. In a statement, President Amir Ghorbani, recently diagnosed with a rare form of leukemia, said he was stepping down to focus his full attention on treatment and recovery. Radiation therapy would leave him too weak to properly fulfill the demanding responsibilities of his office. He will be replaced on an interim basis by opposition leader Roozbeh Esfahmi until new elections can be held. In an unrelated event, General Iraj Firuz, minister of the Guardians of the Islamic Revolution, has been removed in what Iran observers say appears to be some sort of power play. Once again, the major stories of the day: shake-up at the top for Iranian leadership and world financial markets surge up more than two percent. This is BBC World News."

Kristen slowly cut his bonds with more than a little amusement. "Quite a news day when we stop a terrorist's nuclear attack, but we can't even get on the five o'clock news," Ryan mused as he rubbed his wrists to try to get back his circulation. "So what exactly happened? Why didn't they set the thing off?"

"Well, as Director Woods said, they gained the ability to stop it and it wouldn't have exactly looked good from a public-relations point of view to be responsible for a nuclear explosion in one of our allies' own back yards," Kristen replied. "I believe that the leadership in Greece and Turkey would frown on that one – not to mention the fact that they removed the core before sending it back. It took Iran seven years to produce fifty-eight pounds of weapons-grade plutonium. We weren't just going to hand it back to them and then say 'now you go home and play nice.'"

Just then, Alex McCormick walked in and said, "That was a good look for you, all tied up in that chair." He paused for a second and added, "You know, this whole thing will end up in some classified file somewhere, and sometime in the future, some politician might think you deserve a medal or something. But that's not going to happen. Director Woods did, however, want me to give this to you as a reward for service to your country."

Ryan looked blankly at the envelope in Alex's hand. "So what's in it?"

"Two names and two pictures," Alex reported. "One is your mother. I'm sorry to say she passed away two years ago in Montreal." He opened the envelope and handed a picture to Ryan.

"I never thought I'd get a chance to see what my real mother looked like," Ryan said as he stared at the image. He swallowed hard and tears welled up in his eyes. He held out the picture to Kristen. "She was really a beautiful woman," he said. "I wish I had gotten a chance to talk to her, or at least to hug her just one time. So many questions ... I would love to have had some answers."

"I may have the next best thing," Alex said as he removed a second photo. "You have a sister. She's a research scientist in the San Francisco Bay area, at one of the top institutes in the world dealing with childhood cancer. Her name is Susan Danielle. Her address and phone number are on the back of the picture. She never married, but she has dedicated her life and career to her work. By all accounts, she's truly brilliant – and I can only assume that she's much nicer than you."

"Thanks, and right back at you," Ryan said. "Wow, she really looks a lot like our mother."

"Director Woods also asked me to give you this ticket to Los Angeles on a commercial flight leaving this afternoon," Alex said. "The test at the McDonnell Douglas facility has been postponed for a few days."

Looking down at the ticket, Alex suddenly acted surprised. "Son of a gun, now how could this have happened?" he lamented. "Seems that somehow this ticket was issued open-ended to San Francisco with a later connecting flight to Los Angeles. You just can't get good help these days."

Ryan looked at Kristen. "Since I'm in town for the evening, now I can take you up on that dinner invitation."

"And just when did I supposedly invite you to dinner?" she asked mockingly.

"I think it was sometime between pissing off the crew members of the *Al-Jawan* and my explaining how you were the 'beloved of the gods,'" Ryan came back.

"We'll talk about dinner later," Kristen said. "But your sister – she isn't even aware you exist. You need to give her some advance warning. I mean, you can't just show up in someone's life like this. What if she doesn't want to meet you, or believes this is some kind of a con or a fraud?"

"That's something I can't be worried about," Ryan countered. "I mean, it's out of my control. I just want to meet her and talk to her. That's all. After that, I'll just play it as it goes. If she really is my sister, I'm betting she'll also be at least a little curious about me."

Alex laid the von Duckworth folder on the conference table, then placed Susan Danielle's picture and the Carbon One phone on top of it. "Voice command. Find the most probable contact number for Susan Danielle at this time of day." The second number gave the desired results.

"Hello?" a slightly curious voice answered.

"Miss Danielle, I represent an extremely prestigious private endowment which helps fund certain philanthropic endeavors," Alex said. "It is my pleasure to inform you that you have been awarded the 2008 Alexandria Award."

"Never heard of it," Susan declared. "Not interested, and I don't know where you got this number. It's unlisted for a reason. Don't call back."

Just then, Arlene, the redhead with the bad dye job, rushed into Susan Danielle's office. "Quick, turn on KNBR." The screen came to life just in time for them to see the local anchorman give a sappy "two thumbs up" as he signed off for the San Francisco Bay area's newest celebrity.

"Who did you say you were?" Susan Danielle inquired.

Alex's voice came back on the phone. "I can understand your reluctance to answer an unsolicited call such as this. One of my associates, Mr. Ryan Lessley, will be in San Francisco tomorrow evening and he has arranged to meet you at Alioto's Restaurant for dinner. I believe that is your favorite spot. Reservations are under the Alexandria party. Please feel free to bring anyone you wish if it will put you at ease."

Alex hung up the phone and turned to Lessley. "Okay, slugger – now it's up to you."

Kristen smiled and pulled out her cell phone. After she keyed in the number, Ryan heard the response on the other end, it was Kristen's grandmother. "Hi, Grandma ... Yes, I love you, too ... Say, what are you having for dinner tonight? ... Anything I want? Okay, how about that chicken dish you make with the white wine, grapes and mushrooms? You know it's my favorite." Then she looked at Ryan and added, "Oh, and Grandma, set *two* extra plates for dinner. I'm bringing a guest."

* * *

Anatoly Karinkov picked up his phone as it signaled an incoming text message: *Svetlana Dannella (Susan Danielle) Bears in August. The package will be on the move in two days. — Arlene*

Author Bio

Charles "Ed" Gauss, although born in Texas, has spent his entire adult life in Southern California. He is a graduate of San Diego State University and works in a local nursery as he follows his passion for gardening. Two children, four grandchildren and his wife Susan make life more than interesting.

For more information about the author, *The Alexandria Seal* and his upcoming books, follow him on his Facebook page at https://www.facebook.com/CEGauss-479906282212810.